New York Times bestselling author **Jill Shalvis** lives in a small town in the Sierras full of quirky characters. Any resemblance to the quirky characters in her books is, um, mostly coincidental. Look for Jill's bestselling and award-winning books wherever romances are sold.

Visit her website at **www.jillshalvis.com** for a complete book list and daily blog detailing her city-girl-living-in-the-mountains adventures. For other news, find her on Facebook **/JillShalvis**, or follow her on Instagram and X **@jillshalvis**.

Jill Shalvis. Delightfully addictive:

'Fall in love with Jill Shalvis! She's my go-to read for humor and heart'
Susan Mallery, *New York Times* bestselling author

'Humor and heat, and a cast of characters you'll hate to leave behind when you turn the last page . . . the summer's perfect beach read'
Christina Lauren, *New York Times* bestselling author

'Jill Shalvis has a unique talent for making you want to spend time with her characters right off the bat'
Kristen Ashley, *New York Times* bestselling author

'Hot, sweet, fun, and romantic! Pure pleasure!'
Robyn Carr, *New York Times* bestselling author

'Jill Shalvis's books are funny, warm, charming and unforgettable'
RaeAnne Thayne, *New York Times* bestselling author

'Readers will find it easy to root for Shalvis's stubborn, vulnerable heroines to recognize both the decency and compassion of the sexy men who love them and their own worthiness to be loved. This heartfelt tale is thoroughly satisfying'
Publishers Weekly

'A wonderfully touching story about family, love, and second chances that will tug on the heartstrings and take readers on an emotional journey'
Harlequin Junkie

'Fans of the TV drama series *This Is Us* as well as love stories ripe with secrets waiting to be spilled will devour Shalvis's latest'
Library Journal

By Jill Shalvis

Jill Shalvis

THE BRIGHT SPOT

HEADLINE
ETERNAL

Published by arrangement with Avon,
an imprint of HarperCollins Publishers

First published in Great Britain in 2024
by HEADLINE ETERNAL
An imprint of HEADLINE PUBLISHING GROUP

1

Cataloguing in Publication Data is available from the British Library

ISBN 978 1 0354 0721 7

Designed by Diahann Sturge

Lake and tree art © Timo Schmid / The Noun Project

Offset in 10.96/16pt Minion Pro by Jouve (UK), Milton Keynes

Printed and bound in Great Britain by Clays Ltd, Elcograf S.p.A.

Headline's policy is to use papers that are natural, renewable and recyclable
products and made from wood grown in well-managed forests and other
controlled sources. The logging and manufacturing processes are expected
to conform to the environmental regulations of the country of origin.

HEADLINE PUBLISHING GROUP
An Hachette UK Company
Carmelite House
50 Victoria Embankment
London EC4Y 0DZ

www.headlineeternal.com
www.headline.co.uk
www.hachette.co.uk

THE BRIGHT SPOT

CHAPTER 1

Luna Wright awoke to someone nibbling her toes—troubling since she'd gone to bed alone. Well, except for Sprout, her half-deaf, fifteen-year-old rescue mutt, snoring behind her. Cracking open one eye, she lifted her head, eyed her early morning visitor, then sighed and plopped back down. "Dammit Ziggy, we talked about this. It's still dark out." She closed her eyes again, but the bed jiggled impatiently.

With a groan, she sat up. As the manager of Apple Ridge Farm, a small, charming, and let's face it, struggling tree farm and botanical gardens, it was her job to oversee . . . well, everything.

"*Bleeeat.*"

Including their rescue animals, like Dammit Ziggy, their two-month-old orphaned "kid," currently eyeing her with adoration.

"Ugh, you're too cute for your own good." Nudging him aside, she got out of bed. "Stay. I'm just going to the bathroom."

His hooves clicked on the wood floor as he trotted along after her, his expression dialed to: *I'd-feel-more-comfortable-if-we-went-together.*

A few minutes later they exited the bathroom—still together—
freezing in unison as a noise came from her kitchen. Not the still
snoring Sprout. A watchdog he was not. She quickly snatched up
her phone.

"*Bleeeat.*"

"Shh!" She got 911 teed up with one hand, the other over DZ's
mouth. *Please don't be a bear.* "Who's there?" she yelled.

"Shep."

Her farmhand, and she nearly collapsed in relief.

"Is DZ here?" Shep called out. "He ate through the fence again
and got out. You're usually his first stop."

Luna eyed Dammit Ziggy, aka DZ, who nuzzled against her
calf. She looked up when Shep appeared at the end of her hall.
"He ate another post?" she asked.

He nodded. "And then ran straight to you, his mama."

She had to laugh, but it was true. The baby rescues were her
favorite part of this job, and she had a soft spot for DZ, which the
kid—both the goat *and* Shep—knew.

Emergency averted, Shep's gaze caught on Luna's pj's—a
soft, thin camisole and short boy shorts—and he immediately
slapped his hands over his eyes. "Oh shit. I mean crap. I'm sorry,
ma'am." Taking a step back, he tripped over his own feet and fell
on his ass, hands still over his eyes.

He was twenty-one to her almost thirty, so she at least wasn't
corrupting a minor, but his horrified reaction had her turning
back to her room to pull the throw blanket from the foot of her
bed and wrap it around herself. Shep was a good guy and a great
farmhand, able to handle whatever she threw at him, but it'd

taken her six months to get him to call her by her given name and not "ma'am." "Did you hurt yourself?"

"No." He got to his feet with his hands still over his eyes, his Adam's apple bouncing as he swallowed hard. "So . . ." He gestured vaguely toward the door. "I'll just . . ."

"Go? Yes, please, and take DZ with you. *DZ!*"

The goat was eating one of her favorite sneakers. She snatched it back. "Preferably before he eats anything else."

Shep, who looked like the snowboarding bum that he was whenever he wasn't working for her—lanky, lean, rock star hair to his shoulders, long-sleeved T-shirt advertising ski and board wax, high-top work boots unlaced—nodded like a bobblehead.

"I'm pretty sure it's not that bad," she said dryly.

He went beet red. "No, it's *definitely* not bad. I mean, you're put together right nice—" He grimaced. Swallowed again. "Uh, I'm not trying to say you're hot, because that'd imply I—"

"Shep."

"Yeah?"

"*Goodbye.*"

"Right!" He had to come toward her to get Dammit Ziggy, one hand still over his eyes, the other reaching out in front of him.

Oh, for the love of— She passed him, heading for the shower. Sometimes she did YouTube Pilates before work, but . . . well, she hated every minute of it and she wasn't even sure it was working anyway, which made it easy to skip. "I'll see you later."

"Yes, ma'am."

"*Luna,*" she called back.

"Right. Luna. Ma'am."

With a sigh, she shut the bathroom door. She turned on the shower and hopped into the lukewarm water, not waiting for the sixty-second blast of hot, which was all she'd get. Since much of her day was spent outside—that being in the Sierra Mountains in April—she needed that blissful minute. Chilly air or no, spring was in full bloom in Tahoe. It'd been a drought winter, their second in a row, so the snow was mostly gone, the lake already too low, and here at Apple Ridge Farm, they were doing their best to keep the orchards and gardens thriving since their livelihood depended on it.

Twenty minutes later, she was dressed in her usual jeans, boots, and staff sweatshirt. At her side, Sprout wore his usual happy-to-still-be-kickin' attitude, ready to make their morning rounds to ensure everything was as it should be before they opened to the public.

Even when Luna knew everything was *not* as it should be.

A week ago, the owner of the farm, her boss Silas Wittman, had suddenly and unexpectedly passed away. He'd lived eight hours south of Tahoe, in Los Angeles—a fact that had suited everyone since he'd been known as the Grinch, but she couldn't imagine what might happen now.

Five years ago Silas had coaxed her away from a job that had been simply a means to a paycheck. He hadn't been an easy man to work for, long-distance or not, but she'd never regretted taking the position she'd come to love more than anything she'd ever done. Silas had shown up without fail once a quarter to terrify everyone, and had also called Luna bimonthly. He'd been far softer with her than anyone else, answering questions, letting her know she was on track. It'd been . . . comforting, despite his gruff nature. Having him gone rattled her. She'd honestly believed him too tough to ever die.

Would whomever Silas had left the farm to allow them to continue status quo? Or would there be a big shake-up? She had a meeting with the estate attorney later, where she'd no doubt get answers to all her questions good or bad, but at the moment, she felt like that one time she'd gone rock climbing with friends and had gotten stuck a hundred feet above the ground, twirling in the wind.

At her side, Sprout was already wheezing because of his asthma. Heart melting, she scooped up the forty-pound roly-poly sweetheart. "How about a lift?"

He licked her chin and cuddled in for the free ride, the way he had every day since she'd taken him home from the shelter so he wouldn't die alone. That had been two years ago now, and he was thriving.

But now she was the one wheezing as she walked because forty pounds was . . . forty pounds. She adjusted his weight and kept moving, getting another sweet little lick on the chin for her efforts, ensuring she'd carry him forever if need be. Apple Ridge was one hundred and fifty acres, every last corner of the land in use. The wild Sierras circled them in a continuous chain of mountain ranges forming the western "backbone" of the Americas. It was a mix of thick forests, austere rock faces, and lush valleys, and their small corner of it was no exception. The farthest part of the land butted up against a creek. It was there, within hearing distance of the rushing water, that they had seven small cabins—emphasis on small.

Luna lived in the first cabin, and she loved it ridiculously. Employees were in the others. Well, all but the last, which was allegedly haunted by the ghost of someone Silas had once yelled at. Since that list was long, there was no telling who it could be. But ever since one of the seasonal employees had claimed to see a pale, see-through face pressed to the front window several years back, it'd sat empty.

Luna, who'd never seen a ghost herself but wasn't opposed, always looked for a face in the glass. Nothing, so she continued on the trail past the Christmas, cherry, and crab apple tree orchards, past the botanical gardens, slowing at their rescue barn. Inside lived, among others, five chickens (divas, all of them), four goats (the adorable heathens), three pigs (sweet and loving but eternally hungry), two cows (sweetie pies), and a curious emu named Estelle . . . but thankfully no partridge in a pear tree.

Through the open doors, she could see Shep hauling out a bucket of feed for Miss Piggy and Hogwarts, their teacup pigs. At least they'd been told they were teacup pigs when they'd first rescued them at three weeks old. They were now three *years* old and three hundred pounds. *Each.*

Shep looked up and Luna waved. Even from here she could see the scald hit his cheeks. With a sigh, she kept going, heading to the Square, their central location, which held a small farm-to-table café called the Bright Spot, an old horse barn turned souvenir and gift shop called Stella's Place, and the sign-up hut for everything they did seasonally, like hayrides, snow sledding down the two-stories-tall piles of hay barrels, etc. There was also a small coffee shop that had gone out of business and sat temporarily empty until they found a new lessee.

It was the café that she walked to now, the one where they used ingredients grown and foraged on the property, along with goods from other local ranches and farms. Wildflowers bloomed in fat clay pots, framing the porch of the converted old farmhouse, giving it a warmth that would in a few hours be matched by the enticing scents of food wafting out the open windows. Inside would be spotless, the old burnished wood floor gleaming, the shiplap walls smelling of lemon oil, fresh flowers in vases placed on the tables, all thanks to the man named Chef, who ran it.

Luna stopped at the front door, blinking in surprise to see a pic of herself pinned to it with the words *Don't come in unless you finally got some!* written in red Sharpie across the top. "Seriously?" She ripped the photo down, only to find a second one beneath. And a third. And a fourth. "*Oh, come on!*" Setting Sprout on the ground, she yanked down the entire stack and stormed into the café, empty because it was 7:00 a.m. and their front gate didn't open to the public until 10:00 a.m. "Chef, I know you're in here! Show your cowardly face!"

Chef, a dear friend, although soon to be her ex–dear friend, popped his head out of the kitchen with an innocent expression.

As if the man had ever been innocent a single day in his entire life.

He held a chopping knife in one hand and a tomato in the other. "So," he said, gesturing to the flyers in her hand. "Did you?"

"This annoying quest of yours to interfere with my love life—"

"You mean *lack* of love life."

Okay, true. Unfortunately.

"How did last night go?" he asked.

"He didn't show." *He* being her coffee date. To say she wasn't having much luck in the dating world was on par with saying the sky was blue, or summer was hot.

Chef's expression softened. "Honey—"

"No." She jabbed a finger at him. "Don't you *dare* feel sorry for me."

"I don't. You're smart, resilient, resourceful, beautiful—"

She snorted. "You do know that there's no money in the budget for a raise."

"I don't feel sorry for you," he repeated, setting down the knife and tomato to pour her a coffee to go. "I feel sorry for the stupid men who are missing out on you. And yes, I realize I'm one of those stupid men . . ."

Ignoring that, she sniffed the air dramatically. "You know how much I love the smell of your freshly brewed coffee."

"Luna—"

"And you know what else I love? The sound of no one talking to me while I drink it."

He rolled his eyes. "I'm trying to be serious."

She sighed. It wasn't his fault that they'd started dating their freshman year in college and he didn't figure out until his senior year that he preferred men. Love was love, and all that. "I'm fine. It's whatever. But no more blind dates for me. If someone's interested, they're going to need a thousand-word essay on how they will not waste my time."

His smile was charmingly crooked. "Unless they're hot, right?"

"No. The hot ones are assholes."

He put a hand to his chest and pretended to stagger back a step.

"Present company excluded, of course," she said, and lifted her coffee. "Thanks for this. I gotta go."

"Wait." He vanished, then reappeared with a ham bone in a bag. "For Sprout."

Sprout stopped panting and wheezing so his ears, nearly half his height on their own, could perk up.

"It's yours when we get to the office," Luna told the sweetest, steadiest male in her life.

Sprout sighed, but moved under his own steam as they next stopped at Stella's Place. Luna peered in at the once individual horse stalls turned booths, each of which sold a variety of souvenirs and other tchotchkes. "Stella?"

Stella Montgomery, who ran all the booths for the farm, poked her head up from the second booth, where she was shelving some of their locally sourced jelly. "Good night!" the older woman called to Luna gleefully.

Playing the game, Luna smiled. "It's morning."

Sure enough, Stella shook her head. "It's bedtime."

Stella would prefer to be nocturnal. It was rumored she was also a vampire, but since Stella had started those rumors herself, no one took them all that seriously. The seventy-four-year-old had led quite the colorful life, having spent her formidable

years marrying men before giving up the hobby of marriage—
but not men.

She was also Luna's grandma.

Well, her *adoptive* grandma. Luna had been adopted at birth.
She knew nothing of her biological relatives, so she was deeply
emotionally attached to Stella. Stella's daughter, Luna's adoptive
mom, had washed her hands of the older woman for being "difficult," but Luna had refused to do the same. For one thing, Stella
had never let her down. So when Luna's mom had had enough
of her mom's antics, and when no retirement home wanted her,
Luna had happily taken her in and given her a job.

Stella's Place was very popular, mostly because she was so colorful, told fortunes, and sold fun stuff, and people madly loved
all of it. And Luna madly loved her. Just as she loved her entire
crew, and her life here. The problem was, they'd had some good
years, but also some bad, possibly more of those than good. But
they were a Tahoe local and tourist staple, and beloved. Surely
that would mean something to whoever was in charge of their
fate now.

Her chest tightened at the reminder that in a few short hours,
she'd most likely hear that fate, and the future for both the farm
and herself.

Or if any of them even had a future here at all.

CHAPTER 2

At 5:00 p.m., Luna sat in her beat-up truck, stunned. She'd just left Silas's attorney's office and now sat in the parking lot of the local tavern Olde Tahoe Tap, her feet not in sync with her brain. This was what happened when you got life-changing news, which in turn pulled the rug out from beneath your feet, leaving your world in free fall. She glared at the mirror. *"Just get out of the car."*

Her reflection did not, in fact, get out of the truck.

"Talking to yourself again?" came a female voice from outside Luna's open driver-side window. The voice belonged to Willow Green, her best friend since the dawn of time, and the farm's botanical gardens genius.

Luna drew a careful breath. "First off, thanks for the almost heart attack. And I'll have you know, talking to yourself is a sign of intelligence."

"Except you only talk to yourself when something's wrong. Plus you're never late for our weekly drink date, and yet you're twenty minutes tardy. So what's wrong?"

"Nothing."

Willow pointed at her. "You just blinked twice."

"So?"

"So, that's your tell. You're lying." Willow gasped. "Wait. Are our jobs okay? Omigod, please tell me the attorney said our jobs are okay. I just bought this jacket. Do I need to return it and commence panicking?"

"No panicking." Luna was doing enough of that for the both of them.

"Then what's wrong?" Willow put her hand to her heart. "Don't tell me. Silas didn't make my promotion official before he died."

Luna drew in a careful breath because she was about to lie to her very best friend. A few months back, Willow had started asking Luna to see if Silas would promote her to manager, meaning that some of the farmhands would report to her directly. And Luna had actually started to bring it up in her last call with Silas, but he'd stopped her halfway.

"Don't ask me," he said. "Leave yourself room for plausible deniability because my answer is a resounding 'hell no.'"

Because he knew that while Willow was amazing at running the botanical gardens, she wasn't amazing at managing people.

In fact, she was shit at it.

"I'm sorry, Willow," she said softly. "He didn't leave any word." See, that wasn't a regular lie, it was a mercy lie, because she saw no reason to hurt Willow's feelings with Silas gone.

Willow was quiet a moment, then nodded. "Thanks for trying."

Feeling like a jerk, she nodded. "Of course." Desperate to deflect to give herself time to process what she'd learned at the attorney's, she searched for a diversion. She took in Willow's new killer leather jacket, dark jeans, and knee-high boots, making her look as if maybe she just walked off the shoot for the cover of a magazine. "You work in dirt for a living. How do you always look like a million bucks all the livelong day?"

Willow shrugged. "Look like a million bucks, feel like a million bucks." She paused. "Even if on the inside my yoga pose is downward spiral." She opened Luna's car door. "Come on. Suddenly I really need that drink."

"I'm so sorry, Willow."

"Not your fault." She looked Luna over as she slid out of the truck. She wore one of only two dressy outfits in her closet: a black fitted blazer over a silky white tank top, a short black skirt, and her one pair of strappy heels, also black.

Willow shook her head. "You've had that outfit since our junior year in college when you had both a job interview and a funeral for a professor in the same week."

"And?"

"And . . ." Willow gave a reluctant admiring smile. "It still looks great on you. But you've got to dress for the life you want if we're ever going to get to our success pact. Which I now need more than ever to happen."

They'd promised to someday open a B and B together and be their own bosses. They'd been sixteen at the time, working for a veterinarian, shoveling out the animal crates. It'd been a shit job. Literally. But they'd had a lot of time on their hands to dream big. Guilt lancing through her, Luna started walking toward the tavern. The building, just across the street from the stunning Lake Tahoe, had been designed to look like a Swiss Alps village, the walls stone with wood accents, pitched roofs, faux balconies and balustrades, all of it lit with fairy lights, looking welcoming and warm.

Luna was glad they'd decided to meet here. She also really needed a drink, considering the stress and shock bouncing around in her chest from what she'd learned at the attorney's.

Silas Wittman had left her 50 percent ownership of the farm.

Fifty percent . . .

The other half had gone to a man named Jameson Hayes, a business associate of Silas's, and she was to meet this new partner of hers tomorrow morning at the farm.

Oh, and they owed a big fat balloon payment to a group of investors in sixty days for the loan the farm had been given for renovations done five years ago.

But none of that had even been the doozy. Nope, that honor went to the fact that, as it turned out, Silas had been her biological grandfather.

No word, of course, on why he'd kept that a secret. The attorney had said Silas hadn't commented on it, but his personal theory was that her grandfather hadn't known how to approach her after all this time, and was concerned she might even resent his interference in her life at this late date. He'd possibly been worried she'd leave the farm, and he clearly wanted her to feel like she belonged.

So . . . guilt had kept him silent. That was her takeaway, and her head was still spinning.

She'd always been so proud of the fact she'd gotten her job on merit. But she hadn't. Clearly, Silas had brought her here out of a sense of guilt. Why else wouldn't he have also told her who he was? Hell, maybe she'd disappointed him. Or worse, he'd been ashamed of her . . .

And now she'd never know.

Willow's phone rang, but she made no move to pull it from her pocket.

Luna looked at her.

"I'm not answering."

"Maybe it's Shayne," Luna said, looking for any conversation that didn't involve what had happened today.

Shayne had always been their third musketeer. He and Willow had eloped at age eighteen because their parents had forbidden them to.

"Look," Willow said, "some things are just not meant to be."

Truer than she could know. "But you and Shayne aren't one of those things."

"Well, the universe super disagrees with you, so . . ."

"Do you know how I know love exists?" Luna asked.

Willow sighed. "Luna—"

"Remember that barbecue you had five months ago now with a whole bunch of people, and you ate too much and accidentally farted at the exact moment the room got quiet—"

"Oh my God." Willow looked around them. "*Shh!*"

"And Shayne fanned his hand in the air and said 'Sorry, everyone, I just stepped on a frog.'" Luna smiled. "He claimed your fart, Willow. If that's not love, I don't know what is. It was always love at first sight for you two."

"I don't believe in love at first sight. I believe in *annoyed* at first sight." Willow paused. "He called me twice today, and I didn't pick up."

"I know. He came by work to make sure you were okay, but you'd left to go make a supply run. He brought you one of your ridiculously complicated coffee orders. It was very romantic. And delicious."

Willow's mouth fell open. "You drank my romantic coffee?"

"Well, I couldn't let it go to waste."

Shaking her head, Willow opened the front doors to the tavern, music and laughter spilling out. They found two empty barstools.

"He brought me coffee," Willow muttered, still shaking her head. "How is that respecting my request for space? I need it after what he did."

"Bringing you coffee doesn't mean he's not respecting your need for space. It means he misses you. And I know damn well you miss him."

"Do not."

Luna rolled her eyes. "You hate to sleep alone. When we were kids, you'd climb out your window and into mine and make me share my pillow."

"You had a good pillow."

It was much, much more than that, and they both knew it. Neither of them had grown up in the best of circumstances.

"And," Luna went on gently, "two nights ago you knocked on my door at two in the morning."

"Well, your bedroom window was locked."

Luna felt her heart squeeze. "You wanted to have a sleepover."

"Because my feet were cold. You always have warm feet."

"Just admit that you hate to sleep alone," Luna said.

"Fine. That too."

They ordered a pitcher of Hawaiian margaritas because Willow loved an umbrella in her drink. When it came, complete with two glasses and the required umbrellas, Willow poured and they silently toasted. That was the thing about being best friends with someone since the age of six. Sometimes words weren't needed.

Although Luna needed to find the words to tell Willow about Silas's will. Mind whirling, she looked around. The crowd was mostly local this evening, the music an eclectic mix. A few brave souls were even on the dance floor.

Willow took it all in with a grim expression. "I just still don't get it. Shayne and I were happy in New Mexico, and then out of nowhere, he took the interim fire captain's job here without even consulting me."

"I'm not excusing that," Luna said. "But you've been wanting to come back to Sunrise Cove since the day you guys moved away for his first firefighter job in Mammoth seven years ago."

"And instead we bounced to Denver. Then Spokane. And Albuquerque."

"Wasn't that to log the experience he needed to end up back here?"

Willow sipped her drink. "Next convo, please."

Right. She was up. "So—"

"*Omigod*." Willow leaned in close. "Okay, don't look, but just behind you is a hottie suit—"

Luna swiveled on her barstool. Next to her was an empty barstool, and then the "hottie suit," or so she presumed since there was only one man in the place who fit the description.

"I said don't look!"

Yeah, well, she'd never been all that great at following directions. The man was leaning against the bar like he had all the time in the world; tie loose, top two buttons undone on his shirt, hair a little tousled like maybe he'd shoved his fingers through it.

"He's looking over here," Willow whispered.

"Yeah, at *you*."

Willow grinned in delight. "Nope, it's the mile of leg you're showing. I don't know when you finally shaved above your knees in celebration of winter going away, but I approve. And you're even wearing mascara. Didn't know you had any. The last time you used mascara was at senior prom, and you ended up in the ER for poking yourself in the eye."

"It wasn't prom, it was seventh grade, and I wear mascara all the time."

"Name *one* time."

Well, crap. She couldn't remember.

"Exactly," Willow said smugly, then got serious. "Look, you're already wearing your good clothes. You might as well show off, especially since out of the two of us, you're the one with your shit together."

Luna snorted. Whatever the opposite of having your shit together was, she was *that*.

"Just casually turn back and make conversation. See where it goes. Maybe you'll get lucky tonight."

"Oh, no." Luna shook her head so vehemently she got dizzy. "The last time I had a one-night stand, I ended up in a long-term relationship with a guy who three years later realized he was gay."

"Okay, that was bad," Willow admitted. "But you and Chef are still great friends, so there's that. And you've dated since then. Just not successfully. And honey, if there's one thing I'm sure of, it's that you deserve a man who'll give you everything and respect the wonderful, fiery, generous, kindhearted, independent woman you are. Besides, one of us needs to get back up on that horse. It can't be me because I'm still stupidly in love with my stupid husband."

Luna squeezed her hand. "You know he loves you."

"Oh shit." Willow slid lower on her seat. "A bunch of Shayne's coworkers just showed up." She put on her fake smile and waved at a table. "It's a birthday party for the police chief," she whispered. "I forgot that was tonight. I RSVP'd that I couldn't make it."

"They're gesturing for you to join them."

Willow reluctantly got to her feet. "Go flirt with the hottie suit, okay? For me? Just don't talk about the farm."

"What? Why not?"

"Because that's all you ever talk about."

Okay, possibly true. But the farm was her life. "You're just leaving so I won't keep bugging you about your marriage."

"Bingo."

"Come on, you don't have to—" But Luna was talking to air, and guilt swamped her. She'd just let the perfect opportunity to tell Willow walk off. She'd clammed up because the truth was she felt guilty about the unexpected windfall. And there was something else. She was terrified of Willow and her crew looking at her like she was the new Grinch. Just the thought had indigestion bubbling up in her chest, and suddenly she was breathing funny. Panic, of course. It'd been a while since her last panic attack, but she remembered what to do. She inhaled through her nose for a seven count, then held it for four, then exhaled for . . . Crap, was it seven-four-eight, or seven-eight-four?

"Actually four-seven-eight works best."

Startled at the realization she must have spoken out loud, she swiveled to find Hottie Suit looking at her, not with interest but concern. Great. On top of lying to her best friend, she now also made men look at her with worry instead of interest.

CHAPTER 3

Trying to be cool, Luna raised her eyebrows at Suit.

He smiled kindly. "I used to have panic attacks as a kid."

"Oh, this isn't a panic attack." Wow. Such a liar tonight. She inhaled for a four count, then held for seven. Released for eight . . . except she couldn't exhale for that long, so she went back to inhaling.

"Slower." His voice was low and calm as he sat down on the barstool next to her. "Otherwise you'll need a paper bag, or worse, chest compressions."

"Another drink and I might take you up on that," she quipped, her smart-ass mouth taking over, as it always did when she was feeling awkward.

Which was a lot.

His mouth quirked up on one side. "The paper bag or the chest compressions?"

She choked on her inhale. She reached for her drink, but it was empty, and Willow had taken the pitcher with her . . .

Suit gestured for the bartender. "Two more of whatever she's having."

She looked at him. "You're going to drink a Hawaiian margarita with an umbrella?"

He shrugged. "I'm gender secure."

This tugged a laugh out of her. He was surprisingly and effortlessly disarming, and she was *not* used to being disarmed. She had a reputation for being a fair boss, but she was far too jaded to be easily charmed. Or easily anything'd.

The bartender set the drinks in front of them.

Suit took a sip without removing his umbrella and it bumped against his nose. He should've looked ridiculous, but instead he looked like he was in on the joke, which was surprisingly attractive.

"Can we order some apps?" he asked the bartender.

"Sure. What'll you have?"

"What's good here?"

"Everything," the bartender said. "But the sliders and fries are out of this world."

Suit looked at Luna.

"It's true," she said.

Which was how she found herself sitting with a man she didn't know, eating mini burgers and fries that tasted crackalicious.

"I've been to a lot of places," Suit said, "but these curly fries . . ."

"I'm pretty sure they're an illegal substance."

He chuckled, and it was a low, masculine sound that cut through the anxiety she'd felt ever since she'd walked out of the attorney's office earlier.

"I was going to skip dinner and take my exhausted ass straight to bed," he said. "But this is much better."

Luna smiled. "I'm exhausted too, but every time I say that out loud, my step app sends me a message that I've only taken twenty-three steps today." She watched him drag a fry through a mountain of ketchup and eat it with genuine pleasure. "So what brings you to Sunrise Cove?" she heard herself ask. "Business or pleasure?"

"Maybe I'm a local."

"Not in that amazing suit that screams big city, you aren't."

He looked amused. "Business. Although, I'm never opposed to pleasure."

"Me either." She shook her head. "Wait, strike that from the record. My mouth ran off without my brain's permission again. It's been doing that all day. I should've said I have pleasure limits."

He grinned. "Do you want to discuss them?"

Luna laughed again, because damn. Good looking *and* funny. "Let me try that again. I've got serious time restraints regarding fun because I work around the clock. And clearly . . ." She pushed her drink away. "No more refills for me." Mostly because she couldn't take her eyes off his mouth. As in she wanted to do something wild, like have that one-night stand Willow had talked about. "In case you can't tell, I've forgotten how to converse with a man."

"You're better than you think," he said easily. "Do you want the last slider? It's all yours."

Nope, a slider wasn't what she wanted at all. "I blame the Hawaiian margaritas," she blurted out.

"Yeah?" He smiled that crooked smile. "I blame the chemistry."

She almost looked behind her to see who he was talking to. "You're feeling chemistry with me?"

"Yes. Aren't you?"

"I don't know. I'm sort of out of practice at chemistry."

Their knees accidentally brushed together and damn, she *did* feel it. "Okay, maybe a *little* chemistry," she admitted. "Good thing we're strangers and never going to see each other again or I'd be running for the hills. I'm not dating right now."

"What's wrong with dating?"

She shuddered. "Men are what's wrong with dating."

"I'm a man."

No kidding. "Nothing personal, but my last few attempts got me food poisoning, a sprained ankle, and stood up."

He shook his head, like he was maybe apologizing for his entire gender. He lifted his drink. "To being strangers then."

"Who will never see each other again," she repeated, more to remind herself than him.

He chuckled, but nodded his agreement, just as out of the corner of her eye, she accidentally locked gazes with Willow, who beamed and gave her a double thumbs-up.

Luna ignored this and pulled out her cell, currently buzzing with an incoming text. "Sorry, just have to make sure it's not work."

GRAM: Hi, honey, can I say "this meeting got lit" if I mean people are getting upset? And by people, I mean your mother.

Luna snorted and typed back: No, but you can say she got salty.

"Something you can share with the class?" Suit asked, smiling at her amusement.

"My grandma's trying to use the word 'lit' in a sentence."

He laughed. "This is really nice after a shitty week."

She felt a surge of sympathy. "Same."

He cocked his head. "Yeah? Because I'm talking *epically* bad week."

"Again, same."

He gestured to her. "You first."

Deciding she couldn't talk about losing Silas, not yet, she drew a deep breath, aware that on a scale of zero to tipsy, she was a full-on seven. But hell, she wasn't going to ever see this guy again, and maybe that was the whole point. "I thought work was going okay," she finally said. "My boss was miserly with praise, but he let me think everything was fine. I mean, sure, we don't always make our monthly budget, but it wasn't my department. But now . . . now it is."

He was brows up. "You didn't think it was a problem that you don't always end up in the black? How often does that even happen?"

"Hey, we do our best."

He shook his head on a rough laugh. "I mean this with the utmost respect, but here's to never having to work together."

She grimaced. "You're a numbers guy."

"You could say that."

"What else could I say?" she asked.

"I'm in mergers and acquisitions."

She stared at him. "Like a corporate raider?"

"I prefer organizational restructuring," he said with a small smile. "But yes. And my point is, numbers are important. Numbers *balancing* are important."

"I mean, I hear you," she said, waving a curly fry around for emphasis. "I do. I just think there's a lot more that goes into a successful business than numbers."

He was smiling again. "Such as?"

"I don't know . . ." She racked her slightly addled brain. "Joy in the work itself. Fixating solely on profit doesn't motivate the employees to make success happen. Plus, customers don't appreciate being seen just for their revenue. They have choices about where they spend their money, and I pride myself on giving them something they can't get anywhere else. Luckily, I've aligned myself with a crew who feel the same."

"Will they still align with you when you go out of business?"

His voice was teasing, so she took no offense. He was hot as hell, but clearly knew little about people. "We're not going out of business," she said. *Hoped.* "Your turn. What happened this week that made it so rough?"

"I've got to go save a business from ruin by the manager, who's skating by on nepotism and sweet charm."

"Well, that sounds awful."

He shrugged. "I've had worse assignments. Should I be worried about your best friend, who's trying to catch your attention?"

Willow had nearly fallen out of her chair *twice*, and both times Luna had done her best to ignore her. "No."

"She isn't having a seizure, is she?"

"No." Luna shifted slightly so he couldn't see Willow as easily and managed a smile. "So where's home?"

He lifted a broad shoulder. "Haven't figured out where I fit yet."

How many years had she spent feeling like she didn't know where she fit either? All of them, that's how many. She picked up her glass and watched him as she took a sip. He really was very good looking. Leanly fit, dark brown hair, his eyes an intriguing, warm mix of green and gold. And wow, she'd been here entirely too long if she was noticing how warm his gaze seemed. "You're not one of those guys who tucks their wedding ring into their pocket before entering a bar, are you?"

"I'm the guy who gets dumped long before there's a ring," he said wryly. "Well, except the one time when my fiancée walked out my door and never came back." He gave her a small smile when she gasped. "It's okay. It was mostly my fault since I'm constantly on the road. My life doesn't lend itself to relationships." He paused, looking into her eyes. "Your turn."

"I'm not really a jewelry sort of girl, so . . ." She waggled her fingers. "Ring free."

He smiled. "I give you my deep, dark, sad getting dumped story and all you give me back is you're not a jewelry sort of girl?"

"Okay, but this is going to be embarrassing."

He gave her the "let me have it" hands.

She sighed. "Apparently I'm . . . 'too much.'" She finished her second and last drink. "Or not enough." She shrugged. "Depends on who you ask."

When he didn't say anything, she met his gaze, realizing he'd lost the smile. "I hope you rearranged their favorite body parts," he said. "Men are assholes."

"I'm not going to disagree with that." Not ready to go deep again, she went for a subject change. "What do you do to recover from a bad week?"

His smile was suggestive and sexy as hell.

Note to self: *not quite ready for prime-time flirting.* "Oh boy." She fanned a hand in front of her face. "It's hot in here. Is it hot in here? I'm feeling flustered."

He covered her hand with one of his, ran the pad of his thumb over her knuckles. "Just two strangers sitting in a bar, right?"

"Right." She drew a shaky breath. "No one's going to see each other's undies. Which is a good thing because I can't remember if mine are cute today. I guess guys don't worry about their undies being cute."

"How do you know I'm wearing any?"

Hot flash. "I mean . . ." She picked up her glass, but oh yeah, it was empty. Damn. "We can just be whoever we want to be, right . . . ?"

"Absolutely. So . . . who do you want to be?"

And because he seemed genuinely interested, she answered. "How about a smart, witty, charismatic woman flirting with a hot stranger in a bar?"

He smiled, eyes warm and amused. "Do you always say everything you think?"

She grimaced a little. "It's an affliction."

"I like it."

And she liked him. Probably it was the margaritas, but he was everything she'd just said she wanted to be: smart, witty, charismatic, and . . . something she couldn't seem to manage nearly as easily—sexy. Not belonging had been a huge theme in her life, but right then, right there, with him looking at her like she might be the sexiest, funniest, smartest woman he'd ever met, she felt like she *did* belong. The feeling was so foreign, she did something she'd never expected. She leaned in a little to better hear him in the noisy bar, but also because she wanted to kiss him.

Badly.

And then he leaned in too, slowly meeting her halfway, both of them waiting for the other to back off. She knew it wouldn't be him because he broke into what could only be called the hottest smile she'd ever seen, his teeth biting into his lower lip for a second.

Helplessly, she smiled back . . . and then their mouths touched for a teasing, soft, delicious kiss before they gently broke free to stare at each other. He opened his mouth to say something, but desperately afraid the moment would be over, she kissed him again. This earned her a heartfelt groan from the back of his throat and she melted at the sound, wanting more, much more, because the taste of him made her clothes want to fall off.

But that might've been the tequila.

And then while her blood was thrumming in her ears—and elsewhere—he pulled back and sat very still, suddenly looking serious. Maybe he was thinking about the things he wanted to do to her. *She* was certainly thinking about the things she wanted to do to him, so she went in for another kiss and . . . he hesitated. Like *hesitated* hesitated. Horrified, she pulled back, and face hot, she hopped off her barstool. "Sorry. I just remembered I've gotta go."

He caught her hand. "No, wait. You don't understand."

She drew a deep breath. "Are you about to say 'it's not you, it's me'? Because I've heard that one this month already."

He grimaced, ran his free hand through his hair, which explained the tousled look. "Look, I'm sorry. I really don't usually combine business and pleasure. I just didn't expect this, or you, and I can't—*shouldn't*—"

With a rough laugh, she tugged free and backed away. "You don't have to explain yourself. Just strangers in a bar, the end, right?" She dropped some money on the bar and left, pulling up her Uber app as she did since she'd had a few drinks. She'd get a ride for her car in the morning.

Annnd . . . that was a wrap on another day when she'd acted like she knew what she was doing.

Outside in the chilly April night air, she sat on a bench to wait, resting her head back. The night sky was dark with storm clouds.

Same as her life.

And even as she watched, a few lazy raindrops drifted down almost as if in slow motion while her brain churned out flashes of warm lips and goose bumps erupted across her entire body.

She didn't want Suit's rejection to affect her, but it was an unfortunate pattern in her life. When things weren't perfect, when *she* wasn't perfect, people pulled back from her. Her family. Her friends. And tonight, even a perfect stranger.

CHAPTER 4

Willow was warmly greeted at the police chief's birthday party, but it would have been so much easier if she hadn't been. She tried to keep a genuine smile on her face, but it kept slipping. Being back in Tahoe was a mixed bag of emotions. She loved the four distinct seasons. Loved the scent of the trees and the mountains, and the lake she'd practically lived in as a kid.

But she also felt . . . well, embarrassed. She'd left here seven years ago with Shayne, barely a penny to their names, determined to make something of themselves and come back more successful than when they'd left. Shayne had definitely succeeded.

She had not.

She was a logical person, a relatively smart person. She had goals. She wanted to run her own company, and she wanted to be her own boss. But she hadn't achieved either of those things. And yes, fine, she blamed Shayne. One, for moving them around as he kept getting promoted, and two, for agreeing with her years ago, each having been barely raised or wanted by their respective parents, that they never wanted kids. They wouldn't know how to be good parents, they'd said, and had bonded over that.

Only she'd turned thirty this year, and . . . well, the thought of being a mom no longer brought on a full-blown panic attack.

Just half of one.

The thing was, when you were twenty and had goals you hadn't achieved, whatever. There was plenty of time.

But at thirty, it felt like she had a whole lot less time.

It didn't help that Luna seemed to have met her goals. It wasn't a contest, she knew this, but Luna managed the farm and was basically the boss. Plus, she'd hired Willow, which felt a whole lot like a pity job. Willow loved her, loved her so damn much, and she was so incredibly proud of her, but she couldn't handle being pitied.

She'd hoped, so badly, to get a promotion . . .

All around her, people were laughing and chatting, and as she half listened to their banter and stories, she realized *everyone* had grown up and gone on with their lives while she'd been gone. They were all in a good place.

And she was in the same old place where she'd been when she'd left. Feeling a little bit lonely even though it had been her own idea, she turned to go and—

—Bumped into a man in a firefighter T-shirt and jeans. For a beat, they did the awkward dance where both of them tried to avoid a collision.

Finally, he laughed and slid his hands familiarly to her hips, giving her a zing of awareness she hadn't had since the last time her husband—er, her *estranged* husband—had touched her. She drew a deep breath as her heart constricted hard. "What are you doing here?"

Shayne smiled. "I was invited, same as you. Still trying to make the connections with everyone here. Go big or go home, right?"

"Do *not* underestimate my willingness to go home. It's literally my only goal at all times."

Shayne smiled. And he smelled good. *And* then there was how he was looking at her, which made her forget why she was mad at him in the first place. He'd *always* had that effect on her.

"It's good to see you, Wills." His eyes were soaking her up, same as hers. "Maybe I could buy you a drink."

He said this in his bedroom voice. And his eyes were his bedroom eyes, and damn. It melted her bones. So she locked her traitorous knees and jabbed a finger into his chest. "Stop that."

"Stop what?"

"Trying to charm me out of my clothes."

That earned her a full-out grin. "Is it working?"

She blew out a breath. *Yes*, though she'd die before admitting it. "Look, we've talked about this. Sure, we were high school sweethearts, but people change."

"I haven't."

She gave him a get-real look. "We've *both* changed. It used to be I was happy letting you job hop to get the time and experience you needed to land the promotion and the job of your heart. And you did it, you're now interim captain and I'm happy for you. Really happy . . . but I didn't realize it would be at the expense of me, Shayne. I've not been able to get anywhere in a job because we never stayed long enough."

He looked over the crowd for a moment, then back to her. "You know exactly why I left the Swift Water Rescue team in New Mexico for this job."

She did. Swift Water Rescue was like Special Forces. They were specifically and brutally trained, and it was extremely dangerous. Shayne lost two firefighters from his unit last year, and the job nearly killed him as well, which in turn had given her nightmares. Losing him had become one of her biggest fears, and he'd clearly taken her fears very seriously. "I know," she said softly.

"Then you also know that I heard you when you said you couldn't handle me staying in such a dangerous job. I willingly made the change because it makes sense for us."

"But we're not an 'us.'"

He shifted a little nearer, bowing his head close to hers. "No matter if we get back together or not, we're always going to be an us in some form."

She refused to be moved. Not when he'd revised their history slightly. "We both know the real problem. You were offered an interim captain position in New Mexico, where we were already settled. You turned it down, but then took the exact same job in Sunrise Cove." She shook her head. "That sucked for me, Shayne, and worse, you made the decision for the both of us."

"But we both always wanted to get back here, and thanks to the job, it happened."

"Are you not hearing me on purpose?" she asked. "We're back here because *you* made the decision, accepting the job without talking with me first. I loved where we were, and I'd just started my own landscaping business—which I had to give up. For you. Just another of my dreams gone to dust."

His eyes softened with regret. "But you've got a great job with Luna now, and you've always wanted to work together."

"Yes, great, my best friend gave me a pity job, whatever. There's not much flexibility or a lot of options." She paused. "Silas didn't leave any word on a promotion for me."

"Ah, Wills, I'm so sorry." His voice was low, agonized as he tenderly squeezed her hips. "More sorry than I can say. I didn't realize how you felt—"

"Because you didn't want to."

"Because you don't often tell me your real feelings," he corrected gently. "And no, I can't guess them. I've tried. I honestly thought coming back here would make you happy. Can you try to believe that?"

She blew out a breath, hating that Luna had been right. She *didn't* like to talk about her feelings. In fact, she hated her feelings. Hated that she felt so irrational all the time. Shaking her head, she said, "I'm sorry too, but I don't know if we belong together anymore. We've grown apart, Shayne, and want different things."

His eyes registered surprise. And hurt. "You sure about that?"

She realized she had one hand on his chest, the other on his arm. Dammit. Yanking her hands back, she looked around, realizing that several pairs of eyes were on them. "I don't want to talk about this in here."

He gave a nod, though she knew he didn't care what anyone thought. But he led her outside, where they ended up just off the cobblestone walkway between the tavern and the bakery, tucked in a corner under a tall pine tree. She looked up. As far as evenings went, it was a doozy. Just past sunset, which meant the sky was stunning, streaked with shades of purple, red, and orange, all set against a backdrop of staggeringly tall, majestic mountains.

Straightening, she met Shayne's eyes, hooded now, not giving away any of his thoughts. There was a time when she could've easily guessed what was going on in his mind, but he was getting surprisingly good at hiding himself from her, and had been from the day she'd moved out of their little home four months ago, two months after they'd come back to Tahoe.

Shortly thereafter he'd begun staying at the firehouse so she could have their home, because he was a good man. Probably this would be less painful if he wasn't. With a sigh, she leaned back against the tree.

Pressing into her a little bit, making her body hum with anticipation, he braced a hand on the trunk beside her shoulder. "So. Let's talk."

Willow was suddenly realizing she didn't want to talk at all, inside or outside. She wanted something else entirely. So she went up on tiptoes and kissed him, and for one heart-stopping beat, his mouth clung to hers. But then it was gone. When she opened her eyes, she saw that he'd taken a step back. "What?"

He gave a slow headshake. "Every time we do this, I think we're back together and it confuses me."

She drew a deep breath. Okay, so they'd had a few breakup sexcapades. "I'm not trying to confuse you. I just still feel . . ." She searched for the right word. "Messed up. My brain needs more time."

His eyes never left hers. His hand, back on her hip, tightened slightly, his thumb making a lazy sweep that set off a whole bunch of reactions inside. "And your body?"

She flashed what she hoped was a sexy smile and not a needy one. "Needs you."

He dropped his head and studied his shoes for a moment, then tilted his face up to the sky as if searching for words.

"It's not like we haven't slept together since we broke up," she said.

He gave a rough laugh. "We're not sleeping together, Willow. Every time you look at me with those sexy amber eyes, we fall into bed. But not for sleep."

"We don't always fall into bed. Last time it was the supply shed behind the fire station. The time before that was in your truck when we went up to Hidden Falls so you could check on something for work."

He went to open his mouth and she kissed him again. He groaned against her lips, a big, warm hand sliding to the back of her neck, his fingers tangling in her hair as he took over the kiss, which she didn't mind at all since he was so good at it.

"Shit," he muttered when they broke apart for air, dropping his forehead to hers. "We're going to do this, aren't we?"

"Your call," she said demurely.

He gave her a look that was at once frustration personified and yet smoking hot. Then he took her hand in his and tugged her along with him.

And she went gladly.

CHAPTER 5

Jameson Hayes's eyes flew open and he stilled, trying to figure out what woke him. The rhythmic thumping against the wall behind his head was a big clue. It was 4:00 a.m. and the people in the room next to him had to be Energizer bunnies because they'd been going at it since midnight.

Letting out a long exhale, he scrubbed his hands down his face. He'd bought earplugs, but they hadn't been able to drown out the sound of the bed hitting the wall at the rate of three thumps per second. This damn hotel. This damn small Podunk town. This damn whole set of circumstances that had led him here in the first place. The circumstances that had a wave of grief rolling over him, so heavy he couldn't get a grip on it. Or the fact he'd lost the man who'd been a pseudo father to him.

Silas Wittman would be annoyed by Jameson's grief. He'd been about as cozy as a porcupine and tough as steel, but he'd treated Jameson well, teaching him the skills he'd needed to survive, along with other useful things such as compartmentalizing rather than getting derailed by things like messy emotions.

Giving up on sleep, Jameson tossed his covers aside and dressed for a run. Sure, it was only thirty degrees outside, but he'd worked out in far worse conditions. He found a designated trail that led him along the lake and started running. The view took his breath away.

Or maybe that was the windchill factor.

In either case, Lake Tahoe, aka the "lake of the sky," was the purest color of azure blue he'd ever seen. Heart-stopping, really, as was the three-hundred-and-sixty-degree view of the lush mountain peaks that surrounded it, some of them still dotted with snow. The sky was slowly shifting colors from black to dark purples and blues to warm reds and pinks. A slight warming of the day had the rocks on the shore letting off curling tendrils of steam rising into the air.

Jameson wasn't a sentimental man, and as his life was mostly lived out of a suitcase, he didn't collect . . . well, anything. But for the first time in memory, he wanted to stop and take a picture.

He didn't. The reasons why were all sorts of complicated, the biggest being he wasn't exactly happy to be here. He understood that Apple Ridge Farm meant a lot to the local population, and also to the tourists who found it. But as investments went, it sucked. The smart decision would've been for Silas to sell it eons ago. But five years ago, he'd finally located his biological granddaughter and brought her here to run the place.

It'd been a gift to her, and she'd had no idea.

Jameson had never understood why Silas hadn't told her who he was. But then again, Silas had given Jameson so much, and he hadn't understood that either. He'd once asked the old man why him, a perfect stranger? Silas had shrugged and said, "I know

I'm a hard-ass and no one likes me. I couldn't give a shit about that. What I give a shit about is helping the people I believe in. And I believe in you, Jameson."

And, apparently, also in Luna Wright.

Today would be his first time back to Apple Ridge Farm in ten years. He'd been twenty-two then, and Silas had shown him the property he'd long ago inherited from his grandfather. The two of them had stood in the middle of the hundred and fifty acres with an architect and an engineer, Silas beaming with pride as he explained his plan to finally rebuild his family's farming legacy.

And now he was gone and he'd left Jameson 50 percent.

Of course, Silas being Silas, the gift had come with a request that he knew Jameson would never refuse him. A year ago, Silas had come to Jameson with a favor. He'd said, "If something happens to me, go to the farm. Help her either get that place ready to sell or help her save it, whatever she wants, without telling her I sent you. If you tell her what you're doing and why, she'll not trust you either. Give her at least a month, preferably two, of your time, but don't tell her I've asked this of you."

Jameson had pushed back some, asking Silas to just tell her he'd happily come and be there for as long as she needed. Silas had refused. He didn't want her to think that he hadn't believed in her. He said that she'd always, always been on her own, and a lot of that was his family's fault, and he hated that they'd failed her. "This is how I want it done," he'd said. "And you owe me."

Jameson had reluctantly agreed. Of course, that had been back when Jameson had thought the old man would live forever. At the memories, he stopped running to bend over, hands on his knees, sucking in air along with his grief. He'd taken a two-month leave of absence from work, so he might as well settle in and get on with it.

Which is why at 9:00 a.m. sharp, he arrived at the farm for his meeting with Apple Ridge Farm's manager and his new partner.

The front gate was wide open. He knew they let the general public in at ten, but not being the general public, he let himself in. The place was admittedly beautiful. He could see a field of tulips, each line a different color so the entire crop looked like a glorious rainbow. Beyond that were the orchards, with the cherry blossoms in full bloom.

He was still taking it all in when he was goosed. Hands on his ass, he whipped around and came face-to-face with an emu. "No dinner first?"

The emu cocked his . . . *her?* . . . head to the side and just looked at him, eyes warm and curious.

"Are you the greeting committee?" he asked.

The emu's head cocked to the other side.

"I'm going to walk past you now, if that's okay."

Another head tilt.

Moving slowly and carefully, Jameson walked past the massive bird and ended up in the Square, the designated meeting spot. He was waiting for Luna Wright to show up when, shockingly, the sexy, adorable, and possibly unhinged woman from the bar appeared. He hadn't gone home with her last night, but she'd most definitely come home with him. She'd stuck in his head, even though she wore complicated like other women wore perfume.

And he was not a fan of complicated.

At the sight of him, she stopped short. "*You*." She narrowed her eyes. "Are you stalking me or something?"

He had to laugh. She had a way of doing that, he'd give her that much. "I was just about to ask you the same thing."

She craned her neck to make sure no one was around, and even though there wasn't, she still lowered her voice. "It's pretty rude to show up at someone's place of work after you refused to sleep with them."

"I didn't refuse to sl—"

She lifted a finger, signaling she didn't want to hear it. "We're not even open yet, so I'm not sure how you got in, but you have to go. I've got a meeting, though he's a few minutes late." She pulled out her phone and sent a text.

Two seconds later, Jameson's phone pinged an incoming text and he stilled. *Oh shit . . .*

At the same time, her head whipped up, her expression dialed to shock. "What was that? Was that a text? Tell me that wasn't a text."

He looked at his phone. "It's from the person I'm meeting, farm manager Luna Wright."

"Jameson Hayes?" she whispered.

"In the flesh."

"Oh crap." She put a hand to her forehead, like this was the very worst possible thing that could happen to her. "This is bad. Very, very bad."

At the very least. But his never-let-them-see-you-sweat mantra was deeply ingrained. "How about we start completely over, okay?"

"Fine." She gave him a tight smile. "Hello to the person who didn't want to sleep with me."

He let out a low, disbelieving laugh. "*That's* what you're upset about?"

She crossed her arms. "Of course not."

He was pretty sure that was sarcasm.

"Nepotism and sweet charm?" she asked, repeating what he'd said in the tavern about his appointment.

He smiled. "*Not meeting your budget?*"

She tossed up her hands. "How is this even happening? What was Silas thinking, surprising us with all this? And omigod, please tell me we aren't kissing cousins or something."

"We're not related."

She looked relieved, and as much as he'd loved Silas, he'd been a hard man who never gave in to a weakness, *especially* emotion. But what he'd done to Luna, not telling her who he was, was wrong. "You have no other living relatives," he said quietly. "You're the last one."

He saw the flash of disappointment hit her, and then a longer beat of devastation. Last night she'd said she'd been called "too much" and "not enough," but in the little time he'd spent with her, he'd found her to be smart, strong inside *and* out, and funny. She seemed to be able to find joy in the simplest of things, and she was quick with a smile.

More than he could ever hope to be.

"There's really no one else in the family?" she asked quietly.

He gave a slow shake of his head. "I'm sorry."

She let out a whoosh of air and sat on the curb, like her knees were no longer going to keep her upright.

He eyed the dirty walkway and grimaced but sat too. And

yep, right on cue, some of the icy dew of the morning soaked into the seat of his pants.

She slid him a slightly amused look. "That looks like yet another *really* expensive suit and you just sat on a dirty walkway."

"It's fine."

She snorted, then dropped her head to her knees.

Ah, hell. *Say something, genius.* Problem was he'd never been good at this. "Do you know how Silas got this land?" He was pretty sure she didn't, so when she said nothing, he went on. "He inherited it from his grandfather. By that time the farm was no longer operating, but Silas kept it because it was where he'd spent summers as a kid. At that point, his life was in LA, so the land sat. He'd fallen in love and didn't want to disrupt Rose's life by moving her here."

Luna lifted her head. "Rose?" she whispered, looking heartbreakingly desperate for more information about her family.

Aching for her, he nodded. "Your grandmother—he married her. There's not a happy ending though," he warned her. "Silas became a successful businessman, which took him away from Rose for long periods of time. She eventually left him, taking their young daughter, Cami—your birth mother—with her. Years later, understanding what he'd lost, Silas tried to make amends, but it was too late. Rose had died of cancer, and Cami had no interest in him. By then she'd lost herself in opioids, and eventually she overdosed. But when he learned she'd had a kid, he went in search of her."

Luna had stilled. He wasn't even sure she was breathing. "You were working at a food co-op, managing the employees. In college, you'd studied business and, to Silas's shock and delight, agriculture."

She didn't move or say anything.

"You okay?" he asked.

"I'm always okay." She paused. "I know I was born in LA. Why did Cami give me up?"

He did his best to hide his sympathy because he knew he wouldn't want any, and he was pretty sure she wouldn't either. "She was young and single. And not able to care for a baby. She never told Silas, or he'd have stepped in to take you."

"Conjecture," she said, and gave a tight smile. "I also took some law classes. So instead of coming clean to me like a normal human, he lied to get me here, pretended to be just my boss, and then left me this place."

"Well, half of it anyway." He smiled.

She did not. "Right. And you got the other half. The lawyer said I'm to keep on being general manager and you're taking over the finances and accounting from Silas. He also said you'll be here for two months, and then after that, you'll handle your end from LA."

He nodded.

She nodded too, then shook her head. "This is crazy. How is this supposed to work? We're so different."

"If we stay calm and collected, it'll be fine."

"Sorry to break it to you, but calm and collected isn't really my go-to when faced with an impending meltdown."

He was getting that. "Luna."

She looked at him with sky-blue, suspicious eyes. "You sound very serious. There's more."

"About last night . . ."

"Oh great," she muttered, forehead to her knees again. "You want to tell me I kiss bad. Well, excuse me for being out of practice—"

"Luna. Look at me."

"You should know, even in the throes of a breakdown, I don't take orders well."

"Fine. Fair." He drew a breath. "Will you *please* look at me?"

She straightened up again and even gave a small smile. "You said the word 'please' through your teeth. Not used to using the word, I take it."

How did she so easily derail his every thought? "I'm trying to tell you something."

"Oh, right." She waved a hand. "Sorry. Carry on."

She somehow managed to turn him upside down and inside out, and not in a good way. Or at least he was pretty sure not in a good way. "First, the kiss. It wasn't . . . bad."

She snorted. "Be still my beating heart."

He wasn't going to be baited into a discussion of their kiss—which, for the record, had been *holy-shit amazing*. "I'm just saying that I'm sorry it happened, and I hope it won't change anything."

"Wow." She shook her head. "I'm pretty sure me being a bad kisser is less insulting than you being sorry it happened."

He decided it'd be dangerous to tell her just how *not* a bad kisser she was. "We both have jobs to do. In fact, we need to get started."

"You're right. The sooner we get started, the sooner we can be done."

"Exactly. Can you show me the offices? I'd like to get a look at the books." Mostly because the last thing he needed was to spend more time with her, because even without the alcohol, there was chemistry. Maybe even more now that she was dressed simply in jeans with a hole in one knee and the opposite thigh, a sweatshirt with Apple Ridge's logo above her breast, battered boots, and her long hair piled on top of her head. She'd been beautiful dressed up, showing off those long legs that he'd most definitely dreamed about, but the way she looked now was even more attractive to him. A fact he planned to ignore.

Good luck to him.

"We should start off with a tour of the whole property," she said.

Normally when Jameson showed up on a job, he was in a position of power and knew he had the authority to do whatever had to be done. But with Luna, he felt like he had two left feet and zero power. "Sure," he said, trying to bring things back to his comfort level. "Let's make it a tour of the books."

She seemed surprised. "You don't want to see the rest of the farm first? The books are boring. The real heart of this place is the people who run it, along with the botanical gardens and orchards, the cute shops and café, the rescue animals ... All of that is why people come, and continue to make return visits."

Actually, Jameson didn't need to see a thing. Appearances didn't matter. Just because something looked good on the outside didn't mean it wasn't a complete disaster behind closed doors. Not that he could say that to Miss Defensive. "I already met an emu, who might or might not have sexually harassed me."

"Omigod, I'm so sorry. That's Estelle. She was rescued from a traveling carnival, where she was kept on a short leash *and* locked up in a cage. She's been thriving here, and loves people so much. She must've really liked you. I can introduce you to the other rescue animals too. I'll even protect your virtue, I promise."

He hoped the fact that she was teasing him meant she wasn't going to be mad at him for the whole two months. "I've been here before, when your grandfather was making plans to restore this place."

She stilled again, amusement gone, mistrust back. "So you knew him well then?"

There was something in her eyes. Envy? Yeah, and not for the first time, he cursed Silas for not doing this himself. If he'd been honest with her when he'd first found her five years ago, everything would've been easier. But Silas hadn't listened to anyone, not even Jameson, which meant he now got to deal with the very natural emotions Luna felt for her departed grandfather.

Number one being anger, which was clear on her face and in every line of her admittedly beautiful body. "Yes. You could say I knew him well."

"What else would you say about him?"

He didn't want to, but damn, he liked her. "This might go faster if you just ask me what you want to know."

"And you'll answer honestly?" she asked, apparently every bit the cynic as her grandfather had been.

"Always."

"Okay . . ." She nodded. "Was he always closed-minded, tight-fisted, anal-retentive?"

Jameson laughed. "Most definitely."

She looked at him for another beat, then nodded, relaxing slightly. Maybe she'd expected him to take offense, but he knew exactly who Silas had been. And who he hadn't.

"And you worked for him," she said.

"Up until a few years ago, yes."

"How long were you with him?" she asked.

"Since the day he took me in off the streets when I was fifteen."

She blinked. "He raised you?"

"Well, I was mostly raised by then, but he taught me a lot. Also there's the other truth. He didn't find me, I found him. I tried to get a job and lied about my age. He caught me, of course. Instead of kicking me out, he took me in. He was . . ." He lifted a shoulder. "Family."

She inhaled a deep breath, then let it out and met his gaze. "I'm sorry for your loss, Jameson."

Not a single person had said that to him about Silas's passing, and he was startled by how much it meant. "Thank you," he said quietly. "How about you? How was your adoptive family?"

She shrugged. "Good."

"Good?"

"Yeah. I mean, fine. It was fine—" Her phone went off and she reached for it even though she'd ignored earlier texts.

So she liked to change the subject once it turned to her. Something else he understood.

"Dammit," she said.

"What?"

She held up a finger and made a call. "Shep? Hogwarts is over in the orchards eating Willow's tulips again. She said she's having bacon for lunch if you don't hurry." She disconnected and slipped the phone away.

"Hogwarts?" Jameson asked. "As in the Harry Potter Hogwarts?"

"Okay, points for knowing that," she said, looking reluctantly impressed.

"I didn't just appear as a thirty-two-year-old. I had a child-hood."

She laughed. An infectious, musical sound. "Good to know. Hogwarts is one of our rescue pigs. She escaped her pen when one of the farmhands was trying to put suntan lotion on her ears."

He paused. "I'm sure I'm going to be sorry I asked, but . . . *what?*"

"We have to sunscreen the pigs' ears so they don't get sun-burned."

"Huh," he said. "I guess it's better than becoming bacon. How do you catch a pig?"

"Pigs have great concentration. Once they've set a goal, they'll devote all their energy to it—like escaping. Luckily, they never suspect trickery, so they're easy to fool. Shep will set a food trap. Something sweet, so Hogwarts won't be able to resist."

"I wouldn't either."

"Good to know." She hesitated. "So how do you want to do this? Would you like to shadow me today and see how we operate?"

"Really, the books are all I need."

She nodded, stood up, brushed her hands across her backside, then shoved her hands into her pockets. "Right. Wouldn't want to combine business and pleasure."

Damn. He knew she'd taken that statement personally and he

couldn't blame her. He was shit at relationships, even the simple ones, and he felt pretty certain that nothing with Luna Wright would be simple. Before he could speak, she turned to face the Square, which was made of pretty pavers, outlined by a foot-high wooden picket fence and anchored by four poles from which fairy lights were strung. At one corner was the Bright Spot café. Tables and chairs sat out front, the small dining area delineated by large clay pots filled with small but thriving pine trees.

Inside the closest pot, at the base of the tree, sat a goose. A small umbrella had been placed over its head.

"That's Glenna the Goose," Luna said. "She lives with the chickens. Well, except for Hen Solo, who wakes up every day and chooses evil. *She* lives with Tomas the Turkey because he keeps her calm."

"No rooster?"

"One, and Wyatt Chirp is a shy cutie-pie who is terrified of Hen Solo. You won't see much of him. Anyway, Glenna decided to lay her eggs in the planter. So we set her up with the umbrella and food and water so she doesn't have to leave her nest before her babies hatch. Uh-oh."

"What?" he asked, but she was already on the move toward one of the large aspen trees just outside the Square, the heavy branches and full foliage providing shade to the café's tables and benches.

"Give me a boost," she said at the base of the tree, looking up.

He followed her gaze to a branch about eight feet above the ground, upon which sat a small cat.

"Mew."

"I've got you, Fred," she called up, and then looked back to Jameson. "He's fourteen, but he does this thing where he climbs anything and everything, then gets scared to climb down. Link your fingers together and lift me as far as you can. I'll do the rest."

He eyed the branch over their heads. "If you've got a ladder, I could get him—"

"I don't need a ladder."

Okay, then. Crouching, he laced his fingers together. Luna put a hand on his shoulder and a boot into his hands. When he rose, she grabbed onto the branch just below Fred and pulled herself up.

Jameson's eyes skimmed over Luna's boots, following the line of her legs—she was taller than he'd thought—and skated over the curves of her hips. Those curves were tempting, and his short-term goal shifted from the farm's books to trying to forget the delicious taste of her from the night before. Her shirt rose up, teasing him with a glimpse of midriff as he watched her gracefully climb up to get to Fred, who immediately leaped into her outstretched arms and cuddled into the crook of her neck.

Lucky cat.

Jameson assisted them down. Fred squirmed to be free and Luna let him go. "Just like all the men in my life," she said.

Her hair was escaping its bun, a few strands tucked behind her ears, tamed for the moment though a tendril threatened to fall across her cheekbone. He wasn't sure what this attraction to her was about, but he had to get a hold of himself. Needing a distraction, he looked around, his gaze catching on the café. The place's charming entrance had been built to look like a train car.

The "train" windows were clear, and one of them was filled with a handful of people, faces glued to the glass.

"It's an actual train car from the sixties," Luna said. "It was deserted on the very back of the property, long ago abandoned. We added it to the café when it was expanded a few years ago. People love it."

Apparently she wasn't going to explain the faces staring at them. He took another look and they all ducked down in unison, out of sight. "Who are they?"

Luna sighed. "My crew. They're eavesdropping, which is . . ." She cupped her hands over her mouth and yelled, "*Rude!*"

One of them poked his head back up, saw they were still looking, and tried to duck down again.

"Chef!" she yelled. "I can still see you and your big fat head!"

The man rose, grimaced, and then came outside. "Hi, I'm Chef. I run the café. I'm also Luna's ex. And you are?"

"Jameson Hayes," Luna said for him.

"One of the new owners," Jameson added.

Chef's head whipped to Luna.

"Right," she said. "I was just getting to that. We were in the middle of a quick business meeting. Tell the snoopers that everything's okay so they can stop freaking out and following us around."

Chef hesitated. "So . . . everything's *really* okay?"

"Yes," Luna said in a tone that was both boss and caring friend.

Jameson had never had to straddle such a line, and it was not only effective but almost impressive.

"Hey," another man called from inside the café, this one with an unmistakable southern accent. "Can you all talk louder? We can't hear you."

"That's Milo," Luna said. "He's a writer. He does our newsletter and social media. He also wrote a series of pieces about the farm that got picked up by some news outlets last year, and visitor numbers surged. He's helping Chef write a cookbook, and we're all very excited about it."

"He's also my significant other," Chef said.

"Hell yeah I am," Milo called out.

"Oh!" Chef said to Luna. "I met the perfect man for you. I mean, unless *this* man's that man . . . ?" He looked Jameson over, head to toe and back again. "I mean, I certainly wouldn't blame you."

"No," Luna said quickly.

Jameson had opened his mouth to say the same thing, but when she beat him to the punch, he hesitated at the odd flicker of an emotion that felt shockingly like disappointment.

"Okay then," Chef said. "Your perfect date's name is Evan, and he's going to call you for dinner this week. Please don't show up looking like that. Maybe some heels, show a little leg. He's a high-powered and very successful attorney."

"I'm not dating right now," Luna said without looking at Jameson. "And even if I was, I won't date a suit."

"Okay, Luna Always Right Wright." Chef looked down at Fred, who was rubbing against his legs, and picked him up. While he was preoccupied loving up on the cat, Jameson shifted in closer to Luna and whispered, "Last night you were all about the suit."

CHAPTER 6

Jameson watched as Luna turned her head to meet his gaze. "I blame the margaritas."

He laughed.

Chef divided a look between them. "What am I missing?"

"Nothing," Luna said. "Nothing at all. I'll catch up with you later to fill you in."

Chef saluted her, set Fred down in a patch of sun, and then vanished back inside the café.

"So what was that?" Jameson asked Luna.

"Oh." She looked at the café. "I don't want them to worry."

"I meant the lie."

"I didn't lie."

"You omitted the fact that you're the other owner, which is the same as lying. Why?"

She blew out a breath. "You sure ask a lot of questions. Guys never ask questions."

He doubted she knew how revealing a statement that was.

"Then you've been with the wrong guys," he said. "Why didn't you tell your staff about the will?"

"Look, you might not know this about Silas, but he was a . . ."

"Hard-ass?" he supplied.

"*Yes.* And I was the go-between between him and the crew. They're all worried we're going to get shut down or sold, and I'm just trying to give them some peace of mind. If they worry, they won't be able to concentrate on their jobs."

"Even if getting sold is entirely possible?"

She looked away, and he knew she was doing enough worrying for everyone.

"Look, I get it," he said. "You're trying to protect them. But this isn't your family or your friends, it's work." He paused. "Luna Always Right Wright."

"You know why they call me that? Because it's true." She met his gaze. "And they *are* my family."

She might consider them her family and friends, but he couldn't imagine they felt the same. Not when, at the end of the day, she was now their boss. "I get that you're all close," he said, trying not to step on any of Luna's mental land mines. "But—"

"You know what? Let's just get back to our tour," she said. "We can start at the orchards, where, as you know, we sell a bunch of trees every year and make a lot of our annual profits."

When Jameson opened his mouth, she quickly continued. "Honestly, there's no context if you don't see the place first, and the magic of it all."

"Luna, there's no magic in math."

"Fine." She tossed up her hands. "Have it your way." She led him past the café and away from the Square to a building, muttering something about men and tunnel vision as she gestured him inside. He could've said that *she* had tunnel vision as well, but decided to keep that to himself as he liked breathing.

She walked them through a very cluttered front room and down a hallway, where she pushed open a door. The room was small, the desk large. Or at least he assumed that was a desk straining beneath piles of paperwork, though it was actually hard to tell. Even the windowsill had stuff stacked on it. The only thing that didn't was the chair in front of her desk, presumably for guests, although it was currently occupied by a baby goat wearing baby Yoda pajamas.

"Dammit Ziggy," Luna said.

"Dammit who?"

"The goat. His name is Dammit Ziggy." She said this with an utterly straight face, then turned to the tiny thing, hands on hips. "You need to stop breaking out of your pen or no treats for you. Do you understand?"

Ziggy—er, *Dammit* Ziggy—tipped his little head back and bleated to the ceiling in protest.

It was official. He'd entered the circus. He examined the room while Luna scooped up the goat, who set his little head on her shoulder.

Trying not to be moved by that, Jameson looked around. Besides the overabundance of paperwork, there was a horse bridle on a small credenza, next to a deflated Santa and every single one of his reindeer, all against a wall. "Love what you've done with the place."

Ignoring that, Luna gestured him to the now empty chair. He eyed the seat, which was covered in goat hair and possibly, hopefully, dust and not poop pellets.

"It's just dirt." She swiped at the seat a few times. "There. No longer as dirty as the sidewalk. Or the ass of your pants."

His gaze met hers.

She laughed, a light musical sound that drifted over him, and a warmth spread through his belly at the sound. Even if he knew she was enjoying this. A lot. "You looked at my ass?" he asked.

"Just as you looked at mine."

Not knowing what to do with that, he sat.

She did the same, in the chair behind the desk, Dammit Ziggy in her lap. Hard to believe he was envious of a goat, but there it was.

"Here," Luna said, and pushed a big fat ledger across the desk to him. His fingers touched hers. Their eyes locked and he saw his own interest and a good amount of heat reflected back at him as the odd connection between them fluttered into a full-blown gale-force wind.

Dammit Ziggy jumped down from her lap and galloped around the desk. "*Bleeeat.*"

Jameson eyed the goat. He was tiny, the size of a very small dog, and staring at him with brown eyes with sideways pupils that held a lot of hope.

"He wants in your lap," Luna said.

"We don't always get what we want."

Luna snorted. "No kidding."

This had him looking at her. She looked right back before rolling her eyes at him.

"*Bleeeat!*"

"Warning," she said. "He can out-stubborn a mule. And trust me, we have one, so I know what I'm talking about."

Jameson sighed—and when the hell he'd started sighing, he had no idea—and patted his thighs. Dammit Ziggy leaped up into his lap, curling into a ball and closing his eyes.

Luna was grinning. "You're going to be covered in fur, front and back."

"Like you care."

She laughed.

Ignoring both the pretty sound and the fact that her eyes lit like stars when she was amused, he opened the ledger. "Talk to me about this."

"So at the end of the quarter, I mail everything off, ledger and receipts. Silas had someone handle it all on his end, then I'd get the ledger back. On the months we ran out of money, there was a line of credit I could pull from."

Silas had been the "someone" to handle the farm's books. It used to be that Jameson had done the books for Silas's holdings— all except the farm, that is, because for whatever reason, the old man had always wanted to do it himself.

He had a feeling he'd just met the "reason" and her name was Luna.

Oh, the fights he and Silas had over this. Ignoring the memories, good and bad, Jameson took a deep breath and a few minutes to flip through the ledger. There were sticky notes everywhere in neon colors with things on them like *Estelle the Emu's vet bill from swallowing a handful of change* and *raccoon ate through the electrical in the barn again, requiring an electrician's visit.* Jameson stared at the numbers and rubbed the spot between his eyes, where a headache was forming.

"You okay?" Luna asked.

No. No, he was not okay. The numbers were shit, and they were bleeding money in ways that didn't need to happen. He let out a careful breath, every analytical bone inside him twitching. "I see you kept up with Silas's bookkeeping methods."

She looked at him for a beat. "He called me every other week to talk about the bookkeeping and get up to date. Seemed like he liked what I was doing." She shrugged. "So I hadn't planned on changing anything."

He could hear the wistfulness in her voice and realized he wasn't the only one who'd lost Silas, even if she'd been kept in the dark about who he'd really been. "What do you know about the state of the books?" he asked.

"I know we're not a huge moneymaker, but he seemed happy enough. Although I'm not actually sure Silas did happy."

Something they could agree on.

"The attorney told me about the balloon payment."

He nodded. "Without any cushion, we're in a tenuous situation. I'm assuming the attorney didn't tell you about Silas's medical condition, and why there was no money to award you in the will."

She shook her head.

"He had dementia. For an entire year before his death, apparently, though he told no one. Kept it to himself as he made one bad financial decision after another, depleting his cash accounts before wrapping his car around a tree one night."

"I couldn't tell from his calls," she said softly. "Why wouldn't he have told someone?"

"Probably because he knew he'd have lost some of his freedom that he greatly enjoyed. Like being alone."

She was quiet for a moment. Then she drew a deep inhale. "I'm sorry, for all of it. But it doesn't change anything that's going on here. I really hope you'll get to know the place before you pass judgment."

He had to laugh. "Oh, I passed judgment the second I saw the Rudolf the Red-Nosed Reindeer."

"Hey, I lost a storage unit to the botanical gardens this year."

"Did you also lose a vacuum?" he asked, turning another page on the ledger.

"Just wait until Dammit Ziggy wakes up and gets off your lap. Then you'll see something that really needs a vacuum."

He met her gaze. "Can we be serious for a moment?"

"I *am* being serious. Dammit Ziggy and his two siblings were rejected by their mama. For whatever reason, DZ thinks I'm a good surrogate. So I let him hang out here when he wants to."

As stupid as it seemed, that reached him. He knew what it was like to be kicked out at a young age. "I understand."

Luna looked surprised.

"What, you think I'm an uncaring asshole?"

She smiled. "Oh, it's far too soon for me to pass judgment on you."

Touché. "What's with all the Post-it notes? They're on every page."

"Notes for the stuff I didn't know what to do with."

"Isn't there a computer? Any digitalization at all? Where's your—"

"Look." She drew a deep breath. "Yesterday I learned that my boss wasn't just my boss, he was also my bio grandfather, and that he left me a piece of this place. I'm . . ." She shook her head. "Shook. It's hard to think."

He nodded. "I understand that too. But it's not just us involved in the bottom line here."

"Right. The evil coven."

A smile escaped him. "You mean the group of investors who own the loan?"

"Tomayto, tomahto."

He didn't want to be charmed, but he was. "So you understand the situation we're in. The group expects the balloon payment to come in on time for funding the renovations on this place five years ago. With Silas gone, they're circling like sharks, waiting to see what happens. They don't care about staying in with Silas gone. So in sixty days, at the quarter's end, they're going to expect us to pay up or they'll slap a big fat For Sale sign on the front of this place."

"I'd like to buy them out."

This did not surprise him in the least. "Do you have an actual plan for that?"

"My plan is what it's always been. I'm going to do my best."

Jameson was boggled. "Your best?" He shook his head. "You

do realize this isn't a rec league soccer game where there are no losers and everyone gets a participation award, right?"

Her eyes flashed. "Do you have a better plan?"

"Better than *no* plan? Yes." He pulled out his laptop. "We make cuts, for starters. A lot of cuts. Then we go to the bank in town, the one that holds the personal line of credit Silas let you use, and we show them an actual feasible financial plan going forward and hopefully get a loan to pay off the investors."

"And if they won't give us a loan?"

"We could sell."

"That's going to be a hard no." She paused. "And what sort of cuts?"

Ignoring her emphatic not-selling stance, he went back to the ledger. "You've got fifteen regular employees, and up to fifty seasonal employees."

"Seasonal is for planting and harvesting times."

"We're labor heavy," he said. "For instance, I could see the orchards from the front of the café, and there were four guys out there. Three were limbing, but one was just standing around looking at his phone."

"That's Jeb. He supervises the orchards. It's a big job. We do crab apples for fall, Christmas trees for winter, and cherry blossoms in spring. How do you know he wasn't working on his phone? Maybe he was googling something."

"He looked like he was thumbing through videos and laughing. And I'm pretty sure he had a flask he kept taking sips from."

"That's his mom's special hot chocolate. It's freezing out there in the mornings and sometimes he needs a nip to keep warm.

He rarely speaks, is a total introvert, and hates to be bothered, but he's a tree whisperer. Stella had a dream he left and all the trees died."

Jameson just looked at her. He had no idea who Stella was and didn't care.

"He's really, really good at his job. I won't let him go. I won't let any of them go."

He scrubbed a hand down his face. "You've got the ferocity and courage of a lion, anyone ever tell you that?" He turned back to his laptop. "Okay, so you've got six people listed here as farmhands. Besides what we saw in the orchards, what else do they do?"

"Well, there's the gardens too, and they also handle the rescue animals."

"Right, which brings me to the division that brings in zero money," he said, still looking at the ledger. "In fact, the rescues actually cost us."

She crossed her arms. "We're not getting rid of the rescue animals."

He lifted his head and studied her. "What am I missing?"

"Nothing, other than we're not making cuts." She looked away. "I know. I get it. We *need* to make changes, but . . ." She met his gaze again, her own filled with anxiety and worry. "Look, I place loyalty above all else. The employees have all been here forever and are incredibly loyal to me. I can't repay that by letting some of them go because I somehow messed up in managing the farm by not making enough money."

Her enthusiasm and easy charm spread a warmth through

him that he couldn't afford, and he let out a breath. "It's not your fault." And it wasn't. It was Silas's.

She shrugged like she didn't believe him but didn't feel like arguing. "Also, on the subject of the rescue animals, our guests love them. They like that a lot of them wander around and can be petted and fed."

He nodded. "But it's also both an insurance and a legal nightmare. Insurance is a huge hit to our bottom line, a lot of which could be cut if we didn't have them wandering free."

"Not all of them are allowed to wander. Just the ones we're one hundred percent positive are no danger to anyone." She stared at him, steely eyed. Who knew those pretty blue eyes could turn to ice? "Rescuing neglected, abused, and abandoned farm animals is the *best* thing we do here," she said. "If you want a way to negate the costs of that, then let's do an annual calendar. And while we're doing that, we can also let people sponsor an animal, meaning they cover the cost of their care, and in return they get their name on a plaque in front of their pen."

He thought about it. "Genius," he said. "And while we're on this, I want to be clear. I'm not disputing that the rescue animals aren't a worthy cause. I'm simply asking why you need so many farmhands, all of whom seem to set their own hours and work just enough hours to get benefits, but not quite full-time. We could lose a few and have everyone up their hours to full-time status, and *still* save money. And while we're on that, do we pay Milo to do social media? Because his last tweet reads . . ." He accessed his phone. "'Why do cows have hooves instead of feet?—because they lactose.'"

She grinned.

He just looked at her.

"Come on," she said. "Yes, it's an old joke, but it's still funny."

"What it is, if we're paying him, is expensive."

She didn't say anything, which was usually *his* tactic. It was possible he'd underestimated her a little bit.

After a beat, she said, "I assume you're drawing a salary now that you're taking on Silas's job of handling the books." She smiled his own corporate raider smile at him. "I'd be happy to merge your job into mine and handle everything. We'd save your salary."

Okay, so he'd underestimated her *a lot* . . .

Her cell rang. She pulled it from her pocket and stared at it with a frown. "Hello?" she answered suspiciously. There was a pause while she listened. "Who gave you my phone number? Oh, right. Chef . . . Yeah, sorry, now's not a great time, but it's sweet that you called. Thank you and goodbye."

"Evan, I presume?" Jameson grinned. "Smooth. The poor guy never even got his spiel out before you hung up on him."

"I'm not big on spiels."

"You're also not big on suits, apparently. At least without Hawaiian margaritas."

She looked him over without giving a single sign of her thoughts. "I think you've got something stuck to your loafer, or whatever those shoes are called besides expensive."

Jameson looked down. "Shit."

"Exactly."

Dammit Ziggy yawned and stood up in his lap, nearly ensuring Jameson's family jewels never got to the "family" part.

Apparently taking mercy on him, Luna came around the desk and scooped up a very satisfied-looking DZ. "Look, why don't you let *me* do what I do best and run this place, and *you* do what you apparently do best, and . . . wait. What is it that you do best exactly?"

Dammit Ziggy leaped from Luna's arms back to Jameson's lap. He grimaced. "I find vulnerabilities in companies and exploit them," he said, having to crane his neck to the side so the goat couldn't nibble his ear.

"Wow, you've got a *terrible* job," she said. "How about you find our vulnerabilities and *fix* them. You know, use your powers for good instead of evil."

He acknowledged that with a slight bow of his head. "I'm certainly willing to try." But only because Silas had asked, not wanting her to get taken advantage of, even if he had a feeling Luna could take care of herself.

She smiled at him and he was pretty sure the ice encasing his heart cracked just a little. "Okay then," she said. "So I'll leave you to it. *Partner.*"

"Wait," he said as she moved to the door. "You're going to take the goat, right?"

Luna shut the door behind her. He could've sworn he heard her chortling to herself as she walked away.

From his lap, Dammit Ziggy sighed in pleasure and closed his eyes. Well, at least someone here liked him . . .

CHAPTER 7

Luna woke up before her usual crack of dawn. She blamed Jameson. She'd been just fine BTK—*before* the kiss. But ATK—*after* the kiss—she was having trouble. What kind of bad karma had she banked that the man she'd made the first move on turned out to be her new partner?

And don't get her started on Silas hiding who he was from her and then leaving her his pride and joy.

Or that he'd ignored her all her life, and yet had taken in Jameson, a perfect stranger. She closed her eyes. Was she really jealous of Jameson? She did some soul-searching and decided that yes, she was jealous of Jameson for receiving her grandfather's love and affection.

Sprout licked her face and she had to shrug off her feelings to smile at the true love of her life. "Hey, old man. Time to get out of bed."

For the record, he didn't. But she did. She showered, dressed, toasted a frozen waffle—breakfast of champions—and swooped up Sprout on her way out to morning rounds.

Two hours later, she'd dealt with an electrician on an ongoing wiring problem in the main barn and had stepped in to help Shep, who had two sick coworkers today. But sick her ass, she knew they were probably hungover from the party they'd been stupid enough to discuss on their radios yesterday at lunchtime.

She needed to give Shep a raise, because she knew he'd never do that to her. When she'd first hired him three years ago, she'd caught him sleeping a few times during his shifts. Several people had suggested he might be on drugs. But when she'd talked to him about it, it turned out he was homeless and living in his car, and being harassed by cops in the middle of the night for sleeping in public parking lots. Luna had given him one of the cabins to sleep in, and he'd never again fallen asleep on the job. He was now one of her best employees.

Even if he still couldn't look her in the eyes after seeing her in her pj's.

After giving Shep a desperately needed hand in the barn, she'd then had to hunt down Sprout and Miss Piggy, who'd taken themselves on a walkabout to their strawberry patch, where together with Sammy, their fifty-year-old, hundred-pound tortoise, they'd just about cleaned them out of strawberries before she caught them. "Guys! Seriously?"

The culprits, dog, pig, and tortoise, stared up at her, their entire faces dyed red from their feast.

"Gee, I wonder who ate our strawberries?"

Only Sprout had the good sense to look sheepish.

She radioed for Shep to come get the criminals. Sprout wanted to stay with Miss Piggy, so she left to head toward the orchards to see Willow, who'd have chocolate.

She really needed chocolate.

But Willow had gone on a supplies pickup. Damn. Luna was avoiding the office because she knew Jameson would be there. Not mature, but there it was. To say she was still reeling felt like the understatement of the century. For one thing, she'd been under the impression she'd *earned* her job here. Silas had even had her fill out a very long, complicated application for the job—when he'd clearly known he was going to hire her. The knowledge burned. The joke was definitely on her, and even worse, learning that he'd been a blood relation had brought back all those feelings she'd had as a kid, knowing she'd been abandoned before being adopted. She'd always told herself she didn't care, that it didn't matter.

But it did. She'd spent most of her life trying to figure out who she was and where she belonged, and she'd thought she'd found that here. Only now she had to wonder, was she here because she wanted to be or because she'd been manipulated? Before she could decide, her phone vibrated with an incoming text.

JAMESON: I need to talk to you send hey there dammit ziggy hi dammit ziggy hi yes I see you yes you're a good boy but you've gotta stop trying to eat my shoelaces . . .

Laughing, because who hadn't been there with a voice-to-text gone wrong, but that it was buttoned-up-tight Jameson made it

all the funnier. She did an about-face and five minutes later, entered the office building. She was heading down the hall just as
Jameson came out of her office. His hair was standing on end
as if he'd put his fingers through it. Repeatedly. Half his tie was
missing, and if she'd been a betting woman, she'd have laid
down her entire annual salary on the smitten Dammit Ziggy.
Jameson had unbuttoned the top two buttons of his shirt and
shoved the sleeves up his forearms. There were some question-
able stains on his wrinkled trousers, and his fancy shoes were
scuffed and dirty. She thought she'd done a pretty good job of
hiding a smile when he narrowed his eyes at her.

"Everything okay?" she asked innocently.

The fulminating look he gave her only made her smile widen.

"I hear you had a meeting with DZ," she said, "where you dis-
cussed how he is, in fact, a good boy."

"Yeah, about that," he said. "If he ate, say, part of a tie, would
he need to see a vet?"

"Probably not. We'll just check his poop and make sure it all
looks okay."

Jameson grimaced.

"Don't worry," she said. "He once ate Shep's undies and was fine."

"Noted," he said. "And maybe I'll skip ties from now on."

"You can skip the suit entirely, you know."

"So back to the books," he said instead of answering her
smart-ass comment.

Luna was confident in managing the farm. She was. But the
books . . . well, that was her weak spot, and knowing it made her
defensive as hell. "I told you, I do my best."

Unfortunately, Jameson didn't seem to share her favorite personality trait of jumping to conclusions and then getting all defensive at the drop of a hat, because he spoke in that low, calm voice of his, completely void of judgment. "I just wanted to know if you have more paperwork anywhere else that you haven't logged yet."

"Oh." Feeling ridiculous, she took a breath. "Yeah. I've got a stack of invoices in my top drawer that I was going to get to today." Probably. Maybe.

"*Bleeeat.*"

They both looked down.

Dammit Ziggy was chewing on Jameson's laces.

Luna smiled. "Aw, you've really made a new friend."

"More like a stalker. He even follows me to the bathroom." He took in her smile. "You think that's funny? He also ate the toilet paper."

She laughed. "Please tell me you didn't let him drink from the toilet. The other day he dunked his head in and sprayed Willow. She threatened to open the front gate and let him go."

"Did she?"

"Oh, she opened the gate, but DZ knows where his bread is buttered. He took one look at the gate and trotted back inside."

"The gate was wide open this morning too," he said.

"You know, people don't give animals enough credit. None of ours will leave. They love it here. It's like Disneyland for farm animals."

Jameson craned his neck and looked one way and then the other.

"What are you looking for?"

"The cameras. Clearly this is some twisted new reality show, right? It's that, or I've been dropped into an alternate universe."

Taking mercy on him, she pulled the two-way radio from her hip. "Shep, can you come get Dammit Ziggy? Over."

"Will do. Over," he said from right behind her. "What's he guilty of this time? Chew terrorism?"

"Bathroom terrorism. Shep, this is Jameson. He's lead farmhand. Shep, Jameson's one of the new owners."

Shep nodded a greeting and skillfully scooped up Dammit Ziggy in a way so that the baby goat couldn't chew on his ear.

"So *that's* how it's done," Jameson muttered.

Shep smiled. "Took me a long time to figure it out." He looked at Luna. "Don't forget Mrs. Smith's fifth-grade class will be here in an hour, but I've got it handled. Just wanted to remind you."

"Make sure to take pics for Milo to put up on social media."

"Of course," Shep said, and still holding DZ, walked out of the building.

Luna watched them go, a little pensive. The thing was, DZ was actually an excellent judge of character and . . . already madly in love with her new partner. She wasn't sure what to make of that.

"Are the fifth graders getting a farm tour?" Jameson asked.

"No, they come once a week as time allows and they sit outside the animal pens and read to the animals. They love it."

"The kids?"

She laughed. "The animals. But yes, the kids too. Do you know how many have never touched a chicken before? They'll say 'This is the best day of my life,' which is pretty incredible. This whole farm is basically a kindness program. I know it sounds crazy, but it's a good crazy. I'm proud that we march to a different beat here." Her cell buzzed with another text.

GRAM: Do people still say "hella"?

> **LUNA:** Yes, but you have to be in the Bay Area and under seventy.

GRAM: Damn. Youngsters have all the fun.

"There it is," Jameson said.

Luna looked up. "What?"

"Your real smile. I saw it at the tavern. Up until you ran off, that is."

This was a true story. But the tavern had been BTK, up until the kiss. BTK Luna had been full of hopes and dreams.

But today, ATK, she knew the power of it now, her attraction to him, and she'd shoved it so deep she hoped to never find it again.

"Is it a text from your grandma?"

Grateful for the subject change, she turned her phone his way and he smiled. "She sounds like something else."

Yes. He was correct. Her grandma was something else. "Come on. There's something I want to show you."

They walked to the far northeast corner of the property to the water tower, and she started climbing the ladder. She could hear him doing the same behind her and had the ridiculous thought that she hoped her jeans were showing off her assets enough to make him feel like he'd missed out on something good.

Because he had.

"Amazing," he said.

She choked on a laugh, then realized he was talking about the view. Which, okay, was definitely amazing from up here. They could easily see the barns and other buildings, the various pens, the orchards and gardens and the fields growing grass and legumes to feed the animals.

"I come up here sometimes when I need a moment alone," she said softly. Being up here felt sacred, and then she could feel his gaze on her.

"You probably don't get very many of those."

"I do not."

"Hopefully having me here will help."

She turned her head and their gazes locked and held. "Maybe." She pointed out the boundaries of the land. "It probably hasn't changed too much since you saw it way back when."

He shook his head. "It has. It looks . . ."

"What?" she asked defensively.

He slid her a small, curious smile. "Lush. Well taken care of. Valuable."

Well, okay then. "It is all those things. It's also home to a lot of us, and we'd do anything to protect it."

"Noted," he said quietly.

She looked at him to see if he was being facetious, but he wasn't. They climbed back down and walked past a large field with rows and rows of plants growing.

"What's that?" he asked.

"Tulips. People will come from far and wide. For twenty-five bucks they can pick a bucketful."

"No, I meant the animal lying down in the adjacent field. Is it okay?"

"Yeah." She smiled. "That's Kong, our donkey."

"As in . . . Donkey Kong?"

She laughed. "Yes. He loves to lie down in the grass." She hopped the fence. Kong lifted his head and grinned at her approach, baring his buck teeth in all their glory. Luna smiled back and lay down with him. The grass was fragrant and warm and cushy. "How's my good boy?"

Kong snorted and nuzzled her.

Jameson had followed, she could hear his footsteps coming closer. "What are you doing?"

"Cuddling."

"Isn't that dangerous?"

"Nah, donkeys have a natural affection for people and are super gentle. They're very calm in situations that would spook other animals." She kissed Kong on the bridge of his nose.

Jameson was looking at her as if she'd lost her mind. And she absolutely had, but it had nothing to do with Kong. "Do *you* want a cuddle?"

"Yes, but not from Kong," he said, and the air shimmered with that same thing from the other night—hot, dangerous attraction.

"No offense," Jameson told the donkey.

Luna kissed Kong on top of his head and got up, turning to

the man watching her as if she was fascinating—like an erupting volcano kind of fascinating. It made her feel like ruffling his unruffable feathers. "Your cuddle," she said, and threw her arms wide, knowing damn well he'd fold like a cheap suitcase, just like he had at the bar, and pull back.

So it shocked the hell out of her when he closed the distance between them, wrapped his arms around her, nuzzling his cheek against hers, just as she had done to Kong—only the man smelled far better than the donkey.

Also, this was not the hug of a man who'd been indifferent enough to walk away from sleeping with her, so she felt confused as he let the hand between her shoulder blades dip to her lower back and press her closer still. They stayed locked together like that for a long, charged moment, and this time it was she who pulled back first. "Better?"

He flashed white teeth. "Much."

CHAPTER 8

Officially rattled, Luna went back to being Jameson's tour guide. "Okay then," she managed. "Just a few more things to see." She took him to Stella's Place.

"Guests love that it's a renovated barn," she said. "They can buy anything from locally sourced soaps to jellies to candles to—"

"Getting their fortune told?" he asked, pointing to the wooden sign out front.

"It's very popular. People get a big kick out of Stella, she's an attraction here in her own right." She walked through the open double doors, but the place appeared empty. "Stella?"

Nothing, but that wasn't unusual. Stella was nearly deaf from what she claimed had been a wild youth. Luna called it selective hearing. She gestured for Jameson to go through a makeshift doorway at the end of the barn—blocked by a curtain of hanging beads in the colors of the rainbow.

Jameson gamely walked through the beads and stopped short so unexpectedly that Luna ran into the back of him. "What the—" She peered around him and instantly understood.

Stella was on her zero-gravity apparatus, hanging upside down by her bony ankles, arms crossed over her equally bony chest, slightly sunken eyes closed, thin gray hair hanging all around her head like a halo.

"Is she . . ." Jameson moved forward and leaned down to put a finger on her throat, presumably checking for a pulse . . .

Just as Stella opened her eyes and cackled. "Bet you thought I was a vampire, right?" she asked Jameson, who to his credit *hadn't* jumped out of his skin.

He shook his head. "I thought you were dead."

"Aw, and you were worried. How sweet. I bet you were drawn to my aura." She righted herself, holding out a hand. "I'm Stella, by the way. Who are you, Handsome?"

"Jameson Hayes," Luna said. "One of the new owners. Gram, you've got to stop scaring people like that."

Stella's eyes went wide. "*One* of the new owners?"

"*Gram?*" Jameson asked. "As in grandma? The one who sends the texts?"

"Yes," Luna said. "My very favorite person."

"Love you too, girl," Stella said, and hugged her. "To the moon and back." She then turned to Jameson, taking his hand in hers. "So. Owner, huh? You're going to keep us up and running, right?"

"Yes, he is," Luna said, ignoring Jameson's look. She knew he wanted to know more about why she wasn't telling people that she too was part owner, but she wasn't ready to go there. Wasn't ready to be looked at like the new Grinch by the people she cared so much about.

Stella turned Jameson's hand over, running her finger along his palm.

"What does it say?" Luna asked curiously.

Stella closed her eyes and began to hum.

Jameson slid his gaze to Luna. "*Twilight Zone*?"

Luna laughed. He had a sense of humor, who knew?

Stella opened her eyes and beamed up at Jameson. "Your future is up to you."

Jameson smiled good-naturedly. "Nice to know. And nice to meet you."

"Oh, the pleasure was all mine."

Jameson made to go, but Luna stopped him with a hand to his chest as she pointed at Stella. "Hand it over."

Stella sighed dramatically. "I wasn't going to keep it. I was just practicing to keep the skills fresh. I always forget you're the Fun Police." But she handed Jameson his wallet.

He slipped it back into his pocket. "So do you give fortunes, or take them?"

With zero remorse, Stella smiled. "And don't forget *your* fortune," she said to Luna.

Oh boy. Just what she needed. "Not now, Gram, okay?"

"Honey, you can't run from things that are scary."

"Sure you can. Just this morning I ran from a spider in my shower."

"I'm talking about love and commitment."

Luna squelched a grimace and caught Jameson's look of amusement.

Her grandma smiled and gently patted her cheeks. "Sometimes what we need the most is the one thing we keep pushing away because we're afraid." Then she aimed her smile at Jameson. "See you later, Handsome. Come for your fortune anytime."

They walked outside and stood in the warm spring sunshine for a moment. "Speechless?" she finally asked him.

"Utterly."

She laughed. "There's only one known cure. A moment with some more of our rescue fur babies."

"I'm not really much of an animal person."

This was absolutely foreign to her. She'd never met a not-an-animal-person. "What's wrong with you?"

That tugged a laugh from him. "Likely too much to even articulate."

She looked at him.

"What?" he asked.

"I don't know. Most men think they're perfect."

"I'm not most men."

Because that flustered her again, in a way she wasn't sure she liked, she started walking.

"Your gram must've been pretty great to grow up with," he said, keeping pace with her.

"Once when I was a little girl, the two of us got stuck on the side of the road, struggling with a flat. A car with three guys stopped, not to help but to ask for directions to a local golf course. Gram sent them ten miles in the wrong direction."

He smiled. "Like I said, pretty great."

"She's the legend who shaped me." And because his smile was warm and genuine, that flustered her too. So she went back to something safe—being tour guide. She pointed to the orchards. "The trees are our pride and joy here. We grow the best Christmas trees and organic apple and cherry trees in the region. Pretty sure the ledger won't tell you that."

He smirked. "Once we're digitalized, I'll be able to let you know *without* that ledger."

"How?"

"Because I'll be able to departmentalize, analyze the data, and easily see what's working and what's not. That's what I plan to do first. Digitalize." He looked at her. "Assuming that's okay with you, of course."

He didn't have to ask her, they both knew that. But he *was* asking, so she nodded. "Of course." She pointed to the right of the trees. "The greenhouses are new in the past year. They're part of the botanical gardens. Willow Green runs that department."

Willow was at the gate in front of the botanical gardens, eyeing Luna with a brows-up expression.

"This is Jameson. Jameson, this is Willow. She's our agricultural genius."

Willow smiled at Jameson. "Nice to meet you. Excuse us a moment?" She dragged Luna to one side. "Why is Hottie Suit here? I know you didn't sleep with him, you're not glowing."

"No," Luna said. "But you are. Omigod, you were supposed to *talk* to Shayne, not—"

"I couldn't help it!"

"Willow, you're confusing him."

"I'm confusing me too, so it seems only fair that he joins me. Do you know the dumbest thing I ever did as a kid?"

"No."

Willow sighed. "Wished I was an adult. Now tell me what he's doing here if you're not boinking."

"In case you were wondering, I can hear you from over here," Jameson said, and when they both looked at him, he raised his hands. "Believe me, I'm actually trying not to."

"But really," Willow whispered, never taking her eyes off him. "Why is he here?"

"I'm one of the new owners."

Willow gaped at him.

Jameson looked at Luna, clearly once again waiting for her to explain she too was an owner. Luckily Willow's curiosity saved her.

"Well, I hope you're planning on saving this place," she told him. "Because I really like to eat. I mean, no pressure or anything, but don't let us down."

"I try very hard to never let anyone down."

Willow smiled her brilliant smile at him. "Thank you."

Luna was stunned. Willow didn't like new people. *Ever.*

"*Bleeeat.*"

Dammit Ziggy was trotting toward them, picking up speed when he saw Luna. She bent low to scoop the baby up, but he bypassed her and galloped straight to Jameson, where he rubbed his face on Jameson's pant leg.

Jameson looked down. "Did you forget to feed him today?"

"Of course not."

Willow was watching thoughtfully. "You know, DZ's always nice to strangers, but doesn't usually get attached."

"Well, obviously he's confused," Luna said. "The poor abandoned baby." But then Jameson scooped him up and DZ, not looking scared in the least by his past, proceeded to nibble at the man's ear. Damn. DZ most *definitely* liked him. A lot.

But not Luna. Nope. No way. He was a horrible person because . . . She bit her lower lip. Wait. Had she really decided he was a horrible person because he'd turned her down the other night? Okay, so maybe he wasn't *horrible*.

But he did have a stick up his ass. "We gotta go," she said, and started walking, not waiting to see if Jameson and DZ followed. She heard footsteps. No hooves though, which meant that the man who said he wasn't an animal person *was* an animal person because he was still holding DZ.

"Hottie Suit?" he asked.

Grimacing, she kept walking.

"Luna."

"Can't hear you." She kept walking, slowing when they came to a set of three-sided huts, each with wire fencing around it. "The first one houses our guinea pigs," she said, opening the gate. Once they were inside, DZ jumped down to greet his friends. Luna scooped up a guinea pig and set her in Jameson's hands before he could protest. "Her name's Sally."

He stared down at Sally like he was completely unsure of what to do.

Sally stared right back, then opened her mouth and let out an ear-piercing squeal.

Luna laughed. "She's saying hi."

"Guinea pigs are farm animals?"

"Well, no. But we rescued Sally and her family from a meth house out in the middle of nowhere last year. They're super human friendly. Our guests love to hold and pet them."

He carefully stroked Sally's head and she squeaked again, this time in a demand for more.

"It's easy to have the courage of a lion," she said quietly, referring to when he'd called her a lion. "They're gigantic and have claws and no natural predators. I'd rather have the courage of a guinea pig, a two-pound meat potato with zero offensive or defensive abilities, but who will scream at a human one hundred times its size if their lettuce is too wilty."

His smile was small but real. "Noted."

She broke eye contact when she got another text.

"You ever think about throwing that thing in the lake?" he asked.

"Only every day."

WILLOW: He's part owner???? And
does he know he's hot?

Luna put her phone away.

"Anything wrong?" he asked.

"Nope."

He met her gaze. "Good. So you can tell me again why these people don't know who you are."

"They know who I am. I'm the same person I've always been. Luna Wright."

He set down Sally and picked up DZ. "You know what I mean."

Yeah, she did. She just didn't know how to explain. At her heart, she was a people pleaser. Dumb as it was, she needed people, her people, to like her. If she became "the boss," they might treat her differently, close her out. It was one of her biggest fears, and she didn't know if she could survive that, being shut out by the people she counted on for . . . well, everything.

DZ had fallen instantly asleep all comfy cozy in Jameson's arms. Ignoring the little pang that gave her, she sighed. "You know how Silas was kind of a hard-ass?"

"Yes. And no 'kind of' about it. He was absolutely a hard-ass."

"My crew didn't like him," she admitted. "And they love me. And I'm not all that eager to lose the only family who stands by me through thick and thin no matter what, just because I'm the new Silas."

"Your adoptive family doesn't love you?"

"Well, yeah, but . . ." She hugged herself, not liking where this was going. "They love me, and I love them. But it doesn't mean I want to be them. I'm just so very different, and it creates a barrier between us. It's complicated." Why was she still talking? She looked at her watch. "Would you look at the time? We really need to keep moving."

"And people call me a closed book."

"Not the first time I've heard that," she admitted.

He paused, and she liked very much that he thought things through before reacting. But that was it. That was *all* he had going for him. Well, that and his very fine ass. And that he'd been nice to everyone here. And that he was still holding DZ even though the baby goat had shed all over his suit.

"So your crew," he said. "The ones you call your family. You lie to them."

She winced at the hard truth of that. "Not lying, exactly. I just haven't yet disclosed the change in ownership."

"Luna, it's business. It's not personal."

He was wrong about that.

"Let me give you some advice you didn't ask for," he said. "Good business doesn't always line up with being liked. That means you can't do only the things that make other people happy because it'll make your job harder, if not impossible. Trust me, I'm good at this."

Oh great. She was talking to his ego. The surest way to an unproductive conversation with a man. Even this man.

He looked around them, taking in the sights she never, ever, got tired of. The lush valley. The gorgeous still-snowcapped peaks all around them. The sounds of the creek running along the eastern property line and wind rustling through the trees . . .

"Here's what I don't get," he finally said. "Your grandfather, despite his sometimes harsh disposition, was a good man. And a generous one. He left you this property that he loved, and yet you let people think the worst of him, your actual blood relative."

"I'm not *letting* them think anything of him. They've formed their own opinions," she said, even knowing he was right. She needed to fix this. She did. But deep inside a voice kept whispering . . . *how great could he have been when he never told me who he really was?*

Especially when he'd clearly chosen Jameson, taken care of him. But not her, not even after he found her and brought her to the farm.

Maybe . . . maybe the fault was all within her, maybe he hadn't wanted to claim her.

And now she'd never know.

CHAPTER 9

After the tour, Luna went to deal with some issue in the orchards, and Jameson found himself a small corner to work in in the staff break/storage/catchall room, starting the painstakingly slow process to take them into the digital age. In the open like this, he was able to observe everyone moving about. The place was . . . well, fascinating, which was actually the most surprising thing of all.

People came and went, checking the big boards on the wall, which held various schedules for who was where, times of animal feedings, etc. On one hand, it felt messy and unnecessary, because if they had an online global doc, no one would have to stop working to come into the office. But on the other hand, the staff being constantly in touch with each other in person also seemed to make things run surprisingly smoothly in spite of the time lost from leaving their stations.

But for him, working in the busiest room made it almost impossible to concentrate. So eventually he took his laptop outside and sat on a bench in the Square, where two things quickly occurred to him. One, the benches were stone and hard as . . . well, stone. And two, being outside in the stunning sunshine with a brilliant blue sky, puffy white clouds, and pine-scented air so fresh it almost burned his lungs felt like a luxury.

As he worked, guests milled around. A clown made helium balloon animals for the kids who came through. On a unicycle. Personally, Jameson was no fan of clowns, but the unicycle skill was impressive. When he realized he'd been people-watching instead of working for twenty straight minutes, he knew he had to move. Plus, his ass was numb.

He managed to just catch Luna by the hand as she came running through—the woman was *always* on the move—and asked her which employee was in the clown suit.

She looked over her shoulder and smiled. "Oh, that's Bill. He's a volunteer." Jameson must've looked horrified because she rushed to say, "We vetted him, of course. He shows up a couple of days a week for an hour or two. Works for tips."

"And that . . ." Jameson gestured to the left, where a woman was walking a baby cow on a leash. "Who's that?"

Luna smiled, her eyes all soft and warm. "Annabelle."

"Why is Annabelle on a leash?"

Luna gave that magical laugh of hers. "Annabelle's the human. She's with the county animal control and brings us animals that need rescuing. The calf's not only orphaned but also nearly blind, so we're taking her in, the hope being that our grown cow, Mable, will mother her. We take in a lot of animals with disabilities. They're dropped off by owners who can no longer care for them, or locals who find them. We're often their last stop."

Very sweet indeed, but . . . "How in the world do we get any insurance company on this planet to issue us liability coverage?"

"Hey, people care about this place. Plus, our insurance agent's kids love it here," she admitted.

"Seems like everything you do here is related to a connection."

She smiled. "Now you're catching on." She wore no makeup, a slight sunburn on her cheeks and nose. Her hair had been piled on top of her head again, her Levi's faded to what looked like a buttery softness, a radio on her hip, and a pair of dusty black sneaks with bright pink shoelaces on her feet, making her somehow look both sexy and adorable at the same time.

"It's the personal connections that make a place like this work," she said. "We'd be hard-pressed to run at all without the help of caring volunteers and the town."

Personal connections were a weak spot of his. It went along with his deep-seated fear of being discarded, deserted, or forced out. Which, of course, was a self-fulfilling prophecy because ever since being a schoolkid, he'd held himself apart from others, finding it easier to go it alone than to risk being the rescue mutt who didn't get picked.

He was no longer a kid, but Apple Ridge Farm was a group of tight-knit people, and he was all too aware of them being a family.

And him being the outsider.

"Gotta go," Luna said.

"Where to?"

"Payroll. It's not going to write itself."

He'd have been horrified that she was doing payroll by hand, but he'd already noted that and had plans in motion to automate that as well. She'd probably kill him, but she had her lane, and he had his. "Why don't you let me take on all of your bookkeeping roles," he said. "You're busy enough."

She looked at him, surprised. "You'd do that?"

"Of course." It was, after all, self-serving.

She flashed him a warm, genuine smile that just about stopped his heart. "Thanks," she said, and started to walk off. "You're watching my ass as I walk away."

Yeah, he was. He'd slept with her in his head, where she'd worn those jeans and nothing else, and he'd taken his time peeling her out of them. He'd woken up disappointed to find it'd been just a dream, but also relieved because being with her in reality, complete with her crazy life, would drive him out of his mind.

But he sure wouldn't turn down another dream . . .

THAT NIGHT, JAMESON entered his hotel room exhausted and smelling like goat. He went straight to the bathroom and stripped for a desperately needed shower.

It was heaven, at least for three whole minutes, until he ran out of hot water. He toweled off and dropped onto the bed. Grief was exhausting. And damn, so were the changes in his life. He didn't miss home, which was really just a high-rise condo in LA that had come furnished and was completely impersonal. Nor did he miss his solo lifestyle. He had casual friends in LA and he dated here and there, but nothing serious in a long time. And he had no regrets about taking the leave of absence from his job to handle Silas's favor. The work would be there when he was ready to return. He knew this because he was good at what he did. Really good. He liked going into a place, finding the good, the bad, the ugly, and figuring out where the value was.

This didn't mean he was welcomed. In fact, it was usually the opposite. He'd long ago taught himself not to care. Work was analysis, that was it.

But this project was different. It didn't feel like just business, it felt personal. Everything he'd ever had, he'd earned from hard work. Silas had taught him the value of that. Nothing had been handed to him. In his experience, people who were handed things never fully appreciated what they had.

And yet he'd been handed 50 percent of this place.

Too tired to think anymore, he closed his eyes, but even then he could still see his new partner, hands on her hips, those pretty eyes flashing, giving him shit. No one *ever* gave him shit. And there, in the dark, he felt his mouth curve into a smile.

He didn't want to be charmed by her fierce, protective, passionate nature. He wanted to be neutral. He wanted to have no feelings toward the farm one way or the other. He wanted it to simply be an ethereal attachment to a man he'd considered a pseudo father. Swearing, he got up, pulled on sweats, and left his room, heading down the hall to the vending machine.

He liked to eat clean. Well, as clean as he could seeing as he was on the road 24/7. But tonight called for snacks of the saturated-fat kind. He bought a Snickers bar and started eating it in front of the vending machine while contemplating what else he needed. A pack of strawberry licorice sticks—which, hey, were practically a fruit, right?—or a bag of spicy-hot Cheetos?

"Whatcha doing?"

Turning, he found a little girl in pigtails and footie pj's, maybe around seven or eight, staring at him. "I'm eating," he said.

"I wanna eat too."

He was pretty sure a grown-ass man wasn't supposed to feed candy to a kid he didn't know. He looked around, but no one else was in the hallway. "Uh . . . where's your keeper?"

"She's coming."

Good. He put more money into the machine and hit the button for the spicy-hot Cheetos.

They didn't drop. "Son of a bitch—" He broke off and eyed the little girl guiltily. "I mean darn."

She grinned. "Son of a bitch!"

Grimacing, Jameson eyed the machine again. It was a shame it didn't sell booze, as he could use some. Oh well, a pack of licorice sticks it was then.

When they dropped, the little girl jumped up and down, clapping her hands in delight. "I want one!"

"No."

"I want a candy! I want a candy! I want a candy!"

Jeez, for a little thing, she had a set of lungs on her. "If I give you one, will you let me take you back to wherever you belong?"

She nodded.

"Okay, lead the way."

"Candy first."

This kid was going places. "Nice try. But no."

She threw herself down on the floor and started screaming bloody murder. Like *earsplitting* bloody murder.

A woman came running out of her room, scooped up the girl, hugging her close as she glared at Jameson.

He lifted his hands, one holding the Snickers bar, the other the licorice.

Her eyes widened. "Were you feeding candy to my daughter?"

"He said no!" the girl sobbed.

The woman lost some of her righteous anger, but still gave him a dirty look as she whirled and vanished with her daughter back inside their room.

Needing the hot Cheetos bad, he tried once more, pumping a fist in victory when this time the bag dropped. He was eating in bed when something thumped against the wall. And then again. And again, speeding up.

Great. The wall-bangers were at it again.

Then the opposite wall started vibrating with sounds of a gunfight from a TV on at full blast. He sighed and, hands laced behind his head, stared up at the ceiling. How the hell had he gotten here? Oh yeah. It'd been the promise to a dead man. And now his immediate future was locked up in Luna and her band of misfits until he could get back to his formerly scheduled life.

At the moment, that couldn't come soon enough.

CHAPTER 10

Luna walked into the offices the next day, butterflies going crazy in her belly. This morning was their weekly staff meeting for the core crew, and Jameson would be witness to it.

She'd been halfway to a panic attack all night, and with every step down the hallway, that percentage increased. She was at a solid 99.5 percent as she got to the doorway of their staff room, because whether she wanted to come clean about being part owner or not—and for the record, she still did not—she knew if she didn't, Jameson would out her.

Everything would fall apart and no one would like her anymore.

Great, and now her heart thundered in her ears and she was breathing too quickly. She sucked in air for a four count and was holding it and trying to count to seven before releasing it when someone reached around her to hand her a brown bag.

"If you eat the muffin inside," Jameson's voice said in her ear, "you can breathe into the bag after."

She turned to face him. He was wearing another button-down and very nice pair of pants, both of which fit him perfectly, but no tie or suit jacket. *And* he was in work boots. *New* work boots. Nope, that was *not* going to make her smile . . . "We're reforming you."

"I'm trying to fit in."

She snorted.

"You don't think I can?"

She looked at his unbuttoned collar, shirtsleeves shoved up his forearms, which looked tan and surprisingly strong. Then she tipped her head up to meet his gaze and realized something. "You're a chameleon." She pointed at him. "You can change your stripes and colors at will."

"You say that like it's a bad thing. Fitting in."

At this, her anxiety doubled down, because she was about to very much *not* fit in anymore. Her cell buzzed, and grateful for the interruption of her impending anxiety attack, she pulled it from her pocket.

"Is it a text from your grandma?" Jameson asked with charming hope.

She showed him her phone.

GRAM: What does spilling the tea mean?
Not the liquid kind, I don't think.

LUNA: It means giving good gossip.

GRAM: So tonight when I go to your mother's house, I can ask her to spill the tea on where she purchased the stick that's up her patoot?

> **LUNA:** No! Or at least make sure I'm
> there so I can see her reaction.

Jameson was smiling. "Why do I get the feeling you're two peas in a pod?"

She'd never thought of it like that, but he was right, and the knowledge was somehow comforting.

He waggled the muffin at her again but she gently pushed it away, too nervous to eat. "Thank you, really, but I can't eat right now." She paused. "Unless it's chocolate?" she asked hopefully.

"Bran. With raisins."

She blinked. "So you hate me then."

"Of course not. The muffin's amazing. I bought it at the place next to the tavern—Sugar Pine Bakery."

At the mention of the tavern, she remembered their kiss, and promptly started breathing too fast again.

"Would it be easier for you if we go in there as two strangers who didn't meet at the bar the night before I came to the farm?"

"No worries either way," she said, while actually worrying *both* ways, plus a secret third way. Nerves had her taking a bite of the muffin. She froze in surprise, then moaned and took several more bites. "Okay, so you're right about the muffin."

"I'm right about a lot of things."

She rolled her eyes and looked at her watch, shoving the rest of the muffin into her mouth. It was time for the meeting that would inevitably change her life, and *not* for the better. This had her shoving her face inside the now empty bag to breathe.

Jameson waited until she got a couple of gulps of air down, then moved closer and kept his voice low. "It's going to be okay."

"You don't know that."

"What's going on?" Willow asked behind them. "Did she watch a Harry Styles video? She always hyperventilates whenever she watches him."

"I'm fine!" Luna yanked the bag from her face. "*Fine.*" She turned to face Willow, who looked like a million bucks, of course.

Willow must've mistaken Luna's expression because she said, "If you're upset because I'm late while holding a coffee I obviously stopped for, you should know it's much better than me being on time *without* this coffee."

"Agreed."

"We ready?" Jameson asked.

"Almost," Willow said. "I'm just waiting to see if my coffee chooses to use its powers for good or evil today."

"We don't want to rush that choice," Luna explained to Jameson. She peeked into the staff room. The rest of her crew were already there: Chef, Milo, Stella, Jeb, and Shep. Feeling sick, she put a hand to her belly.

"Hey." Willow ran a hand up her arm. "What's wrong?"

"Nothing." She managed a smile, even as her stomach churned. She stepped into the room and looked at everyone. "I know we usually open with the week's progress, but I need to talk to you all first." She could feel the weight of Willow's stare, along with her concern, but Luna couldn't go there right now or she might start crying. "Can everyone take a seat?"

This took longer than it should have. It always did. Because first, everyone needed to pour themselves coffee or tea. And then there was a discussion on the latest episode of *Survivor*, and the inevitable debate over which of *them* would make the best survivor. Luna always maintained it'd be her, but no one ever believed her. Currently, everyone's money was on Chef, because he could cook.

Whatever.

When she realized everyone was actually sitting, looking at her, she drew a deep breath. "Okay, so I've got some news."

"Oh my God," Chef said. "Is this about the farm's future? Were you just pacifying me when you assured me it was all okay?" He put a hand to his chest. "Silas left instructions to shut us down." He looked at Jameson. "You're not shutting us down, right? Shit. Silas gave me gas when he was alive, and now he's dead and I *still* have gas. I need Tums. Does anyone have Tums?"

"I've got some, baby." This from Stella, who started rooting through her bag, which was the size of a suitcase.

Chef took a handful.

Milo looked at him, amused. "Can we give Luna the floor again, or do you have another dramatic performance for us this morning?"

Stella shushed them. "My darling Luna's going to tell us that of *course* we're not being shut down and losing our jobs."

"We're not," Luna said.

"Then what?" Willow asked.

Luna took a deep breath. "Silas wasn't just our boss, he was also . . ." She swallowed hard. "My biological grandfather."

Utter silence for three seconds. Then mayhem erupted, with everyone speaking at once.

"*Hey*," Luna said.

No one listened.

So she climbed onto the table and gave a sharp whistle.

The room fell silent for a single beat, then Stella spoke into it. "Why, this is wonderful! You've always wanted to know a blood relative." She was beaming for her. "When did you find this out?"

Luna dragged in another deep breath. "At the reading of his will."

Willow drew in a sharp breath. "Okay, first of all, I'm with Stella on discovering a blood relative." She said this genuinely, but then shook her head. "But you found out right before you met me at the tavern, *three days* ago, and you didn't tell me? I thought we tell each other *everything*."

Luna opened her mouth, but Willow went on. "It's because you feel sorry for me. First a pity job, and now keeping things to yourself. Wow."

"Your job isn't a pity job," Luna said. "Are you kidding me? Not a single person here could do your job. And I know, because we all tried before you moved back to Sunrise Cove six months ago. And I didn't mean for it to be a secret. I just . . . needed a minute."

Willow looked at her watch. "You've had a whole bunch of minutes! Someone bring up the calculator on your phone pronto! What's three days of minutes? And don't forget to double it for the bullshit factor."

"Is this a business meeting?" Jameson asked. "Or high school recess?"

"I know," Milo said. "Sometimes it's hard to tell."

Chef hadn't moved or taken his eyes off Luna. "Are you seriously telling me that penny-pinching, grumpy old man was your grandfather . . . this whole time?"

"This whole time," Luna said.

"And you kept it a secret from us?"

"It's only been three days since I found out," she said.

"And like you've never kept a secret," Milo said to Chef.

"I've *never* kept a secret from you."

"Are you sure? Because let me tell you, you haven't experienced true heartbreak until you've been thinking about your leftovers all day and then come home to find that someone *ate them*."

"*I'm* the one who made the food!"

"And you made it for *moi*."

Chef sighed.

Willow had a hand to her heart. "I feel your pain, Milo. You think you know someone, but then your best friend of over twenty years tells a perfect stranger things she hasn't told you."

Luna sighed. "Jameson only knows because . . ." Well, here went *everything*. "I inherited the other fifty percent ownership of this property."

Utter silence again.

And here it came, her biggest fear. They were all going to hate her now, just like they'd hated Silas. "But that's actually good news," she said, trying to spin it. "Because we can all stay together."

"Actually," Jameson said, pulling out his laptop, "in two

months, the farm owes a balloon payment to a group of investors who covered the extensive renovations here five years ago. According to the terms, if we don't make that payment, they can force us to sell."

"Of course we're going to make the payment," Luna jumped in with, sending Jameson a quick glare. Seemed like the years he'd spent with her grandfather had given him Grinch tendencies as well. "We can fix this."

"Just how short are we?" Stella asked. "Because I could go back to my previous profession—"

"*No!*" Luna said, then had to forcibly soften her voice. Her grandma's previous profession—decades prior—had been marriage. A lot of them. "No," she said again, more quietly. "We'll figure out a way to make this work. Right, Jameson?"

"With a new business plan, hopefully." He patted his laptop.

Luna was beginning to hate that laptop.

"Honey," Chef said, looking hurt. "Why didn't you tell us it was this bad?"

She looked at the man she'd loved and had at one time actually thought she might marry, who'd *always* supported her. And she was letting him down. "I've got a plan."

Chef smiled. "I knew you would."

Milo nodded. So did Stella and the others. Well, everyone but Willow and Jameson. "I'm all ears," he said.

Luna was good at thinking on her feet, really good, but she knew this had to be great. "The most important thing to remember is that we're awesome at our jobs and people love this place. We can invite the investors out here to see for themselves just how beloved the farm is to the entire Tahoe area and beyond. They'll see the potential. Then we'll ask for an extension on the balloon payment, or get our bank to roll it over into a loan. If we just stick together, we can't go wrong."

"Just keep in mind that neither an extension nor a loan is a given," Jameson said. "Not in today's market."

Everyone took their eyes off Luna, to whom they'd always looked to solve any and every problem no matter how big or small, and turned expectantly to Jameson instead.

"Okay then," Chef said. "So what's *your* plan?"

And so it began. The family that had always looked to her for direction now had a new leader, and she couldn't even blame them.

"My plan," Jameson said, sitting there calm and steady, emoting a confidence that couldn't be faked, "would be to think-tank this with all of you. In my experience, the people who work the business have the best ideas for how to fix things."

Oh, he was good. Asking for their opinions meant that maybe they'd talk his ear off all damn day long, and probably nothing would get accomplished, but also? If he actually listened to them, they'd follow him anywhere.

Just like they'd followed her up until this very moment.

Willow raised her hand. "I've been thinking about this idea since I came on board. We could rent out the gardens for events. Weddings, wine parties, things like that."

"Excellent idea," Jameson said.

Brilliant idea, one Luna should've thought of. *One slice of humble pie to go, please . . .*

Shep cleared his throat. "Right now, we hand out food for people to feed the animals. We could charge for the food."

"I like it," Jameson said.

Stella raised her hand next. "I sent my idea to Luna a while back."

"Uh, maybe now's not the time," Luna said quickly because she knew what was coming. A train wreck.

"I'm all ears," Jameson said.

Stella beamed. "We need to add some new equipment. We've got benches in the Square and also at the botanical gardens, but they're made of hard stone, and people of a certain age need a little cushion if you see what I'm saying."

Luna relaxed, because that wasn't what she remembered her grandma's idea being.

"This whole place is bordering on ageism," Stella said. "You're missing an entire demographic of sixty-five and older. For instance, we also need a machine that dispenses things like ibuprofen and Metamucil."

There it was . . .

Chef choked on his tea. Shep and Jeb grinned. Milo and Willow laughed. And *everyone* turned in unison to see Jameson's reaction.

To his credit, he didn't laugh at Stella. "That would be . . . *interesting*. I'll put that on our list of things to consider."

"And Viagra," Stella added. "Viagra in the vending machine."

"I wouldn't be mad at that," Milo said with a smirk. "But how's Viagra going to help the farm make money?"

"Oh it won't," Stella said. "But it'd help my social life."

Jameson was looking at her with an admirably straight face. "The Viagra, while . . . interesting, is a no-go. It's illegal to dispense drugs." He looked around with what might've been a flash of desperation. "Anyone else? Anyone?"

Luna leaned into him. "Hey, Bueller, need the brown bag?"

He rolled his eyes. Good to know she was rubbing off on him. "We could charge for parking," she suggested.

Jameson nodded. "We could also up the entrance fee by twenty percent and still be competitive with other attractions in the area."

Good point, but 20 percent seemed too much. "Ten percent."

Jameson nodded. "I'll take it."

Shep raised his hand. "What about adding a farmers market?"

"*Yes*," Chef said. "With food trucks. Everyone loves a good food truck."

Luna straightened. "Hey, that's a *great* idea. Why didn't you say something about it before?"

Shep shrugged. "I put the idea in the suggestion box a month ago."

Everyone's head swiveled to Luna. Right. The suggestion box. The one she'd put up several years ago, which had been used by the crew to tattle on each other, so she'd stopped looking. Her bad. "You could've just told me. We're all open with each other here."

There was an awkward silence and Luna felt her stomach sink a little. *They weren't all open with each other?*

"A farmers market is good," Jameson said into the awkward silence. "It's also a big step. Let me run some numbers to see if it's viable, although off the top of my head, for this venue, during the late spring and summer months, it makes a lot of sense. But . . ." He looked at Chef. "It'd cut into the Bright Spot's revenues."

Chef shook his head. "It's a different clientele. More foot traffic means more money for all of us. And to be honest, I could take off whatever days we run a farmers market. I wouldn't mind having some more personal time . . ."

Luna stared at him, shocked. "You eat, live, and breathe the café. What do you need personal time for?"

He looked at Milo and smiled. "A life."

Luna's love for him had shifted over the years they'd been together. It was now a deep, abiding friendship sort of love. A family love, because she absolutely considered him blood. But it was still hard to know he'd so easily moved on to have successful relationships while she hadn't managed a successful anything.

Jameson nodded. "Food trucks are great, so that's going on the list too. Low overhead for us."

"One of my friends is the sole ghostbuster in the area," Stella said. "She travels around to fairs and sets up a booth. She's very popular. I'm sure she'd be thrilled to come in as often as we want her." Again she pointed to Jameson's laptop. "Write that down too."

Jameson dutifully typed something. Whether it was about Stella's friend or a smoke signal asking for help was anyone's guess.

"Oh!" Chef said. "My boyfriend is a social media influencer and he always says if you can get them to spread the word, you're golden."

Milo blushed.

Chef laughed and reached for his hand.

"I think this ends our so-called business meeting," Luna said dryly.

Everyone stopped to talk to her on their way out.

"I feel like we're in good hands," Chef said, nodding toward Jameson.

"I like him," Shep said.

Stella nodded. "He's the nicest, and so cute too."

"Agreed," Milo said. "Do you think he's got a six-pack?"

Jeb, of course, said nothing. But he looked at ease, and if he had a problem about anything, he'd have at the very least texted Luna on the spot.

Chef leaned in and whispered, "Let me work some magic on your hair and set you up with him."

"No!" She drew a deep breath, refusing to run her hand over her hair to check it, or to tell Chef that Jameson had already turned her down, because *both* were humiliating. "*Don't you dare.*"

Willow was last. "Are you okay?" she asked with genuine concern. "Silas being blood really is a huge deal for you."

"I'm okay," Luna said quietly. "Thanks, and I'm sorry—"

"Nope. Don't apologize for something you did very purposefully."

Luna winced at the truth of that. "I just . . . needed a moment."

Willow nodded. "And now so do I. I need some time and space."

"Hey, that's what you told Shayne, and now you two are separated."

"Well, if the shoe fits . . ." Willow started to walk away but paused. "Tell me the truth. Did you ever really ask Silas for that promotion for me?"

Luna sucked in a breath.

Willow's eyes went cold. "Yeah. That's what I thought. Thanks for the vote of confidence."

"No, you don't understand. Willow—"

"Just answer me this. Now that you're in Silas's shoes, are you going to give me the promotion?"

Luna's stomach hit her toes. She couldn't bring herself to lie again, but nor could she give Willow what she wanted, it would never work. "Listen—"

"No. Never mind." Willow turned to go, but then whirled back. "Oh, and for the record?" She nodded toward Jameson. "I like him. Certainly a lot more than I like you right now."

When she was gone, Luna turned to Jameson, who'd been silent, just watching and taking in everyone's reaction.

"What was that about?" he asked.

"She's always wanted to be a manager, and asked me to see if Silas would promote her, but . . ." She grimaced. "While she's amazing at a lot of things, managing people isn't one of them. Silas said hell no."

"So you're protecting Silas? Why not just tell her he said no?"

"I'm not protecting Silas. I'm protecting Willow. It would crush her."

"Okay," he said, nodding. "And the smoke curling out from the top of your head?"

"That's all for you. You should've talked to me first before we had an open-table discussion. I've found with too many cooks in the kitchen, you only end up with a grease fire."

"Okay, yes, you're right and I'm sorry. But the place is already in flames. *And* they had some valid ideas." He paused. "For all your open kindness, for how much they all care about you, why have you never asked them for help?"

She looked away, disarmed by his easy apology. "I like to rely on myself."

"But you've got a great crew. You never have to rely on only yourself."

"You're just saying that because *you* came off as the good guy today and I came off as the person who after all this time of gaining their trust, broke it."

He shook his head. "You were just trying to protect them. They'll understand that."

"Says the guy who's probably never had to earn someone's trust or love in your life."

"You have no idea." Before she could ask what that meant, he nodded his head toward her office. "Can we go over some things?"

She led the way. Inside her office, he moved to the window that overlooked the Square, and beyond that the beautiful orchards where cherry blossoms were in full bloom. Leaning against the sill, hands in his pockets, he murmured, "I forgot how pretty it is here."

"You sound surprised."

He turned to face her. "Nothing surprises me. At least not anymore."

"Not even the idea of putting in a Viagra-dispensing machine?"

That earned her a smile. "Okay, maybe that." He ran a hand over his jaw, which she was starting to realize was a tell. He was going to say something that he wasn't sure would be well received.

Damn. She really should've stayed in bed today.

CHAPTER 11

Just say it," Luna said to Jameson, feeling impatient because . . . well, because he looked better than any man had a
right to. "Say whatever it is you think I'm not going to like. I'm
not a special snowflake."

He met her gaze, reluctant amusement in his. "I've noticed.
And I'm grateful, as you're the perfect person to be managing
this place. You're pretty kick-ass, I hope you know that."

Something weird happened low in her belly at the compliment. "And . . . ?"

"And . . . you know we're bleeding money here. That we need
to tighten the belt. The way I see it, we have only a few options."

"Such as you leaving, trusting me to fix things on my own?"
she asked with a sweet smile.

He smiled. "Good to know where you stand, but no. We're in
this mess together. And there's a time limit on this."

"The balloon payment," she said.

"That, and the fact that my max leave without losing my job
is two months."

She tried to figure out how she felt about this and settled on offended. "This isn't some hobby for me, Jameson. It's a full-time job. More than a full-time job."

"I know. You work twelve-hour days, and I'm in awe of all you handle."

He was in awe of all she handled?

"But," he said.

Oh great. A but.

"We're barely breaking even, Luna. And that's not going to just go away. Back to our options. One, we work together. Or two—which sucks, but it is an option—you could sell your fifty percent."

Look at that, she was offended *and* ticked off. "Let me guess. To you?"

"Or the investors."

She stared at him. "You don't even like it here."

He didn't bite. Nor did he lose his cool the way she did. "Because I loved Silas," he said calmly. "And he loved this property."

Right. The grandfather who'd never even told her who he was. "Well, I've got two responses to your two options. One, it's never going to happen. Two, never ever. And three, you're a jerk."

A corner of his mouth quirked. "I thought you only had two responses."

"Oh, I've got many, *many* more than two, but I'm trying to be polite and keep my opinions to myself."

"Good to know." His eyes never left hers, those green-gold eyes that seemed to see everything, even the stuff she didn't want anyone to see. "Let me give you another option," he said.

"It's the one where everyone loses their job because we lose the farm."

She blew out a breath. "Okay, fine, we work together. But I'm not going to like it."

"Noted."

Great. Fantastic. Perfect. Frustrated, angry, and, dammit, a little scared that he was right, she stood. "This has been fun, but I've got a million things to do." She headed to the door, then sighed and turned back, telling herself to be adult about this. "I meant to ask you yesterday. Where are you staying?"

"I've spent the last few nights at the Sunrise Cove Inn," he said. "In a room between seventy-year-old newlyweds with thirty-year-old stamina, and a guy who watches true-crime shows at full volume all night long. I was going to spend some time today looking for a short-term rental."

Well, you asked . . . She tried to keep her mouth shut, she really did, but he was going to be here for two months and she couldn't in good conscience make him pay for a place when they could put him up. "Take one of the cabins for now. They're small, and not anything to write home about, but better than a hotel."

"Great, thank you," he said, seeming genuinely relieved.

The exact opposite of what she was feeling. She opened her desk and pulled out a key. "Come on. I'll walk you as far as the cherry blossoms. I've got to talk to Jeb."

Ten minutes later, she stopped at the fork in the trail, the botanical gardens straight out in front of them. She could see Willow out there, on her knees in front of a row of baby raspberry bushes, gloves on her hands as she worked in the dirt doing . . .

well, Luna had no idea what exactly, something no doubt to make her plants happy to grow for her. Willow had the greenest thumb of anyone she knew.

Luna had the *blackest* thumb on the entire planet. She couldn't grow a thing, but she knew how to manage the people who could.

Willow looked up.

Luna waved.

Willow did not.

"Problem?" Jameson asked.

"Yes." *And it's you* . . . "I've got to go. Stay on the trail as it winds up behind the orchards, then around the hugest pine tree you've ever seen and then up a small hill. There are seven small cabins. Yours is the last one. Um . . ." She wrestled with her conscience some more. "You should probably know, that one's rumored to be haunted. It's also the closest to the woods."

He took the key. "Worried about me?"

She was worried that her cabin wasn't far enough from his.

He gave her a small smile, like he could read her thoughts. "I'm too tired to hear any ghosts," he assured her. "Plus, I like the sounds of the woods. It's been a long time since I was here."

"With Silas."

He nodded.

"And he raised you."

"I was raised by my mom." He looked away, off at the beautiful orchards, though she was pretty sure he wasn't seeing them. "She passed away from untreated pneumonia when I was fourteen."

"You said Silas took you in when you were fifteen. Who did you live with for that year in between?"

"Couch surfed, stuff like that," he said vaguely. "Then one day I tried to get a job taking care of the lawns at Silas's properties. Got caught lying about my age." His lips curved slightly. "He gave me a job anyway, and room and board."

Her heart skipped a beat at the implication of what he'd said, and what he hadn't. Maybe she'd always felt like the square peg in a round hole when it came to her parents, but at least she'd never been on her own as a teenager for an entire year.

"Don't feel sorry for me," he said quietly. "I don't deserve it. Plus, you didn't exactly have the perfect life either."

"I always had a roof over my head and food to eat."

"And love?" he asked. "Did you always have love? Because I did. Maybe not from my father, but certainly from my mom. And then Silas." He tilted his head. "Or at least his version of love."

Uncomfortable with the direction this conversation was going, she started to walk off, but she couldn't do it, she just couldn't wrestle her conscience into submission. "Make sure to lock your door, okay? Bears like to break in and eat raspberry tarts left out on the counter."

"Only raspberry tarts?"

She saw the light of humor in his eyes. "You jest." *And why was that so attractive?* "But one day last year, after I'd just bought a four-pack of the most *amazing* raspberry tarts, I had to rush back to the office to solve a problem. When I got home again, there was Winnie-the-Pooh standing at my counter inhaling the tarts."

His brows shot up. "And you . . . what?"

"Yelled at him and waved my arms until he went out the same window he'd climbed in. But it was too late. The tarts were gone."

He laughed softly. "Most women would be focused on the close call with a bear, but not you."

She shrugged. "California black bears aren't aggressive. And I *really* needed those tarts."

"Courageous, as well as stubborn *and* overbearingly protective of those you care about," he said, still smiling. "So, the moral of this story is to also lock your windows along with your door?"

She snorted. "No, it's to always eat the raspberry tarts first thing. *Never* save the good stuff for later."

He laughed again. And damn, he had a really good laugh. Guilt for giving him the haunted cabin swamped her enough to do an about-face. "You know what? I'll walk you."

They headed up the path in what she hoped wasn't an awkward silence. "You confuse me," she finally admitted.

"How?"

She hadn't meant to say the "you confuse me" out loud, but she had, so she faced him. "Sometimes it seems like you're flirting with me."

"Because I am."

She almost tripped over her own two feet. "So . . . you can flirt with me, but not sleep with me?"

He winced and started to say something, but she closed her eyes in mortification. "Please scratch that from the record." She started walking again. The next time she spoke her thoughts out loud, she was going to cut off her own tongue.

When they got to the cabins, they both eyed the first six,

which were clearly fairly well tended. Neat front walks. The seventh looked a bit neglected. Jameson didn't say a word, but Luna's guilt grew a teeny-tiny bit as she inserted the key in the door handle—only it wasn't locked. The door swung open to reveal Shayne Green, Willow's estranged husband, sprawled out on the couch watching TV.

"What are you doing here?" she asked.

"It was my day off." Shayne sat up with a yawn, tossing the remote aside. "Sorry. I didn't want to hang out at the fire station anymore, or go home to an empty house."

"I understand." And she really did. Willow had only been mad at Luna for a few hours and she missed her already. She couldn't imagine what Shayne was going through. "Shayne, this is Jameson Hayes, part owner of Apple Ridge. And Jameson, this is Shayne, newly minted interim fire chief for Sunrise Cove."

Shayne got up and shook Jameson's hand, and they nodded to each other in that word-miserly way men had. Shayne's phone beeped. He looked at the display and grimaced. "I've gotta get to the station." He one-arm hugged Luna, brushing a kiss to the top of her head. "Tell Willow . . ." He seemed to falter for words.

"You could come to poker night and tell her whatever you want yourself," she suggested.

He shook his head. "I promised her some space, and I'm trying to honor that promise even if it kills me. Just tell her hi and that I miss her. But be sure to duck when you say it."

"She'll come around."

He gave her a small smile, tugged playfully on a loose strand of her hair, and left. Luna turned to find Jameson watching her with an expression she couldn't place. "What?"

"You're a good friend."

After what had happened with Willow regarding a promotion, or lack thereof, she wasn't sure that was actually true. Which was probably what was causing the panic simmering at a low boil in her gut.

"Want to talk about it?" he asked.

"About what?"

"Whatever you just thought about to make you sad."

"No." Hell no. She mustered a smile. "Anyway, good luck, and don't forget, put all the food away, *always.*"

"I'll be fine."

She headed to the door, then paused. "Purely out of morbid curiosity, if you get eaten, what happens to your half of the farm?"

He let out a low laugh. "How about I don't get eaten?"

She rolled her eyes at the both of them and opened the door.

"Luna?"

She looked back. "Yeah?"

"For the record, I *did* want to sleep with you. *Desperately.* Still do." And then he shut the door, leaving her standing there stunned.

CHAPTER 12

The next morning, Willow stood in line for coffee at the same little coffeehouse she went to every day for her caffeine pick-me-up. Normally she and Luna met there to sit for a moment and bitch about life, but there was no sign of Luna. And anyway, Willow didn't want to see her.

So why are you here at your usual time?

The line was long, but it always was. That was the price she willingly paid for coffee that tasted better than anywhere else on the planet. In front of her stood a woman with two little girls wearing matching candy-striped leggings and bright red sweaters streaked with dirt. Their ponytails were loose, their hair wild. And they were arguing.

"Mommy, she touched me!" Thing One said.

"Mommy, she's looking at me!" Thing Two said. "And I gotta go potty!"

Mommy seemed like maybe she needed coffee more than her next breath. When she caught Willow looking at her, she sighed. "'Have kids,' they said, 'it'll be fun,' they said." She shook her head. "I haven't gotten to the fun part yet. I think they lied about the fun."

"Mommy! Hurry!" Thing Two was now doing the potty dance.

The woman looked at Willow with desperation. "I'm sorry, but you look like a nice person, and I've got a bathroom emergency. I'm going to leave Charlotte to hold my place in line. Can you keep an eye on her?"

"Uh . . ." Willow looked around for an adultier adult, but the girls' mom was already vanishing into the restroom. Panic filled her as she eyed Charlotte, aka Thing One.

Charlotte eyed her right back. "Where do babies come from?"

Willow choked on her gum. "Seriously?"

Charlotte shrugged. "I asked my older brother and he said babies come from trees." She gestured out the window at the trees lining the lot. "But I don't see any babies in them, do you?"

Dear God. This was so above her pay grade. "Uh . . . maybe they're up higher than we can see."

When Charlotte's mom showed back up with Thing Two in tow, Charlotte was still craning her neck to see higher up in the trees.

"What are you doing?" her mom asked.

"The babysitter said babies *do* come from trees, and maybe we can't see them because they're too high up."

The woman turned to stare at Willow.

"Okay, that's not exactly how the conversation went," Willow said, but it was too late. The woman grabbed her girls' hands and marched out of the shop.

Willow made a mental note to buy Shayne a case of condoms.

Several customers received their coffees and everyone in line shuffled forward. So close now. She glanced at her watch. Normally, this was her favorite part of her day, but not today. Today she felt hollow inside, like she was missing something as important as a limb. And that limb's name was Luna, dammit.

Everyone at Apple Ridge had easily accepted the news about the new ownership. And it wasn't like Luna had done anything wrong, but . . . well, to be selfish about it, it negated their dream, the one that Willow had been carrying in her back pocket for a really long time.

But both Luna and Shayne had their own dreams now, their ducks lined up in a row all nice and neat.

Willow didn't even have a single duck.

The door to the coffee shop opened and in waltzed Luna, wearing jeans, work boots that had seen better days, and a sweatshirt that had a tractor on it and read: *Keep Calm and Farm On*—looking cute and pretty, and absolutely clueless about it. And as she did every single day, she headed right for Willow.

Willow stared at her. "*No cutting.*"

"Love your sweatshirt," someone behind them said.

Luna beamed. "Oh, thank you. We sell them at Apple Ridge Farm."

"I love that place!"

Mandy, the barista, was waving at Luna. "Your order's up, hon!"

Of course it was. Luna always ordered hers ahead of time because she hated to wait. Willow didn't because she hated her coffee not piping hot. But the real truth was that Luna's people skills knew no bounds, and even though she was a complete mess half the time, people always embraced her with open arms. Always.

That wasn't the case with Willow, and she sighed, knowing she needed to try harder with people. A lot harder.

Luna ran up to the front to get her coffee, then came back to Willow holding two cups. "Here," she said. "I got yours too. Let's go."

Willow took the cup—she was angry but not stupid—and followed Luna outside, but stopped short of going to one of the open tables with her. "I've got to get to work."

Luna stopped too and turned to face her. "Look, about yesterday—"

"No." Willow shook her head. "Not going there." She took a sip of her coffee and made a face. As always when Mandy was working, her order was completely wrong.

"I got us scones," Luna said, and waved the bag.

Willow's mouth watered. "Blueberry?"

"Pumpkin."

Oh, thank God. Blueberry would've swayed her and her hips couldn't afford it. "No thank you."

Luna's smile faded. "Please, will you sit for a minute?"

With a sigh, she sat.

Luna looked relieved. "I wasn't sure you'd be here."

"Yeah, well, I wasn't sure either." Willow shook her head. "No, that was a lie. I wanted to come because I wanted to see you grovel."

Luna's expression never changed. She'd walked into the place worried, and she still was. "Would that help?"

"Yes." *No.* Willow knew it wouldn't, but damn. Her emotions about the situation went so much deeper than she'd realized. And it wasn't even about being angry. It was the hurt beneath it that killed her. They'd had each other's back now for over two decades, through thick and thin, and there'd been a lot of thin. Their childhoods had bonded them, and while they didn't always agree, Willow couldn't remember a single time when they'd fought. The thought made her feel a little sick.

Luna blew out a breath. "I'm sorry I didn't tell you at the tavern. I meant to." She set down her coffee and looked away. "I guess I wasn't ready to tell anyone about it."

"Since when am I just anyone?"

"You're not." Luna turned back, putting her hand on Willow's. "You're not," she repeated softly. "I'm just still trying to process it all." And then her eyes filled.

Damn. Luna never cried, never, and Willow ached for her. Turning her hand over and entwining their fingers, she took a deep breath. "Okay, I guess my hurt feelings can take a back seat for a hot minute, but only because I get that this is life changing for you."

Luna swiped away her tears with her free hand, never letting go of Willow, and she felt her eyes sting. Luna's adoptive parents were well-meaning but older, and though they'd loved her in their own way, her life had been filled with stringent requirements to achieve in areas important to them but not to Luna. As a result, she'd often been seen as a failure. They'd never understood why she wouldn't want to be in the medical world, as they were. Willow had watched Luna spend her teenage years struggling to fit into the role they wanted her to fit into. She'd been there when Luna had tried to get her sealed birth records opened, but couldn't. She'd seen Luna get her heart broken by men because she didn't understand unconditional love. Still didn't.

Not that Willow had learned that from her parents either.

They were two peas in a pod in that way. In most ways. But there was one major difference. Luna operated on emotions, giving in to her feelings for every decision. Willow was the opposite. She did her best to completely ignore her emotions, especially now that she and Shayne were done. She gently squeezed Luna's hand. "Do your parents know about Silas?"

"I don't know. I also don't know why Silas didn't tell me," Luna said softly. "According to the attorney, he was sick for months and knew the end was near, and he never told a soul. What could possibly have kept him from telling me?"

At a loss, Willow shook her head.

Luna tossed up a hand, but only one because she still had a death grip on Willow's. "Why didn't he want me to know? If he'd told me even after he'd first gotten sick, we could've at least had a few months to get to know each other as family."

Willow thought of her own mom, who'd also been tough and distant like Silas, no reason given. "Sometimes we don't get to know the why. And maybe when Silas hired you, he planned to tell you, but somehow the moment never came, and then it was too late. Maybe . . . maybe his gift of ownership was him trying to apologize for his shortcomings and hoping you could get to a place where you understood."

"Maybe," Luna said, clearly doubtful.

"When you received his job offer, you were floundering. Remember? You'd been unable to find a job that suited you, and you were unhappy. He fixed that for you."

"Yeah, he did. But all the things he didn't tell me are sort of overshadowing that now." Luna stood up.

"You're leaving?"

"Have to get back to work."

"You're the boss now," Willow reminded her, and ignored the little stab of jealousy, because being the boss, being her own boss, had been all she'd ever wanted. "You've got another few minutes. After all, you wasted all our time making everything about you."

Luna snorted, but sat back down. "You mean after you told me to stop pitying myself?"

"That's not what I said."

"It's what I heard."

"Okay, fine," Willow said. "You're pitying yourself, when you've got everything you could ever want right now."

Luna started to open her mouth, but Willow held up a finger. "Including your new guy. I mean, I get it. He's hot in a very sexy nerd sort of way."

"He's not my new guy."

"Uh-huh. Is that why you've been wearing mascara?"

Luna flushed. "Hey. Once you start a new tube, you gotta use it up."

"I saw you kiss him, remember?" Willow said.

then came closer, setting down the coffee and scone on her workshop table. "What's wrong?"

"I just got in a fight with Luna."

"You two never fight."

A few tears escaped and she sniffed. "I guess there's a first time for everything."

His hands were on her arms, running up and down. "Oh, babe. I'm so sorry. Want to talk about it?"

She swiped at her tears. "No."

"Because you're still mad at me?"

"Because you're being nice. And you know I hate when you're nice while we're arguing."

Shayne sighed and dropped his hands from her. "I guess I'd hoped after the other night—"

"You thought because we had sex, everything would be fixed and we'd be happy?"

He gave her a small smile. "Babe, news flash. All you gotta do to make me happy is show up. Maybe naked. Maybe with food."

She choked out a laugh that might've also been a sob.

"Hey," he said softly, tilting her head up. "Talk to me."

"Silas was Luna's biological grandpa, and when he died, he left her half of the farm."

"Wow. *Nice.* And . . . ?"

"*And* she didn't tell me! Instead, she waited until the staff meeting and told us all at the same time. And then on top of it all, Silas said no to my promotion and she wasn't even going to tell me about it."

With a sound of understanding, he pulled her into his arms and she caught herself going willingly, then froze. What was she doing? When was she going to learn how to stand on her own two feet? Every man for himself and all that, and she stepped back.

"So we can't even hug now?" he asked.

"The whole point of our separation is for me to figure out who I am, and yet once again I'm leaning on you as a crutch. Literally, in fact." She turned away. "You know what? I can't do this now."

"Then let's talk about it over dinner."

"We don't have dinner plans."

"But we could."

She could see in his eyes that he was hoping for a repeat of the bar incident, and she was tempted. Oh, so tempted. But that would only make things worse. Their problems had never been in the bedroom. "I feel lost, Shayne. And confused."

"Join my club."

She stared at him. "What are *you* confused about? You're the one in the driver's seat. You've never even asked me to be your copilot."

He tossed up his hands. "This again? You wanted me to take a less dangerous job, and I did."

"You could've taken it where we were, in New Mexico!"

Shayne's patience was endless, always had been, but he shoved his hands through his hair. "You and I both know this was the better career path. And I thought we were honest with each other, no matter what."

"What does that mean?"

"Do you have any idea how good you are at pretending nothing hurts you ever? I still can't tell if you're hurt that we're not together."

Her jaw dropped. "*Shayne—*"

But he was already walking away. "Enjoy your scone and coffee."

Alone, she sank onto a bench and pressed the heels of her hands to her eyes, her chest aching. It really pissed her off that she was crying. Like Luna, she wasn't a crier. Never had been. Her childhood had beaten that out of her.

Someone sat next to her and she dropped her hands, her heart leaping with painful hope that it was Shayne, back to somehow help her fix them.

Instead, Stella handed her a small pack of tissues. "I warned you that the stars weren't aligned in your favor, and that this week wasn't the week to make any complicated decisions."

Willow leaned back and stared up at the sky. "I didn't make the decisions. The decisions cornered me."

"Did the decisions corner you about having a baby?"

Willow sat up straight. "*What?*"

"Aren't you pregnant?"

"No!" She put her hands to her stomach, which, okay, wasn't exactly flat. "It's called one too many scones, jeez."

"Sorry. The cards told me—"

Willow relaxed back with a rough laugh. "You and your tarot cards."

"They're rarely wrong."

"Well, they are this time." Which she hoped was true because she didn't want to be pregnant.

And since when she'd started lying to herself, she had no idea.

"Parenting isn't bad," Stella said. "I mean sure, it's a lot like drowning except when you finally surface for air you immediately catch on fire . . ."

Willow snorted.

"No, but really, having a kid can be nice. Mine turned out to be a bit of an uptight asshole, but hey, no one's perfect." Stella met Willow's eyes. "Not Shayne. Not Luna. And not you either."

Well, wasn't that the screwed-up truth. "What should I do?" she whispered.

Stella gave her a warm hug. "Sorry, baby. My cards don't tell anyone how to live their life."

Right. So she was all on her own then. She should probably get used to that.

CHAPTER 13

At the ungodly screech of what *had* to be a possessed rooster, Jameson shot out of bed and bashed his shin on the bed frame. He was still hopping on one foot and swearing when there was a second cock-a-doodle-do that sounded like it was right there in the room with him, but when he turned on the light, he was alone.

He'd just survived his second night in the "haunted" cabin without seeing any ghosts. Unless ghosts screeched cock-a-doodle-do. He decided to go for a run. With his heart still trying to burst out of his chest, he pulled on sweats, opened the cabin door, and came face-to-face with a massive rooster, who spread his wings, ducked his head low, and charged.

Reacting without thinking, he raised his arms and yelled, "*Back!*"

The rooster pulled up short and leveled an eye at him, but slowly backed away.

"Terrorizing the local fowl?"

He turned and found Luna looking like maybe she wanted to

laugh. "You've got it backward," he muttered. "And what the hell was that thing?"

"Wyatt Chirp. He's actually super shy and sweet. He was just looking for a handout."

"Shy? *Sweet*?" he asked in disbelief.

"Yep." She crouched low and made a clucking sound.

Wyatt Chirp came running back, wings extended, making continuous happy sounds as he basically threw himself at her.

Luna caught him and scratched his chest. Then she pulled something out of a pocket, which Wyatt Chirp gobbled up, then clucked out a possible "thank you" and left.

Jameson had to laugh. She was the prettiest Dr. Dolittle he'd ever seen.

"Did you sleep okay?" she asked.

"Sure. Except for the ghost."

Her mouth fell open and he grinned.

She shook her head. "Funny."

"Hey, I'm a good time."

"Are you though?"

This made him laugh. "You're still mad at me."

"I don't get mad. I get even."

He wasn't sure what it said about him that he liked her grumpy side. He also liked her pissed-off side. They made her real. But his favorite was her playful side, because it brought out his, which he didn't get to use often. Fact was, he liked *all* her sides, which spelled nothing but trouble. "You start work early."

"At oh-dark-thirty," she said. "Shep and Jeb have two guys out today, so I'm lending a hand."

"On top of all your other roles."

"Yes. Well, except for the accounting that you took over, so thanks for that because it saves me a lot of time."

"I'm here, I'm going to pull my weight."

"Appreciate it," she said. "We all tend to handle whatever's needed."

"Who handles your . . . *whatever*?"

Was that a blush hitting her cheeks? Stepping closer, then closer still, he bent his knees a little to better see her face. Yep. A blush. He laughed softly. "I'd give my week's salary to know what you're thinking. Preferably in great detail."

She rolled her eyes. "Like I'm going to dignify *that* with a response." She started to walk away.

"Luna."

She shot back.

He smiled. "I'd be happy to handle your . . . whatever . . . any day of the week."

She studied him for a long moment, then shook her head. "You had your chance."

"And if I said I'd like another?"

"Then I'd say it's a bad idea."

No kidding. It was a *terrible* idea. Didn't stop him from wanting it though. Or wanting her.

"We're polar opposites," she said. "I'm a people pleaser, and you're . . ."

He smiled. "Not? You're right. But there's a compromise in there somewhere."

"Yeah, and it's called love and happiness, which neither of us is any good at."

He laughed ruefully because he recognized the truth when he heard it. When she was gone, he took that run, then showered, dressed, and headed out. A few minutes later, he walked into the office building, looking for a place to work. He'd tried the staff room—too crowded. He'd also tried the front room. Too small, too cluttered, and whenever he did sit there, any guests who wandered in tended to turn to him like he was the receptionist, usually wanting to know where the restroom was.

He acquisitioned a folding table he'd seen leaning against a wall in the hall, taking it to Luna's office. She had a walk-in closet just behind her door. Possibly his shower in his cabin was bigger, but it was private. Unfortunately, it was also filled to the gills, this one with file boxes dating back a decade. Stacking them more neatly against one wall, he was able to make enough room to squeeze in the folding table. He snagged a chair from the staff room and voilà . . . he had a makeshift office. Sure, he had to climb over the folding table to get in and out, and in doing that twice already had bashed his sore shin, but the quiet was worth it.

He was working away when he heard the now familiar "*bleeeat*" and then tiny hooves trying to climb up his legs. With a sigh, he scooped up Dammit Ziggy—in SpongeBob pj's today. "I think you should've been named Houdini."

DZ set his head on Jameson's chest and looked up at him with a content expression on his face, and he knew he was in trouble. Ignoring the warm feels spreading through him, Jameson shifted the goat so he could work with him in his lap. DZ instantly fell asleep, drooling on Jameson's jeans.

Yes, jeans. He'd given up on professionalism.

He went back to work on his project of taking the farm into the twenty-first century. For the millionth time, he wondered what the actual hell Silas had been thinking, leaving the farm's bookkeeping on paper only, no backup system . . . It went against the grain of everything the old man had ever taught him. The only thing he could think was that Silas had enjoyed the secrecy of it all, keeping this place separate from everything else.

And the more time he spent here, the more he understood it. He'd come into this thinking he'd put in the time he'd promised, then he'd sell his portion, or encourage Luna to sell to the investors.

Now he wasn't so sure. If it wasn't so absolutely crazy to even think it, he might be scared that the place was actually growing on him.

He heard footsteps coming his way and looked up just as Stella peeked around the open closet door at him.

"Here, Hot Stuff." She set a hot coffee on the corner of his makeshift desk. She eyed the goat in his lap, and then Jameson's long legs bent awkwardly, bumping up against the table. "You good?"

"I've worked with less room before." Which was true. He never knew what kind of space he'd find to work in when he was sent into a company. Hell, once in a particularly hostile situation, he'd worked in his rental car for weeks on end. "I've never had an emotional support goat before."

She laughed. "I *knew* it. I *knew* you had a sense of humor. It was written in the lines of your palm."

"Speaking of palms, you're pretty quick with yours," he said. "You're very good."

With a wink, she turned to go.

"Stella."

She shot an innocent smile his way. "Has anyone ever told you that your eyes are gorgeous?" she asked.

He held out his hand, wiggling his fingers.

"Damn." But she handed over the pen she'd just stolen. "I must be losing my touch."

He simply smiled. "No, I'm just also very good."

She tipped her head back and laughed.

Ten minutes later, Milo came by to see if Luna was in and went brows up at Jameson behind the door. "Honey, never let anyone put you in the closet." Then he set a book on the table.

#FollowMe, by Milo Young. "It's about my experiences as a social media influencer," he said. "I hope I'm not being presumptuous, but you seem like the studious type who enjoys reading, so I thought I'd kiss up and thank you for letting me park my ass here for free and write."

"I look like the studious type?"

Milo grinned. "Actually, some might say you look like an uptight accountant, but hey, not judging. I think nerds are sexy as hell."

Jameson didn't know where to go with that, so he took another direction. "You park your ass here for free?" He already knew the answer. He had it on his list of things to discuss with Luna on a day he felt like being murdered.

Milo flashed a smile. "Well, yes. But I'm dedicating my book to the farm, and my social media and newsletters bring in lots of visitors, so . . ." He gave a finger wave, murmured "toodles," and was gone.

"He's pretty, isn't he?"

Jameson looked up just as Chef set a small brown bag on his desk. "A breakfast sandwich," the guy said. "Five stars, if I say so myself. Hope you're not looking after your cholesterol."

Jameson made a show of looking past Chef. "Is there some sort of schedule to spy on the new guy, or are you all just insanely nosy?"

"Both." Chef smiled. "Don't be insulted. It means we like you. Well, I like you. And Stella and Milo like you. Pretty sure Willow doesn't give a shit about anything right now, which has nothing to do with you. And Luna . . . Well." He shrugged.

"Well what?" He didn't know why he asked. Clearly the circus was getting to him.

Chef's smile faded some. "She's been through a lot, so she holds back with anyone new. I blame her parents and the exes who hurt her."

Jameson stilled. "Exes hurt her? Plural?"

"Emotionally."

"Just as bad," Jameson said, fighting his inner caveman, who wanted to track down anyone who'd caused her pain.

"Well, you know what happened with her and me," Chef said.

"And though I had to be true to myself, I hated that it hurt her. I still love her, you know. So much." He shook his head. "But the ass who came around after me was way worse."

"How?"

"Wanted her to change who she was." Chef's jaw tightened. "Gaslit her for a little bit into thinking she wasn't enough, but you can't fool Luna for long. She dumped him when she realized what he was doing to her confidence. It left a mark though."

Jameson drew a careful breath. "Where is he now?"

"Long gone, and don't worry, *way* ahead of you." Chef smiled darkly. "He came into the Bright Spot one day and briefly left his phone unattended at the table. I changed his mom's name to the girl he cheated on Luna with. Later, we heard through the grapevine he sent his mom a dick pic."

Jameson smiled his approval. "Creative."

"Oh, it gets better. Milo went into his IG account and posted a story as him that read: *I'm an asshole, don't date me*, and then we turned off his notifications."

That gave him a rough laugh. "Remind me to never get on your bad side."

Not two minutes after Chef left, Luna walked right past him to her desk, yelling over her shoulder, "Who left my closet door open? Shayne said we need to keep this door closed! Fire hazard—"

Jameson stuck his foot out to stop the door from closing on him.

Squeaking in surprise, Luna yanked the door open again to stare at him behind it, her mouth dropping in shock. "*What are you doing in there?*"

Before he could answer, the radio on her hip crackled. "Luna, darling, your mom's on the phone again," Stella said.

Luna groaned and pulled the radio off her hip. "Take a message."

"No can do," Stella radioed back. "She says if I don't put you through, she's going to show up here."

Luna face-palmed. "The last time she was here, Kong pooped on her new shoes and I can't hear that story again. Tell her no!"

"You know I'd do anything for you, honey, but she's still not speaking to me. I sorta, um, dated her best friend's father, and he gave me the diamond necklace that Donna had been hoping to get. I mean, honestly. I can't help that she was always mean to him and he didn't want her to have it. Or that I'm so irresistible."

Luna sighed and hit herself in the forehead with the radio a few times. "*Dammit.*"

Dammit Ziggy lifted his sweet little head, eyes sleepy as he blinked at Luna questioningly from Jameson's lap.

"Not you, baby," Luna said soothingly, and hit speaker on the phone on her desk. "Hey, Mom. I thought we agreed you wouldn't call my work unless it was an emergency. My cell phone works, you know."

"You never answer your cell, and this is an emergency. Stacy from Bunco told me you haven't applied for that job with her son yet. Luna, it's a *huge* medical group. You'd be assisting the staff and making excellent money with a great benefits package. You could even go back to school and—"

"Mom." Luna closed her eyes for a beat. "I've got a job."

"That's exactly it, Luna. It's a *job*, not a career. And in ten years you're going to look back and regret that you didn't get yourself a grown-up career."

Wincing for her, Jameson stood up to give her some privacy, swinging one leg over the table to climb out. Luna shook her head, waving him to sit back down, signaling she was almost done.

"Are you going to come to dinner this week?" Luna's mom asked.

"I'll try, but we're super busy here. Several team meetings. Thanks for calling, Mom. Talk soon." She disconnected and dropped her head back, staring at the ceiling.

"I didn't hear about any team meetings," Jameson said.

"That's because there aren't any." She let out a long exhale. "I'm probably going to hell in a handbasket. It's not her fault I'm the family screwup."

"You're not a screwup. You're just different from your mom."

She looked at him, eyes curious. "And you? Are you different from your mom?"

He smiled. "Very."

"She was a good mom?"

"The best." His smile faded. "But I wasn't always a good son."

She looked at him for a long beat. "I bet she knew you tried."

"I hope."

She looked away. Hesitated. "I'm not the best daughter either. My mom means well. We just don't see eye to eye. I mean, she loves me. She really does. But she's also going to be the one staring down at my open casket asking my cold, dead body if that's really what I'm wearing."

"Your grandfather used to ask me that too."

That earned him a full-bellied laugh. "So *that's* why you're always dressed so nice."

"Not today."

"I noticed." She eyed him. "Nice jeans."

"Right back at you," he said, and she blushed again, which given how tough she was really cracked him up.

"So what are you doing in my closet?" she asked.

"Working. Quietest place I could find."

She sighed. "Wish I could say the same. Besides being myself *and* one of the farmhands today, I've got a busted water line in the irrigation system at the botanical gardens, which means we had to turn the water off, which also means that the public utility department's gotta be called to get out here ASAP or plants are going to start dying. I've also got a meeting with a possible new tenant for the empty space in the Square." She ran a hand over her eyes like maybe she was exhausted.

There was something about her that made him want to solve all her problems. It made no sense. She was the most capable woman he'd ever met. "I could take your meeting, or call the PUD for you. Or both."

She dropped her hand and gave him a look like maybe he hung the moon. "You'd do that?"

"Partners, right?"

"Thank you," she said with feeling. "I'll take the meeting if you don't mind making the call. It'll take longer than you think to get through. Just don't let them walk all over you. Because if they sense a weakness, they will."

"There's not a weak bone in my body."

She laughed, and he went brows up. "Sorry," she said. "I don't mean to insult your manhood or anything, but we *all* have our weaknesses. Even you, tough guy."

He smiled. "You let me know when you find it."

Looking intrigued, she ran her gaze over him, and this time she didn't blush.

Progress.

CHAPTER 14

When Luna left, Jameson called the Tahoe PUD and began the painful process of dealing with an automated system that kept kicking him to the curb. "Agent," he said for the twentieth time.

Disconnect.

"Customer service," he said next time.

Disconnect.

"A LIVE PERSON," he said loudly on his fifth attempt, like the automated system cared.

Disconnect.

In a last-ditch effort, and more than an hour into the effort of reaching someone, he hit all the numbers and the pound sign and the star sign a million times. He was just about to hang up when someone said, "Tahoe Water Public Utilities Department."

He blinked. "Are you a real person?"

"Last I checked. How can I help you?"

"We've got a busted water line at Apple Ridge Farm, in the botanical gardens," he said. "We need someone here ASAP."

"Sorry, sir. We're working about two weeks out."

He rubbed the tension spot between his eyes. "That would leave us without water in the fields and shut us down, not to mention threaten the life of the gardens and orchards."

"So do you want the appointment in two weeks or not?"

He ground his back teeth. "Yes." He climbed over his make-shift desk with DZ under one arm. After passing the goat to Stella in the front room, he headed outside to find Luna to let her know about the PUD. He was halfway to the barn when he saw her in her truck coming toward the barn from the other way. The truck was old and beat to hell, bouncing her around on the dirt road, but she didn't seem to mind. In fact, her smile as she pulled up—executing half a donut while she was at it—to park next to another truck said it all.

Then she hopped out, and damn. Everything about the sight— the sun making her hair shine, her eyes flashing with good humor, and those long, long legs as she closed the distance to the group of men waiting on her—really did it for him.

Not having seen Jameson walking the trail toward the barn, Luna stopped to talk to Jeb and a few other guys with him. Jameson had met Shep and Jeb, but not the others. She hugged one in a way that told him they were very familiar with each other, and as he got closer, he could hear her words.

"Marco, how's your wife, how are those gorgeous babies?"

Marco grinned wide and pulled out his phone, presumably to show her pictures.

"I can't believe how big they're getting!" she gushed, looking at the phone. "So adorable . . ."

One of the other guys also showed her pics, and just when he wondered if anyone was going to get any work done today, she stepped back with a sweet smile and said, "Hey, thanks for listening to the changes we're making, guys. It means a lot that you understand we've got to work harder and smarter if we want to stay in business. I so appreciate all you do." Catching sight of Jameson, she excused herself, climbed the fence between them with an ease that was sexy as hell, and looked at him expectantly.

"The PUD is two weeks out," he said.

"What? *No.*" She whipped out her phone and stalked off. "Thanks for trying," she called over her shoulder. "Don't worry about it, no one else here can get anything from them either."

"But you can?"

"Well, duh."

He had to let out a wry laugh as she left him in her dust. Feeling like he'd failed at a basic task, something he wasn't used to, he went back to Luna's office to work, but found Stella in there making some calls. He ended up in the Square on a bench, which was every bit as hard as Stella had complained about in their staff meeting. But it was quiet, so he stayed out there with his laptop and a soda, a burger, and fries he'd ordered to go from the café. He was deep in the work when he realized he had company. Three humongous crows stood near his feet, in a line, and stared up at him with their large, beady black eyes like three godfathers waiting for their payment for allowing him to sit there.

He tossed them some fries.

They shared, eating neatly and thoroughly, then stared at him some more.

"That's it, guys, sorry. The rest is for me."

They flew off.

He went back to work, but two minutes later the crows were back. The first one dropped a piece of foil at his feet, the second a shiny silvery pen missing a few pieces, and the third a wrinkled dollar bill.

"They're making a trade."

Jameson craned his neck as Luna came up to him, a wheezing Sprout trotting along at her side, her faithful steed.

"If you keep trading with the crows, they'll keep bringing you stuff," she said. "If they bring you something you like, give them a bigger portion and they'll keep bringing that thing to you."

He picked up the wrinkled dollar bill and tossed them more fries.

She smiled. "Now they understand what to do. Bring you money."

He had to laugh. "Sounds morally gray . . ."

"You *probably* couldn't be charged with stealing. Maybe an accessory though . . ." She sat next to him and Sprout plopped at her feet in a warm sunspot. Luna brazenly stole a fry from Jameson's plate, dragging it through his neat dollop of ketchup before popping it into her mouth.

No one had ever done that, eaten off his plate, and . . . he liked it.

"Oh my God," she moaned, and he really hoped she kept stealing his food so he could hear that sound, that sexy purr from deep in her throat again. That, or screw the french fry, he wanted the chance to make her purr himself.

Milo, sitting on a bench across from them, called out, "Babe, you're doing it again, having sex with a french fry."

"Sorry." Luna, not looking sorry at all, grabbed two french fries this time, and once again drowned them in ketchup. "And sorry I'm stealing your food. I skipped breakfast and lunch. *Starving.*"

Jameson pushed the plate with half of what was left of his burger over to her.

"Wise decision," Milo told him. "We had maybe twenty seconds left until she turned into a very different person."

"Don't listen to him." She met Jameson's gaze. "You sure you don't mind?"

Her hands were shaking a little and she was pale. "I'm not hungry," he said, and waited until she was in the middle of inhaling his burger while running through her work emails and texts with her free hand, multitasking in a way he knew he'd never managed . . . "Luna."

She gave him a go-ahead gesture with her burger hand, still scrolling with her other.

"Did you get anywhere with the PUD?"

She chewed and swallowed. "Dammit! They didn't call me back. Son of a—" Wiping her mouth with a napkin, she hit a number on her phone and stared at him as she waited for the connection. Specifically at his mouth, which brought visceral memories of when that mouth had been on hers, of the sweet little whimper she'd made when his tongue had touched hers—

"Hi, Sharon," she said, her voice a little husky now, like maybe she knew his mind had gone to the same place as hers. "Can I

speak to Bob, please? It's Luna at Apple Ridge. Yep, I'll hold."
She stuffed in another two bites before wiping her mouth
again. "Hey, Bob. Guess what? I've got another busted pipe at
the main, which is your territory— Yep, right at the same place.
Your people already turned off the water but I need your guys
out here to fix. Yesterday. The new boss is an even harder hard-
ass than the previous one." She smirked at Jameson. "Yeah, a
real a-hole. So save my life and get out here, please? Yeah? Aw,
you're my favorite." She listened, then laughed. "You bet. I'll
have Chef box you up his famous strawberry pie—of course
from our own strawberries."

She hung up and had the good grace not to gloat as she went
back to demolishing his lunch.

"How did you do that?" He shook his head. "I was on hold for
a total of two hours and got nowhere."

"Everyone's got their own will-do-anything-for-you button.
You just gotta know what it is."

"Yeah? What's yours?"

She smiled. "You're going to have to work a lot harder for that
information."

Willow walked by. "Hello, Jameson," she said, pointedly ignoring Luna, and sat with Milo.

Jameson looked at Luna. "What was that?"

"Nothing." She narrowed her eyes. "Why? What have you
heard?"

"What would I hear?"

"I don't know. How would I know what you've heard until you
tell me what you heard? Who was it, Stella?"

"Hey," Stella said via the radio. "Hurtful."

"Dammit," Luna said. "My stupid radio keeps getting caught on my belt in the on position." She adjusted it and looked at Jameson. "It was Chef, right? He gossips like an old man at a poker game."

"No one told me anything," Jameson said.

"Uh-huh." Her phone had been buzzing in her pocket this whole time. Her radio was also squawking, and she paused to handle all of it, something about a garden snake in the barn, and something else about Hen Solo on the loose chasing two teenagers who'd tried to shoplift lip gloss from Stella's shop . . . Her life made him dizzy.

"Excuse me," she said, and was gone.

Jameson went back to the office and reclaimed his closet. When his stomach growled, he looked up. It was 6:00 p.m. He went in search of sustenance and found Willow and Shayne in a serious lip-lock in the staff room. He quietly turned around and headed out. He'd just passed the Square when he saw Luna standing with a man next to a Tahoe Water Public Utilities truck. The man looked stern and kept shaking his head, and as Jameson moved closer, he caught their convo.

"You were right, Cutie-Pie. There's a big problem, one I can't possibly fix today. I'll come back with all the needed equipment soon as I can, I promise."

"By then I'll have a dead botanical garden," she said. "Think of the bunnies who eat all my flowers, Bob. We both know your sweet little Kylie loves to come see the bunnies. You going to tell her that they're all dead because you didn't have time? How's that going to go over?"

Bob, looking pained, sighed. "My boss'll have my hide if I fix this for you right now instead of the other five emergencies we've got today."

"And my boss will have *your* boss's hide. You know how much philanthropy we do, how much we give back to the community. Plus"—Luna sweetened her smile and leaned in a little closer—"I've got two tickets to the Warriors game next Thursday night with your name on them."

Bob gasped. And if he'd been wearing pearls, he'd certainly have been clutching them. "You better not be messing with me. You know how I love the Warriors."

"I do," Luna said. "So, do we have a deal?"

"You drive a hard bargain, but yeah, we've got a deal."

Luna gave Bob a brilliant smile. She'd effortlessly charmed the guy. And maybe, possibly, Jameson as well. It was fascinating to watch her work. She connected with people, making everyone a friend for life, something completely out of his skill set.

She looked up then, saw him, and waved him over. "Jameson, meet Bob from the PUD. Bob, you're really going to like Jameson even if he's a numbers guy and a suit."

"I thought we already established that I'm in jeans today," Jameson said.

"Don't think I don't know that it's only because Dammit Ziggy kept chewing on your suit's pant leg."

"At least I'm adapting."

Luna smiled. "That's news to me. I wasn't aware that Y chromosomes could adapt."

Bob grinned. "So *you're* the new hard-ass boss."

Jameson gave Luna a side-eye.

"I was just kidding!" she said.

Right.

"You also said he was so uptight he squeaked when he walked," Bob said helpfully, and smiled at Jameson. "Which is what they need around here. They work hard, and are so great for the community, but I've got a feeling they could use a hand up in the area of actually making money."

One hundred percent true story.

Luna rolled her eyes. "Maybe I should call someone else to assist me with our water main."

Bob laughed so hard he had to bend over, hands on his knees.

Luna sighed. It'd been a desperate, empty threat and everyone knew it. She looked at the time. "Oops, gotta go. I'm meeting the new tenant with a contract in five. We're finally filling that little shop adjacent to the Bright Spot."

"Something good, I hope?" Bob asked.

"A candy shop."

"Yes!" Bob pumped his fist, then watched Luna walk away. "That there is one of the best women on this planet."

Jameson was also watching her go, thinking *yep*. And she also had the best ass on the planet.

"Be careful with her," Bob warned. "She's family."

There was that f-word again. "We're just partners."

"Whatever you say, man. Just know that she deserves the world, you know what I mean?"

Jameson found himself nodding, but he wasn't sure he knew

even a fraction of it. She was very good at the illusion of being open, but she was even more closed off than he was, and that was saying something. What he did know was that he'd seen her people skills now, and how she easily—if not reluctantly—had folded him into the network. In his past jobs, if someone had a connection, they wouldn't have shared it. But Luna was the real deal, and genuine. Holding her connections close to her chest had probably never occurred to her.

Nope, the only things she held close to her chest were her emotions.

He made his way back to the closet. If Luna was still working, he'd do the same. An hour later, she finally appeared, looking like she'd been through the wringer. She was in different jeans, a flannel shirt over a cami, damp hair up in a messy topknot, emphasis on messy. Which maybe was his new favorite Luna look. He really wanted to know what it'd feel like to kiss her again, to unleash all that fiery sass and passion his way. "You changed."

"Yep, that's what happens when your orphaned calf thinks you're her mama and wants you to lie down with her. In her own poop."

He grimaced, but then manfully took a deep inhale. "You don't smell like poop."

"Which was the point of my thirty-minute shower." She paused and appeared to be biting back a smile. "At my mom's." She shrugged. "She did say she wanted to see my face. Task complete."

He laughed. "You've got a little evil in you. I like it."

"So do you."

No doubt. She grinned at him and the familiar jolt of aware-ness streaked through him. "Warriors tickets?" he asked.

"Yep. One of the players has a house on the lake, and his wife and kids come to the farm all the time. She gave me the tickets a few days ago."

"Sweet of you to pass them on to someone else."

"Nothing sweet about it. I have no regrets bribing Bob so we can be operational."

"But it shouldn't come from your own pockets."

She met his gaze. "Don't you get it yet? I'd do just about any-thing for this place."

He knew that, and in a world that didn't value hard work as much as it used to, he found her mesmerizing, and so fascinating he was having difficulty keeping himself in check.

"Have you seen Willow?" she asked. "She's still hiding from me."

"She and Shayne were swallowing each other's tonsils in the staff room earlier."

"And they think they're separated."

"Someone needs to tell their lips."

"It won't be me." She met his gaze. "She's still mad at me, both for not securing her a promotion and for how she found out about Silas leaving me half the farm."

"And you think that's my fault."

"Well, it's not *not* your fault." She gave a small headshake. "Never mind. Why are you still in my closet?"

"I couldn't find another place to work."

She bit her lower lip. "I'm sorry. I didn't think. I'll find you a space."

Stella stuck her head in the open door, craning her neck to see Jameson. "Hey there, Hot Stuff. I'll share my desk with you anytime."

Jameson managed to keep his blank face on, barely. "Thanks. But I'm really okay in the closet."

"That's just physically though, right?" Stella asked. "You're not like *in* the closet closet, are you? Because Luna's not getting any younger, and we're all sorta shipping you two." She paused at Jameson's blank look. "Shipping is when others, such as everyone on this farm except you two, secretly wish to see you in a romantic—and hopefully sexual—relationship."

"Gram!"

"Right. Mind my own business." Stella grinned. "It's just hard to do when I'm as talented of a fortune teller as I am."

"Stella, raise up your phone, we can't see," Chef said.

Stella held up her phone, which revealed she was on a FaceTime call with not just Chef but also Milo.

Luna face-palmed.

"Tell Jameson I can permanently reserve a table for him at the back of the café," Chef told Stella. "That way I could look at his pretty face all day long."

"He can hear you," Luna said dryly. "And why are you all chatting instead of working?"

Jameson's question would have been why were they on the phone when they were together all the time? In his experience, people went into work and then raced out of there the second their time had been put in. Sooner if they could get away with it.

But they obviously really liked each other here. In fact, everyone had been kind and generous with him.

"*Out*," Luna told her grandma.

Stella, clearly not taking offense, leaned in to kiss her cheek, and then left.

Luna looked at Jameson. "You didn't leave."

"I assumed you weren't talking to me."

She plopped into her chair with a laugh. "Men should bottle up and sell their cockiness."

Jameson ignored that. He wasn't cocky. At all. Okay, maybe confident, but ever since he'd stepped foot inside Apple Ridge Farm, he could honestly say the only thing he was confident about was that he had no idea what he was doing here. "They're good people," he said.

"I know." Luna opened her laptop and began typing.

Okay. Message received. He watched her for a minute, noticing that while she was sexy as hell in a girl-next-door-with-an-edge sort of way, she still seemed so tired. She hid it well, but he suspected she worked way too many hours handling everything on her plate. Work that was probably enough to keep three employees busy, not just one, but she never seemed to complain. They might be polar opposites, but he could see just how valuable she was to this place. Hell, she did more in a day here than he could've ever figured out how to manage.

"Why are you staring at me?" she asked, eyes still on her screen, fingers still typing.

"I was hoping to get a word with you."

"Oh? Should I step into your office?"

He smiled. He wouldn't mind her stepping into his office. He'd plop her ass on the desk, step in between her legs, and—

"What's on the agenda?"

Right. Business only—his doing. God, he was stupid. "I've been entering everything from the ledger into our new program. We need to discuss this past month's numbers." He turned his laptop to face her.

She came over to see better and he realized she smelled delicious. "What language is this?" she asked.

He smiled. "Math."

"Funny. Tell me what I'm looking at."

"Lots of negative numbers. Too many. To get out of the red, we need to trim the fat."

She sighed. "How?"

"For starters, we could cut a meal a day from the employees. Or all of them. We pay well, we don't need to provide three squares as well."

"It's one of their benefits."

"Okay, then we've got to make the really difficult decision to cut some of the employees."

She straightened up. "We've been over this. We're not firing anyone."

Their gazes met and held, and there was a banked fire in hers. "Fine," she said. "We cut their meals—" She broke off when his phone began buzzing. "Oh bummer," she said, scooping up Sprout. "I'm going to give you some privacy." She snapped her fingers. "Come on, Dammit Ziggy, you too."

Dammit Ziggy lifted his head from his perch on Jameson's lap. "*Bleeeat*," he said lovingly into Jameson's eyes.

"Traitor," Luna said, and left without the goat.

Jameson stared at the call coming in from Brett Stephens, one of the "coven," as Luna had called them. Brett had been a partner with Silas over the years on many investments, which wasn't to say they'd been friends. They hadn't. But they'd enjoyed each other's ability to make money. Brett also happened to head up the investment group that held the loan Silas had taken out for the farm's renovations.

"Hayes," Brett said in greeting. "How's it going, kid?"

Kid. Jameson was thirty-two, and at six foot two, towered over Brett by a good seven inches. But he supposed that since Brett had known him as the fifteen-year-old street rat Silas had taken in, first impressions never went away. Jameson had to purposely relax his every muscle, including letting his shoulders down from where they'd ended up at his ears at just the sound of Brett's voice. "It's going," he said, not letting out another word. If Brett wanted info, he'd have to ask for it.

And Jameson had no doubt Brett wanted info. The group had a lot of money in Apple Ridge Farm, and without Silas beating them back, the lions were circling.

"I'll cut right to the chase," Brett said. "We want to buy your fifty percent. And to be honest, we want Luna's fifty percent too. I figure the best way to do that is for you to bring your fifty percent on board, and then we'll have the leverage to force her out. The farm's barely breaking even thanks to her inefficiency."

"Luna is the perfect manager for this farm. She's gifted at what she does, has good intuition, and no off switch."

"I didn't ask for her qualifications. And frankly, I expected this to be a no-brainer decision for you."

None of this was a surprise. And yeah, maybe Jameson could even understand why it might've been an attractive offer before he'd come here. But he was here now, and couldn't see himself being a part of the reason Luna got forced out. He knew the group had no interest in the farm. The land though . . . that was worth more than the money they had in the place. They'd raze the farm and build something. And get even richer.

"You there?" Brett asked, sounding annoyed.

Since it was a bad idea to ever show one's hand to Brett, he said, "I'll think it over."

"Don't mistake this for any sort of bailing-you-out thing," Brett warned. "We both know that the farm will sink fast without Silas. So either you start earning a lot of money fast, or you sell to us. Either way, at the end of the quarter, we intend to have our money from that balloon payment. We won't want to hear any sob stories about how the farm means so much to the employees. We just want our money. Oh, and the offer won't be on the table for long. Don't go down with the ship."

Jameson knew the ship was already taking on water. But if anyone could make this work, it was him. That wasn't him being cocky, as Luna would accuse him. He simply knew the ins and outs of the financial world, and what could be saved and what couldn't.

"Look," Brett said, "we all know you. We know what the old

man did for you. The best thing you can do for him now is to get out alive while you can. Don't prove his time and efforts with you a waste of time."

It was always Brett's way or the hard way. And the hard way never ended well if you went up against him.

"And if it makes you feel better," Brett went on, "our offer will be fair market value—minus the balance on the loan. You'd both get a very big fat check."

"And the employees?"

"Collateral damage," Brett said. "You know the drill. You're not new at this."

True story. He'd never let himself think about the people whose jobs he'd dissolved in the past. What kind of man did that make him? He'd always hated regrets, but in that moment, they nearly swamped him.

A regret isn't written in ink until you refuse to learn from it.

His mom had said that to him, how many times? Too many to count. Just thinking about her squeezed his heart. All this time and he still missed her more than he could say. Would she be proud of him? He'd like to think so. But he knew one way to honor her memory and be the best man he was capable of being, and that was to do the right thing for this farm.

Silas had pulled in his favors and asked him to be here, but the old man had also given him an opportunity to belong somewhere, to be a part of a self-made family, and he was going to take advantage of every gift the old man had given him, unknowingly or otherwise.

"Son, don't confuse sentiment with sensibility," Brett said into

Jameson's silence. "Take the check and move on. Or step into the ring with us and reap the benefits when we raze the farm and build something new and hugely profitable."

Silas had poured a lot of surprising heart into this place to keep it open, maybe out of some sort of romanticism, but possibly also as an obligation to his granddaughter. Either way . . . "I'm going to take my chances here."

Brett's voice turned cold. "Then the day the balloon payment's due, we'll expect our payment in full, or we'll force you *both* gone."

And they would.

But Jameson couldn't sell the crew out. He couldn't sell Luna out. Bottom line, he refused to be the next guy to disappoint her. Which meant they had to pull this off, or it would truly be game over.

CHAPTER 15

Later in the week, Luna felt exhausted to her soul, but she still gamely walked into the Shore Club, the restaurant for her and Chef's monthly "exes" date. The deal was that she got to pick the place and he got to pick the attire—though he always chose dressy.

Every month she grumbled and tried to get out of it, even though she always found herself relaxed, laughing, and having a great time, because with Chef there was absolutely no pressure, and the food never failed to be amazing.

Okay, it'd failed a few times. Like the time he'd made her try escargot.

And oysters.

They'd agreed maybe she didn't want her horizons broadened that much.

She was in the second of her two dressy outfits: a long-sleeved, midi-length dress of a soft jersey material that clung but also somehow made her feel like a million bucks. Maybe it was the kick-ass boots Willow had given her for Christmas. Maybe it was because her mirror had told her she was actually having a good hair day for once.

Or . . . maybe it was because she'd started to realize that her fears of everyone looking at her differently because she'd become an owner of the farm had proved to be false. Happily confident, she strode through the restaurant, but that confidence faltered when she caught sight of Chef, handsome as ever, sitting with Milo and . . . another man in a suit. And not the suit she'd been thinking about all day either.

She stopped at the table and tried to smile, but given Chef's expression, it'd probably been more of a grimace. "I didn't realize this was going to be a party." *Or a double date . . .*

Chef just smiled.

The suit stood. "Hi, Luna. I'm Evan. We got disconnected the other day, so when Chef invited me to dinner . . ."

"Nice to meet you," she said, because in spite of herself, her mom had drilled manners into her at an early age. Then she turned and gave Chef a pointed look.

He returned it.

They all sat, and when Chef and Evan began to talk about which wine they wanted to try, Luna turned to Milo and whispered, "How did you get dragged into this?"

"Free food." He smiled. "My favorite kind."

Over the next hour she gave it her best, and the company was admittedly lively and fun, but she wanted her bed. "I think it's time for me to—"

"Order dessert," Chef said smoothly. "Their peach flambé has got to be tasted to be believed. Almost as good as mine."

Luna kicked him under the table. Hard.

To his credit, Chef manfully held in his response, though he did reach under the table to rub his shin.

But damn if he wasn't right. The flambé *was* out of this world.

"I hear there's a comet tonight between ten and midnight," Evan said. "Anyone want to find a place to watch for it?"

Here was the thing. The date had already lasted over five years, and yes, Evan was kind and funny and looked great, but he wasn't the right suit. And at that shocking realization, she abruptly stood.

All three men looked up at her. "You okay?" Milo asked.

"I'm sorry. Migraine coming."

Evan stood up too. "I could drive you home."

"No, I'm fine. Truly. But thank you. Tonight was . . ." What was a suitably nice word, but not so nice that he'd ask her out again? "Pleasant."

Chef face-palmed.

Milo had to work to hide a grin behind his wineglass.

She grimaced. "I'm sorry, Evan. Meeting you was . . ." Shit. She honestly couldn't think of a good word. Maybe she really was getting a migraine.

"Pleasant?" Evan asked with amusement lurking in his gaze.

She sighed and gave a rueful smile. "Yeah." And when she got out to her car, she was still shaking her head at herself. She drove directly to the local convenience store and bought a rack of cookies, which she ate on her way home. It wasn't until she parked at the farm that she realized she'd forgotten her coat at the restaurant. She texted Chef to get it for her because no way was she going back.

Chilled in the brisk forty-five degrees, she quickly walked the trail to her cabin, missing Willow. She wondered what she was up to tonight, which put a pang in her gut. Since when didn't they know each other's every move?

She looked up at the gorgeous night sky, well-lit by a blanket of stars and a near full moon. It seemed alive. The view, day or night, summer or winter, never, ever failed to lower her blood pressure and calm her down.

But it also might've been the cookies.

Suddenly not ready to go to bed, she passed her cabin. Milo's cabin was still dark. Stella had a light on, but Luna didn't want to rehash the evening, so she kept moving, past Jeb's cabin, then Shep's. The sixth had two farmhands in it.

The farm's property line lay just behind the last cabin, Jameson's, which was also dark. Just beyond that, she could hear the creek. She loved to sit on her favorite rock and listen to the water rushing by. She could think of no better way to further unbusy her mind.

Well, okay, she could think of *one* way, but that involved a lot of nakedness and preferably another person. "And," she muttered, coming to the end of the path, stepping off it to get to her rock, "you gave up dating, so you need to get used to this no-sex thing."

At the sound of someone choking out a laugh, she froze. She knew that sexy laugh.

Jameson was sitting on a rock, *her* rock. Grinning. She jabbed a finger in his direction. "That's *my* spot."

He scooted over for her, but nope. Not going to sit that close to him. He'd had his chance.

"Rough night?"

"No. Well, yes. But no."

"That clears that up."

She went hands on hips. "Why are you out here?"

"Some lucky son of a bitch tied a sock on the door handle of the cabin. I assume it's Shayne."

Luna's first reaction was irritation at Shayne and Willow. Her second reaction was a wistful sigh. She wouldn't mind needing a sock.

Jameson laughed softly. "Been a while, huh?"

"So long I can't remember."

"Same."

Their gazes locked and held. "Maybe," she said, "that's because when someone throws themselves at you, you say 'no thanks.'"

He gave a small shake of his head. "That had nothing to do with you. I wanted you. Badly. But I can think with two body parts at the same time, and tend to weigh what is the right thing versus what I want."

Hmm. "So just how long has it been since your last relationship?"

"A year. We were together for two years. We were engaged, but then one day I came home from a trip and she handed me back my key and walked out the door." He looked over at her, saw her horrified and sympathetic expression and shook his head. "Don't feel sorry for me. It was my own fault. I traveled all the time, was hardly ever home, and Julie had to keep pushing the wedding date back. Finally, she got tired of me not being able to give her what she needed, so she left."

Unable to help herself, she reached over and squeezed his hand. "It had to hurt."

"It did. But it wasn't the right time for me, and she wasn't the right woman. No one should have to change who they are to be loved." He squeezed her hand back. "Which, given how deeply you still care about Chef, I'm guessing you understand."

She smiled wryly. "Very much so."

He went brows up, like he was waiting for something.

"What?" she asked.

"Now you."

"Now me what?"

He smiled. "You know what. When someone opens up to you, it's customary for you to open up back."

"You already know about Chef."

He nodded and gave her a "go on" gesture. She hesitated. If she was being honest, she was embarrassed. "Believe me, there's nothing good in my romantic history, and I *really* don't like to talk about it."

"Okay, so what *do* you want to talk about?" he asked.

"Why it's been so long since you got some. A year's a long time."

He shrugged. "I guess I'm not really a one-night-stand sort of guy."

There was something incredibly sexy about that. *Why* was there something incredibly sexy about that?

He smiled. "It bodes well for me that you're surprised."

She laughed. "Well, surely those loafers were chick magnets."

"Hey," he said with mock defensiveness. "What did my loafers ever do to you?"

She took a good look at him in his down jacket and jeans, now sporting a hole over one knee, which she knew Dammit Ziggy had started for him, and work boots. "I guess you *can* take the city out of the guy."

"Hey, I'm adaptable. And I like it here. For a long time my life's felt . . . dark." He met her gaze as if he expected that to scare her off.

It didn't. Maybe because she understood it more than she wanted to. "The farm and all the inhabitants in it are so colorful and full of light, it's hard to not become a part of it," she said softly, moved by his admission.

One corner of his mouth quirked up. "Yeah. For me, it's your smile." He laughed when she bit her lower lip because she liked hearing that, way too much. Tipping his head to take in the sky, he said, "I've been . . . everywhere, but I've never seen a night sky like this. It feels so untouched, and without any city lights, the stars shine brighter than diamonds."

"Yeah, I know." She looked up and was moved enough to sigh, which had her shoulders lowering from her ears. Or maybe that was Jameson. Seemed like he was even better than cookies. "You should see it during a lightning storm. The streaks of lightning flash and light up the entire sky."

He pulled off his jacket. Beneath, he wore an unbuttoned plaid shirt over a well-worn T-shirt, snug to his chest, loose over his abs. She was still staring when he tugged her down beside him and wrapped the jacket around her shoulders.

It was warm from his body heat and she snuggled in, grateful. It was a struggle to *not* press her face to her arm and inhale his scent. She failed.

When he caught her at it, his eyes darkened, clearly both amused and turned on. And suddenly she felt the same. "Was it hard to get over losing Julie?"

"I thought so at the time. But with hindsight being 20/20, we weren't right for each other. How about you, with Chef? Did he break your heart?"

"I thought so at the time," she said, using his words, making him smile. She shifted to get more comfortable and their arms brushed. She would really like to know why every time they accidentally touched, she felt a tingle of awareness up the back of her neck and down, spreading throughout her entire body. "But now I'm realizing that I loved being with him because it felt like mac and cheese."

"Mac and cheese," he repeated, sounding confused.

"Yeah. You know, comfort food. He made me feel safe and secure and anchored. It's why I hired him on here. I thought I needed him, because . . . well, you know."

"Mac and cheese."

She smiled. "Exactly. But I'm so much happier with what we are to each other now. Family. Like siblings."

"Anyone since Chef?" he asked.

She pretended to be very busy studying the sky.

"You could just say 'none of your business,'" he said lightly.

She grimaced. "It feels a little bit like your business," she admitted, surprising herself.

"Nice to know. And I'm all ears."

Her phone buzzed and he gave her a small smile. "Saved by the bell."

She snorted as she read the text.

"Stella?" he asked.

"Yep. She wants to know, and I quote, 'How do I cancel a meeting with my boss?'"

"But . . . *you're* her boss."

"Yeah. I'm trying to figure out what to say."

"Ask her to provide a list of her complaints and say you'll add them to the next staff meeting agenda."

"Oh you're good." She sent that exact text. A few minutes went by with no response and Luna beamed at him. "Anyone ever tell you that you know your stuff?"

He shrugged. "Fewer than you'd think."

She leaned back and stared up at the sky some more, aware that he was looking at her profile. "What?"

"Why do I get the feeling that dinner with Chef didn't go well?"

"Chef invited Milo." She blew out a breath. "And Evan the Suit."

"And . . . ?"

"He just wasn't my type."

He hesitated, as if wanting to be careful with his words. "Sometimes, I feel like I see something familiar in your eyes."

"You're not a fan of suits either?"

The corners of his mouth tilted slightly. "Something deeper," he said.

"Like, you too have a stomachache from too many cookies?"

His mouth quirked again, but he apparently wasn't going to let her joke this away because he said, "We've got the same core wound, which means we understand each other."

Luna had a therapist tell her once that her thing was abandonment. That's what her adoption represented to her, that her bio mom had abandoned her. At the time, she hadn't believed it. After all, she'd been adopted immediately and her basic needs had always been met.

But as it turned out, there were other needs she didn't know she had. Such as acceptance, and as a result, she'd spent a whole lot of her life coasting on surface emotions. It suited her. It kept her heart safe. But she couldn't coast with Jameson. She had to be on her toes and stay alert to keep him from sliding beneath the protective walls around her heart. After all, nothing good could come of her giving in to temptation and being stupid enough to sleep with him. *Especially* if he wanted to talk about their deep, dark issues. Nope, she'd buried it all deep, thank you very much. So she was surprised when her mouth took over and asked the question she wasn't at all sure she wanted the answer to. "Did this core wound ruin your relationships?"

He shifted on the big rock, long legs stretched out in front of him, leaning back on his elbows, head tipped to the stunning sky. "Probably."

Her heart tightened hard, and to give herself a moment, she mirrored his position.

"Look." He pointed upward, to an amazingly bright star with a faint fuzzy tail—no, not a star. The comet, and the beauty of it took her breath. They watched until it vanished behind the inky outline of the mountains.

The wind rustled the trees, and here and there an animal called out into the dark. "I'm glad Silas found you," she said with a little shoulder nudge.

He smiled, she could hear it in his voice as he nudged her back. "Me too."

"And you're here to protect his asset," she said. "Which is now your asset too."

"And yours, which means I'm here to protect you too."

She turned and met his gaze. "From the coven?"

"From whatever you need protecting from."

She stared at him. "I don't need protecting."

"I'm starting to get that."

A low, throaty female moan came from the cabin, and Luna straightened her spine, her eyes narrowed. "Oh, for the love of God." She climbed off the rock and strode straight across the path to Jameson's door and pounded on it.

After a long moment, Shayne opened up, no shirt, no shoes, hair rumpled, and lipstick on his mouth. He braced one arm against the doorjamb, the very picture of sated male.

"Seriously?" Luna demanded, trying to see past him. "*Willow!*"

Willow came to the door buttoning her jeans. "What's up, Luna Always Right Wright?"

Luna ground her back teeth. "What are you guys doing?"

"Fighting," Willow said.

"Naked?"

"Maybe that's how we fight. Plus, I don't have to answer to you after hours, especially since we're not speaking. In fact, I'm not speaking to *either* of you." She gave Shayne a pointed look.

He just smiled at her. "You were speaking to me plenty just five minutes ago."

"That was cabin talk only! And what happens in the cabin stays in the cabin, Shayne! We agreed!" With that, she gave him a nudge, making him take a step back, onto the porch.

Then she slammed the door on all of them.

"Well, damn," Shayne said.

Luna looked into his mournful face and shook her head. "What part of wooing her with your words didn't you understand?"

"*She* called *me*."

"Oh my God." Luna tossed up her hands. "Men are so dumb."

"Hey, you're on her shit list too."

"Great, because you're *both* on mine. This cabin is still Jameson's. You can't just lock him out."

The door to the cabin opened again and Shayne's shirt, shoes, and keys were tossed out. With a sigh, Shayne scooped everything up. He looked over at Jameson, quietly taking everything in with that quiet, calm way of his. "Sorry, man. But I don't think she's coming out."

Jameson shrugged. "I always wanted to try camping. Maybe now's a good time."

"It's a cold night," Shayne said.

"I'll be okay."

Shayne nodded and looked at his phone for the time. "I've got an early shift. I'm just going to head to the station and get a few hours of sleep."

When he was gone, Luna looked over at Jameson. "You're not really going to camp, are you? Because what if you get bitten by a coyote, or if a bear wants to eat you for a snack?"

He grinned. "You think I'm a snack."

She rolled her eyes.

"I'll go back to the hotel."

She sighed. "My couch has a pull-out bed and it's free."

He smiled. "So the jeans and boots really *do* work for you."

"You did hear me say couch, right? *Not* my bed."

"That's okay. I'm a third-date kind of guy anyway."

CHAPTER 16

At four in the morning, Jameson sat in Luna's kitchen, the only sound his fingers hitting his laptop's keyboard. Oh, and the high-speed buzz saw that wasn't a buzz saw at all but Sprout snoring in his lap. He himself should be tired too, but he'd never needed much sleep. Tonight, he felt especially restless.

And uncharacteristically stressed out.

Looking at the numbers for the farm, running them every possible way, he wasn't sure he could save the place. It felt like the most important project of his life, and yet for the first time since college, failure was on the table.

He hated, *hated*, the thought. He'd made a promise to Silas that he'd help Luna whichever way she wanted to go, and he didn't break promises, especially to the man who'd given him everything.

He planned to give everything of himself in return, but not just for Silas.

In the beginning, he'd felt like the outsider. But at nearly two weeks in, everyone here treated him the exact same as they did each other, like he'd been here forever, like he was one of them, leaving him genuinely thrown by their generosity of spirit. He had little to no experience being part of a crew like this, but he liked it. In fact, he liked it a whole lot. He wasn't exactly sure how he fit in, a numbers guy who'd never operated as part of a team, but they were trying. And so would he.

A sound pulled him out of his thoughts. A sound he couldn't quite place. He rose and set Sprout on the chair before moving into the dark living room, where he hit the light switch.

And froze.

As did Luna, who wielded a baseball bat like she wasn't afraid to use it, complete with bed head and no pants. She was choked up on the bat, her T-shirt also hiked up to nearly the promised land, her mile-long legs and feet bare.

"Might want to put the bat down," he said. "If you lift it even a fraction of an inch more, I'm going to know what color your undies are."

Luna tossed the bat on the couch and tugged her oversized black T-shirt down her thighs. "How do you know I'm not commando?"

"God-given talent. The bat's a nice touch."

She snorted. "I thought you were a bear."

He smiled. "Were you coming out here to save the muffins on your counter, or me?"

She bit her lower lip.

"You forgot I was here." Endearing, but hard on the ego. "I was working. I'm sorry if I woke you."

"No, my stomach did that. How do numbers take up so many hours of the day?"

"Well, for one thing, I don't just throw the receipts into a ledger and hope for the best."

She laughed. "Cute. I need a snack."

He smiled, and she pointed at him. "You are *not* going to be my snack."

But she was tempted, he could tell.

She moved past him and into the kitchen, where she rustled around, coming up with a family-size bag of BBQ chips.

"That's not going to hold you long. Do you mind?" he asked, gesturing to the fridge.

"Help yourself."

He emerged from the fridge with tortillas, cheese, an avocado, and a tomato. "Grilled quesadilla okay with you?"

She looked surprised, this kick-ass woman who took care of everyone and everything in her world, as if maybe no one ever offered to take care of her. "Sounds fancy."

"No, just good."

"As long as you don't use those peppers on the counter. Shep grows them and he's constantly leaving me a few, and I can't bring myself to tell him how much I hate them."

"I do too."

She graced him with a huge smile, as if now she suddenly felt bonded to him. Not over their loss of Silas, or being business partners, but because he hated peppers too, *that* made him trustworthy. Good to know where she stood. He located a pan and cut up the tomato and avocado. The kitchen was small, but instead of feeling cramped, it felt . . . intimate.

Luna had hopped up to sit on the counter, settling in with her legs swinging back and forth over the edge, watching with ravenous ecstasy as he flicked on a burner to heat up the pan. He thought about giving her incentive to want him as much as she did the food, but he wasn't sure he'd win over the quesadilla.

Sprout watched too, suddenly wide awake.

"You cook a lot?" she asked.

"Not nearly as much as I used to."

"Why did you stop?"

"I used to cook for me and my mom because she was always working." He paused for the gut punch he felt every time he talked about her. And it came, but so did a soft smile because the memories of her were all so sweet. "And when I say *cook*, I mean easy stuff."

She smiled. "Like quesadillas."

"And ramen. And anything else you can do on a budget. We were poor as dirt, but it took me a long time to realize that. She never let it show."

"Sounds like she was amazing."

He nodded. "Amazing, scrappy, fiery, and passionately protective." Then he found another smile. "Like someone else I know."

She cocked her head to the side in confusion and he chuckled. "You, Luna."

She looked like she was running back his words in her head, trying to decide if she was pleased or not. Then smiled. "I'd have liked her then."

"Yes."

She opened then shut her mouth.

"Since when do you hold back your words?" he asked.

"Do you really think I'm all those things?"

"Yes," he said seriously, wanting her to believe him. "You're brave and gutsy and tenacious. You surprise me, and I haven't been surprised by anything in a very long time." She was also definitely his particular brand of kryptonite, not that he planned on admitting that. He waved the spatula at her.

"What?"

"You know what," he said. "Now you tell me something."

"Such as . . . ?" she asked warily.

"I don't know. What was your home life like?"

"Well . . . I was an only child, and my parents adopted me later in life. They're doctors. Not scrappy or fiery. Serious. Very serious. And maybe protective. But not passionate, not really. They were good to me, *are* good to me, but I've been a disappointment. They wanted me to do what they do. But not only did I fail o-chem in college . . . that life, it was always too restrictive for me. Too many rules, too much of having to fall into line."

He smiled. "And you don't fall into line."

She laughed. "Not willingly anyway. So as you can imagine, I didn't quite fulfill their expectations."

To hide the sympathy she would hate, he busied himself with

scooping the quesadillas onto two plates. Then pushed one toward her. She took a bite and let out a "yummy" sound.

"They should be proud of you, running this whole place," he said quietly, enjoying the sight of her in that T-shirt on the counter, eating like what he'd made was the best thing she'd ever tasted.

"They are proud. In their own way."

She didn't look at him as she said that, and he wanted to hug her. "Expectations are hard," he said.

"What's harder is *unmet* familial expectations."

He nodded the truth of that. "Your grandfather had a lot of expectations for me."

She laughed. "He only came once a quarter, and that was for the best. He always had Milo shaking in his boots and Chef burning food. Once Stella came into the café when he was eating and told him his future was going to be lonely if he kept being so grumbly, and that she was willing to make him less lonely if he was interested."

Jameson choked out a laugh picturing that. "What happened?"

"He told her he preferred his own company, so he didn't give a shit. And then shortly after that he vanished, and so did Stella. Didn't think anything of it until the next morning when I realized his car was still in the lot."

Jameson choked on a bite of his quesadilla. "Him and Stella . . . ?"

She shrugged. "Neither of them ever said. But the next morning he actually said goodbye to everyone when he left. I asked Stella about it and she said a real lady would never kiss and tell."

They both shuddered at the mental image.

"You make a mean quesadilla," she said. "Thank you."

"Anytime."

Their gazes met and held, and that weird charged-air thing happened again.

"So," she said after a long beat. "What were you working on?"

"Trying to figure out how to pay all the bills this month."

She leaned in and looked at his screen. "Why are the tractor barrel ride and the haystack slides highlighted?"

"The insurance liability coverage is killing us. I spoke to the adjuster. We can cut the bill down by limiting liability."

"But the visitors love the tractor barrel ride and the haystack slides."

"No, the visitors love you guys," he said. "Luna, to make this work, we need to find more ways to make money, and also cut the fat. All of it. We gotta go as lean as possible."

"You can't just math away the experiences our visitors get here," she said.

"And you can't sweet-talk a ledger filled with red into miraculously turning black and profitable. Ten minus twenty will always equal a negative number." He paused and looked at her. "Look, I'm just trying to honor your wishes and find a way to keep all the employees. I know how much they mean to you."

"I've been thinking about that," she said. "Would it help if I cut my salary and we rented out this cabin? I could move out."

Damn, his heart melted for her. "We're not dislodging you. You already don't make nearly as much as you should. In fact, you've been underpaid. I've been thinking too. We make more money off the orchards than anything else. Why not get rid of the second barn and free up some acreage for more space to plant."

"You mean Stella's Place?" Luna immediately shook her head. "Those shops make us money, and people love the goods. Stella's put five years into the business. And, well, if we lose the barn and she has to go live with my parents, there will be bloodshed."

"The shops are underperforming. We're going to have to make some hard decisions, or *everyone's* going to lose their business."

"I know." She hopped off the counter and walked toward him, not stopping until her bare toes touched his. Then she brushed a kiss to the underside of his jaw. "We'll figure it out."

He caught her hand as she started to walk off. "What was that?"

"A good night kiss."

He gave a slow shake of his head and slowly pulled her into him, giving her plenty of time to say no. When she didn't, he kissed her. Not on her jaw, but on that delicious mouth of hers. She made that sound he loved and tried to climb him like a tree. When he pulled back, she gave a soft whimper of protest. He smiled into her dazed face. "Now *that's* a good night kiss."

"And more," she murmured, voice husky, her fingers touching her lips as if to hold on to the taste of him.

He smiled. "Not so cute now, am I?"

"Try sexy as hell on for size," she muttered, and pointed at him. "Stop it."

He lifted his hands in innocence, making her laugh.

Then she set a hand to his chest. "We'll figure it out," she repeated, but this time he knew she wasn't talking about the farm. And then she vanished into her room.

"How? How will we figure it out?" he asked of the kitchen, which didn't answer.

AND SO THE nights went for the next week. With Jameson often working late and Luna not being a great sleeper, they often ran into each other late at night, usually in the kitchen.

He'd asked if he should go back to his own cabin. She'd looked at him for a long moment, then shaken her head. Fine by him, he enjoyed her company even if it wasn't of the naked variety. He had no idea why she hadn't kicked him out, she tended to keep her own counsel, but he was grateful.

There'd been more kissing and touching, but it hadn't gone further. It was almost as if they both felt gun-shy and afraid to mess up their tenuous connection, not to mention their partnership.

One late night after Luna had gone to bed, he took a shower, having to slide aside a few bras that were drying on the shower rod, all of which were lacy or silky, and skimpy. He thought about her wearing the sexy lingerie beneath her jeans and T-shirts, and the shower took a little longer than he'd intended.

After, he realized he didn't have any clean clothes for the next day—unless he wanted to go back into a suit. Instead, he headed to the washing machine in the kitchen with an armful of clothes, and shoved everything into one load, whites and colors together. He could almost hear his mom's voice admonishing him in his ear. Smiling to himself, he sat at the table in knit boxers and went back to his laptop.

An hour later the clock struck midnight as he pulled out a pair of jeans from the dryer.

He was just pulling them up when he heard footsteps coming his way. He knew exactly what to expect now, and still, as she rounded the corner in her pj's—tonight a cami and the tiniest shorts he'd ever seen—she stole his breath.

She stopped short, as if him shirtless in her kitchen had taken her breath as well.

"Couldn't sleep?" he asked.

"Hungry."

So was he, but not for food. Still, he made her a quesadilla and handed it over.

"These have become an addiction."

He opened his mouth to say he felt the same about her, but just then she pulled her quesadilla in half, and when the cheese stretched between the two sides, she snagged the melted strings of cheese—with her tongue.

"Don't you think?" she asked.

He'd lost track of their conversation. That's what happened when the blood in his brain drained for parts south. "What?"

"There's got to be something we can do to fix this." She licked some cheese off her thumb with a suction sound that didn't help matters any. She finished eating, then sighed in exhaustion.

Living on the farm as he was, he'd become privy to her schedule, which was rising before dawn to help feed the animals, making sure they were all taken care of, making sure everything was cleaned up and looking good for the people who would pay to come in, and so much more. In his greatest imagination, he couldn't have managed a day in her life. "You're not okay."

"No. I'm stressed." She put a hand to her chest. "I need to alleviate some of it."

He raised a brow as she rifled through a laundry basket on top of her dryer, producing a pair of sweats, which she pulled on. Then she reached into the dryer and threw something at him.

One of his shirts. He'd sorta hoped this would be going the other way. "What are we doing?" he asked.

"I know the perfect thing for stress."

"So . . . my night's about to get better then?"

"Follow me, funny guy."

He'd probably follow her right off a cliff, which wasn't as shocking as it should've been. He was somehow getting used to the fact that he was incredibly attracted to her, enough to allow himself to wonder how things might work if they gave this thing between them a go.

Taking his hand, she led him down the path toward the animal barn. Inside, they walked past the emu pen. Estelle stuck her head over the gate to eye Jameson, and he just managed to resist covering his ass with his hands.

Luna laughed, and he was wondering why this was the place she'd chosen to improve their night when she let them into the baby goat pen.

DZ and his two siblings were all in pj's, the three of them looking adorably sleepy as Luna grabbed a lantern off a hook and turned it on, setting it in the middle of the pen. "Sit," she said to Jameson.

"In the hay?"

She plopped down and crisscrossed her legs, patting the spot next to her.

By this time, Dammit Ziggy was losing his mind, bouncing in front of Jameson, bleating to be picked up. So he sat and DZ hopped into his lap. His two sisters, Mini and Pearl, were in Luna's, and she was cuddling them both, laughing softly as they nuzzled her.

She'd been right. Sitting with baby goats in the middle of the night was incredibly relaxing. So was being with Luna. With hay in her hair and in those big baggy sweats, he probably couldn't have found her body if he'd tried, and she *still* looked edible. One of the goats licked her chin and she laughed again, her eyes smiling and sparkling in the light of the lantern. His thigh was pressed to hers, and without allowing himself to think, he wrapped his free arm low on her hips and leaned into her. "You're beautiful."

She laughed this off. "You need glasses."

No, he didn't. Hell, he could see her with his eyes closed. Because he knew her now. She was tough as they came, and resilient as hell, but this farm was a huge strain on her and he was as guilty as everyone else in her circle of not looking past her easy strength to see it.

When the goats had fallen asleep again, he turned to Luna, rising to his feet, pulling her up with him. Taking her hand, he moved them out of the pen and into the night where he walked her to the cabin. In her kitchen, he set water to boil for the tea she loved.

"I don't want to lose any employees," she said softly. "Or the rescue animals. We're all they have."

He turned to her and, putting his hands on her waist, lifted her onto the counter she'd been leaning against. She spread her knees in invitation, and unable to resist, he stepped between them, hands on her thighs, dipping his head a little to look into her eyes. "I know. And I really hope it doesn't come to that."

"I can't fail."

His heart ached for the responsibility she'd put on herself. And again he felt pissed off at Silas for letting her take all this on herself. Sure, he'd given her a job, an important one. But he'd underpaid her, and had left her in a tough if not impossible situation. "What can I do for you?" he whispered.

She stared at him. "A hug would be nice."

He wrapped her up in his arms.

"Thanks," she breathed, leaning into him, relaxing as if he was giving her comfort.

She was certainly giving him comfort, the way she hooked one arm around his neck, her other around his back, squeezing like he was her only anchor in a rough storm. And he relaxed into her with only one thought in his head.

She felt like home.

She pressed her face in the crook of his neck, her breath warm on his skin, and the air seemed to shift around them as the hug went from comfort to something else entirely.

And still she didn't let go. Instead, she lifted her head slightly so that her every exhale brushed over his jaw, and then right beneath his ear, which he'd never realized until he shivered was a *go* button for him.

"Still not a fan of working together," she whispered, and he was pretty sure she was gliding her mouth over that sensitive spot on purpose now.

He could only manage a nod.

"And we should definitely never sleep together since we're working so closely. Right?"

When he didn't answer, she lifted her head and they stared at each other as a heated beat went by. "Right?" she whispered.

He gave a slow headshake, then kissed her. Long. Deep. Until they were both pulling at clothes.

"This is probably really stupid," she whispered, tugging his shirt up.

He took over, pulling it the rest of the way off. "One hundred percent accurate."

They stared at each other some more. "Luna, your opinion is the only thing that matters to me. Do you want this?"

She let out a rough laugh. "Can't you tell?"

"I need you to say it."

"I want this," she said readily. "I want you, Jameson." And then she fused her mouth to his.

CHAPTER 17

Pressed against Jameson from chest to knees, Luna looked him in the eyes, suddenly *very* sure how she wanted to spend what was left of the night. Back BTK, she'd been feeling alone and a little lost. Very lost. ATK, the loneliness had retreated a bit. She had a feeling that if they took things to the next level, that loneliness would be eradicated entirely. "I know you're already sleeping here," she murmured. "And I know we haven't gone out three times unless you count when I ate your burger, and sitting on my rock, and tonight playing with baby goats . . . but I'm pretty sure the couch thing is getting old. Conveniently I have room in my bed. I mean, if you're interested."

"I think we both know just how *interested* I am. But—"

"Oh my God." She shoved him back a step, embarrassed to her core. When would she learn to not put herself out there, basically begging to be hurt?

Jameson came right back, hands on her hips, eyes intense. "There's nothing I'd rather be doing than spending time with you, Luna, don't ever doubt that. You've been starring in my fantasies nightly." His voice went low. Gruff. "The things we've done to each other . . ."

Her pulse kicked into high gear. "The but. I need to hear the but."

"*But* . . . I just want to put it out there for the both of us to remember—I'm leaving at the end of next month."

"I remember." The pang in her gut suggested otherwise, but she ignored it. "And? Because I also sense an 'and.'"

"*And*," he said, holding eye contact the way he always did, "there are things you don't know about me."

This time her heart skipped a beat in shock. "Like . . . you're a criminal?"

He gave a barely there smile and shook his head. "No."

"You hate animals."

The hint of a smile grew. "No."

"You don't recycle."

With a rough laugh, he dropped his head for a beat, then lifted it again. "I like you, Luna. I like you a lot."

A warmth hit her chest. As far as things about him she didn't know, she could get behind this one.

"I like your spirit," he said. "I like your guts, and your inability to give in or give up."

She snorted. "You mean stubbornness."

"Yes." He paused. Smiled. "And let's not forget your bad attitude."

She rolled her eyes, but he stepped up close and personal again. "It makes you real. And real is my very favorite thing about you." He tipped her head up to his and kissed her softly. "I also like the way you make me smile."

"That sounds . . . friendly," she decided.

"Believe me, I feel *very* friendly toward you."

She laughed, but he didn't. He looked deeply into her eyes. "Real truth?" he asked.

"Yes, please."

"You treat me like a human being. You trust me. You accept me, as is. You've given me your friendship, and make me feel as though I have value, that you care about me." He cupped her face. "You have a beautiful heart."

She had no idea why she felt so damn moved. They were just words. But her heart rolled over in her chest and exposed its tender underbelly. "Right back at you," she whispered. "All of it."

His eyes warmed, but still he hesitated.

"Don't worry," she said, "I know it's just for tonight."

"Believe me, I'd take more, but it'd make me a selfish bastard. I don't want you to get hurt because of me."

She didn't want to think about that, so she took him by the hand. "I understand the terms and I'm signing on the dotted line." She led him into her bedroom. It was small but neat, and the dark wood bed was her very favorite piece of furniture in the entire cabin. Cozy with warm bedding, she couldn't wait to see him in it.

So she gave him a push, smiling when he let himself fall back—taking her with him. Lying beneath her, body sprawled out for her perusal, he looked hot as hell and she wanted to ride him like he was the mechanical bronco that she and Willow rode last month at a bar in Reno. To that end, she straightened and started to pull her clothes off.

He stopped her, his hands covering hers and holding on. "I've been looking forward to this for a long time. Don't rush me."

"We can go slow next time."

His eyes heated. "I like the way you think." He slowly slid off her sweatshirt, then kissed his way from her bare shoulder up her throat, making her shiver. "But since nothing in life is guaranteed, I'm taking my time with you. I want you completely out of your mind for me by the time I'm inside you."

She had to laugh. "Did you forget how long it's been for me? I'm already out of my mind!"

With a grin, he rolled them until she was flat on her back with one hundred and seventy-five pounds of sexy, focused man pinning her there. It was a thrill, and when he kissed the soft, sensitive skin just beneath her ear, she gasped with pleasure.

"Love that sound," he murmured against her. "What else can I kiss to get you to make it again?" When she didn't answer, couldn't because he'd robbed her of the ability to speak, he took his mouth on a hot, wet, thorough tour to the hollow of her throat, making her writhe beneath him for more.

She had her hands inside his jeans now, trying to get him naked. "Jameson."

"Right here." He had her sweatpants off in a single heartbeat. "Mmm, and what about here . . ." Lowering his head, he kissed everything he'd uncovered before making a home for himself between her thighs, and she definitely kept making sounds. She couldn't help herself. "I especially love the way you look like this."

"At your mercy, you mean."

"You've got that entirely backward." He hooked a couple of fingers in her bikini undies and slid them aside, making way for his mouth.

"Omigod."

She felt him smile against her hot skin. "No. Just me."

She huffed out a breathless laugh. "Jameson . . ."

"There you go. I've got you, Luna."

The combination of that low, husky voice with his knowing fingers and tongue drove her right out of her mind in shockingly little time. She might've been embarrassed if he hadn't been making some yummy noises of his own, saying things against her like "you're so soft" and "damn, you're beautiful . . ." and "the way you taste . . ."

When she was boneless, he rose up to strip off his jeans when suddenly he went still while also swearing rather impressively under his breath.

"What?" she gasped. "I didn't catch you with the zipper, did I? Oh God. I'm sorry!"

He was shaking and she tried to get out from beneath him, but he held her close, which was when she realized he was laughing.

"So . . . I didn't just unman you?" she asked, eyes narrowed as he laughed even harder. She went hands on hips and narrowed her eyes. "I don't know why me worrying that I've robbed you of ever having children is so funny."

He wrapped his arms around her. "Do you know how long it's been since I laughed like that? With a woman? In bed?"

"Wow. First you laugh at me, and now you want to talk about other women?"

His grin was back and he gave her a very hot kiss that had her relaxing again before depriving her of his mouth to say, "Never." He kissed her again. "*Never* have I ever laughed with a woman in bed."

Oh. Oh, damn, he was good, because she melted into a puddle of boneless goo. "Jameson?"

"Yeah?"

"*Now.*"

"I would." He kissed his way along her jaw to that spot beneath her ear that drove her so crazy. "But I don't have a condom."

She froze. She was glad one of them was thinking, and it certainly wasn't her. Then she remembered. "*I do!*" Wriggling free, she ran to the living room where she'd dumped her purse earlier. She rifled through it until she found it at the very bottom of the bag, long forgotten until now.

When she ran back into the bedroom, Jameson was sitting up, looking sexily rumpled and hot as hell in nothing but her sheets.

She showed him the condom and he laughed again, and yeah, she could get used to that sound. "Okay, yes," she said. "It's bright blue. I got it as a party favor like a year ago, but it qualifies as a solution to our problem."

His eyes softened and so did his smile. "Come here, Luna."

That voice. If he kept speaking to her in that voice she'd probably do anything he asked. When she got close, he snagged her, pulling her into his arms. Even though the only light in the room came from the dim glow of her living room light down the hall, she could see his gaze roaming her face. He seemed to be looking for something, so she did her best to look confident and not needy.

"Luna."

"Jameson," she said in a low voice, mimicking his tone.

His mouth quirked and then he kissed her, but when she tried to deepen it, he pulled back a fraction. He had a forearm braced on the bed on either side of her head, his hands cupping her face, his fingers sliding into her hair. "You're sure?"

It was the first time she'd seen him vulnerable, and that's when she knew. She was falling for him. Falling scary fast and deep, with no life preserver in sight. "Did you not hear how long it's been since I've used a condom? Yes, I'm sure." And in case he needed show-not-tell, she wrapped her legs around his waist and tightened. Huh, look at that, Pilates *was* working out for her. "Now, Jameson."

She was already breathing heavy in anticipation when he lowered his head, but instead of kissing her on the mouth, he dragged wet, hot kisses down the side of her throat, along her collarbone and south, sending goose bumps dancing over her skin.

It felt amazing, he felt amazing, and she sort of accidentally bit his shoulder to keep him moving. Chuckling, he gave her the lead, and the two of them wriggled to get into a good position, bumping into each other, laughing and swearing as they tried to line things up.

Finally, he sat up, sheathed himself in the bright blue condom while she touched every part of him she could reach. Then he had her straddle him, slowly letting her sink over him until he was in as deep as he could go. She couldn't speak, couldn't breathe, could only feel. When she rolled her hips to his, he stilled, head back, eyes closed, a look of sheer ecstasy on his face. Then he opened his eyes and looked deep into hers. "Once isn't going to be nearly enough, Luna."

With that shocking statement, he began to move, and just like that, she didn't feel so lost. She felt . . . found.

She had no idea how much later it was when she opened her eyes. Jameson was watching her, the sheet slipped low on his hips, giving her an incredible view. Then their eyes caught, the moment stretching between them. She hesitated, unsure how to proceed because he looked serious. Much too serious for a man who'd just had his mouth on every inch of her. But then his lips curved in an intimate smile and her heart flipped over in her chest.

Pushing her hair from her face, he pulled her tight against him, pressing a kiss to her temple. "Do we need to talk about it?"

"Oh, definitely not." She shook her head, like it was no big deal.

When it was a big deal. The hugest deal. He'd just taken her apart and put her back together again with such erotic ease and care that she didn't even know what to do with it.

He came up on an elbow and ran a finger along her temple, around the shell of her ear. "Around you, logic vanishes."

She smiled. "You're just frustrated because there isn't an equation for feels. You can't math this."

He looked at her for a long beat, and then nodded. "I can't math this."

"Don't worry, I'm right here if you get scared."

"What if I'm scared now?" he asked, hands gliding over her body, renewing the flames.

"It's okay." She leaned over him. "I've got you . . ."

Much later, she opened her eyes when the bed shifted. Jameson vanished, then came back with two bottles of water. She smiled as he handed her one. "Staying hydrated?"

He toasted her with his bottle. "Safety first."

She laughed as he leaned down and brushed a kiss across her lips, his fingers gliding over her stomach.

"You staying?" she whispered.

He flashed a crooked smile. "You're naked. Where on earth would I go?"

CHAPTER 18

Several days later, which felt like two years thanks to a surprise spring snowstorm that dumped five inches of snow, plus Miss Piggy giving birth to three piglets, Luna was just about done in. It was 6:30 p.m. before she was able to rush home with Sprout to grab a quick dinner before the crew's regular poker night.

Her cabin was empty. No Jameson. She hadn't made it back to the offices before calling it a day, so he could still be working. Or maybe not. She pulled out her phone, stared at her thumb hovering over his contact, then shook her head.

Sure, they'd had a great night. Okay, a few of them. But they'd also said this wasn't going anywhere because he was leaving. Not wanting to be a stage five clinger in their non-relationship relationship, she shoved her phone back into her pocket and made herself a quick PB&J for dinner. She also fed Sprout and then tucked him into bed before leaving to head to poker night, which was at Stella's tonight.

Even though they all worked together, most of the time they

were too busy to breathe, much less hang out, so she loved that they did this. She was early, but she hadn't gotten to see much of her grandma this week, and she missed her. Expecting Stella to be puttering around setting up, she stilled in surprise at the sight of her and Jameson sitting at the palm reading table—which was also their poker table—but instead of cards and poker chips, there were spreadsheets.

"But the tourists love the local artisan jewelry," Stella was saying.

Jameson nodded. "I'm not suggesting eliminating it, but you're only getting ten percent on consignment from the local jewelry makers."

Stella shrugged. "They're the ones who do all the work."

"Not true. You're displaying it, you're handling the advertising, and you do all the sales work. Upping your percentage is not only fair, it increases your profitability in a large way. I suggest forty percent."

Stella took this all in with unusual concentration, while Luna felt her heart swell at Jameson's expression. He wanted her gram to succeed. And she realized she hadn't been at all sure of his intentions to be on their side until that very moment.

"The jewelry takes up valuable real estate in here," Jameson said. "You could be selling more apparel, which is your real moneymaker." He showed her a different sheet of paper. "I did some analysis using previous sales numbers. If you'd used the space for more clothing racks this past month, here's what your income could've been."

"Wow." She shook her head. "But my friends constantly tell

me that out of all the places they sell their art, I sell more than the rest combined."

"Because I guarantee you, they're paying forty percent to their other sellers. Or more."

"Huh." She nodded. "Okay, I hear you."

He smiled at her and pulled out another sheet of paper. "This is your square footage rearranged. The way it's set up right now, you're losing too much space. Worse, you're also being taken advantage of on the consignment stuff, and I don't like to see that. You deserve better, Stella."

Luna thought so too, and that Jameson was not only looking out for someone she loved dearly, but that he'd also printed out everything because he knew Stella would prefer that to looking at a screen, actually choked her up. There he was, spending his time helping out a stranger, really, and making a difference. Something she hadn't managed to do.

Why hadn't she thought to check in with her people about how things were going, to see if she could help improve their profits? Watching Jameson do exactly that had the wall around her heart cracking slightly. He could've thrown his lot in with the coven and forced her out. But he hadn't. In spite of it being all about numbers and math for him, he'd set that aside enough to wade in and help her try to save the farm.

"The thing is," Stella said, "I love working and promoting local artists. I never wanted to make money off of them."

"Do you also love eating?" He smiled. "I know it goes against the grain, but you're a businesswoman, and you're a hell of a good one. You can be that *and* their friend."

Stella beamed. "I knew from the moment I read your palm that you were going to be a special addition to our family."

The briefest beat of surprise crossed his face. Surprise and . . . he was moved, she realized. She wondered at what cost his cut-throat world had been that such a simple comment could touch him.

Stella looked up, caught sight of Luna, and beamed. "Darling! Right on time, as usual."

"I'm fifteen minutes early."

Stella smiled at Jameson. "She's always early. If she's not early, she panics. It's not her fault, it's an OCD thing. I blame my son. He's so tight with his time and affections, not to mention his money, that he squeaks when he walks."

Jameson met Luna's gaze, eyes warm. "Nothing wrong with caring enough to be early."

She drew a deep breath against the fact that her heart skipped a beat. "I don't panic," she said. "And it's not OCD. It's just a po-lite thing. Being late is rude." She sent her grandma a long gaze.

"Eh, time is fluid," Stella said on a shrug. "And in here, in this shop? We're on the universe's time, so no one's late. Jame-son came over to offer some suggestions on how to make more money. Isn't he the sweetest, kindest thing?"

Jameson grimaced. Maybe he'd never been called sweet or kind before. Or maybe he was just wondering what time it was in the universe's house.

"He's got serious special talents," Stella said.

No kidding. She'd been lucky enough to experience some of them firsthand.

"Tell us some more, Jameson," Stella said, pouring him some tea.

"*Wait!*" Luna leaned forward and sniffed the tea.

"Honestly," Stella said. "I hardly ever make shroom tea anymore."

To his credit, Jameson didn't look alarmed, but he very slightly did push the tea away.

Stella sighed. "It's just chamomile! I hope you don't mind, but when you put your hands on the table, I read the veins on the back of your hands. They say you're not drinking enough, and that you're retaining water."

Luna choked on her own tongue.

Jameson slid her a glance.

She smirked.

He gave a rather impressive eye roll. Because Jameson was perfect, and they both knew it. Not an ounce of water retention on that bod anywhere. And she should know, as she'd had her hands and mouth on every inch of it. Repeatedly.

"And you," Stella said to Luna. "I had Chinese food earlier and I got a fortune that was meant for you, not me." She pulled it out of her pocket and handed it over. "Read it out loud."

Luna unfolded it: "'Are you the one in relationships who makes the spreadsheets, or the one who mocks the spreadsheets but still benefits from them?'"

Jameson snorted, then took a sip of tea to cover it up.

"Not funny," Luna said.

"Let's agree to disagree," he said.

"Okay, well, here's a fortune for *you*." Luna looked him in the eye. "Everyone talks about how bad social media is for your mental health, but what about Excel?"

Stella grinned. "Nice one, honey."

Jameson rolled his eyes. She was rubbing off on him. He stood. "We can finish this later. I don't want to interfere with your poker night."

"No worries," Stella said. "We've got plenty of time. Everyone besides Luna will be at least thirty minutes late. We'd love you to stay and play. Wouldn't we, Luna?"

Luna met Jameson's gaze, and if she didn't know better, she'd have thought he actually *wanted* to be invited. By her. Problem was, she wasn't at all sure she wanted him to see the worst of them, and poker night *definitely* brought out their worst, but she knew he had no social life here in Sunrise Cove. She wasn't sure a man like Jameson ever got lonely, but she nodded. "Do you play poker?"

"You worried?"

She smiled. "You're bluffing, so no, I'm not even a little worried."

Jameson returned her smile with one that held a deceptive mischievousness, and possibly trouble with a capital *T*. "It's been a very long time since I played."

Good. She wanted to beat him. Actually, when he smiled like that, she also wanted to kiss him. And, well, other things. But beating him in poker worked too.

Stella smiled at Jameson. "Thank you. I appreciate your ideas and will try every one of them. Anything to draw more people in and help the farm stay afloat. Excuse us a moment?" And then she stood up and tugged Luna along with her to the back of the barn and the teeny-tiny room that had once been for tack and other equipment but was now her office. "Okay, spill," Stella said.

"Spill what?"

"What's going on between you and your sexy new partner?"

She had to work to keep her expression even because her gram could read her like a book. "We're working our butts off to figure out a way to keep this place afloat."

"Uh-huh. And I can see you've got that pat little story down for whoever asks. Now tell me what's really going on."

Luna sighed. "I'm not really sure."

"Okay, let's try this. What do you *think* is going on?"

Oh, nothing except that she was falling for someone she had no business falling for.

Stella smiled. "Never mind. Your eyes say it all. He's a good choice for you, honey. He's strong, inside and out. He's incredibly intelligent, resourceful, protective, *and* he's got a sense of humor. I mean, he has to, to put up with all of us. But I think my favorite thing is the way he looks at you."

"Like he wouldn't mind smothering me with a pillow in my sleep?"

Stella laughed. "Honey, we *all* feel that way about you every now and then."

"Thanks, Gram."

"I'm talking about the fact that he looks at you like maybe you're lunch. I hope you plan to do something about that. If I was thirty years younger—"

Luckily, the front door opened again, and the sounds of Milo's and Chef's voices came through.

"Look at that," Luna said. "Time to get started!"

"*Chicken.*"

"Sticks and stones . . ." Luna headed out there and was hugged by Chef and Milo. Then she realized Willow was behind them and she sucked in a painful breath. Her BFF was wearing her usual poker night T-shirt. Actually, they all were. Luna's said: *No One Cares What You Folded!*

Willow's was: *POKERologist—Bluffing Specialist.*

"I'm so happy to see you," Luna said softly.

Willow shrugged. "I'm only here because I need some new candy. I intend to bleed you dry."

Luna felt a relieved smile split her face. "You can try."

For a beat, Willow looked just as relieved, but then she lifted her chin. "For the record, this changes nothing."

Luna pretended that didn't hurt. Normally that wouldn't be hard. She was good at pretending. But as this was Willow, her ride-or-die, she had to swallow hard. "Understood."

Willow nodded and put on her lucky poker hat—her Mike Trout baseball cap, because he'd once thrown it to her at a game—and lifted her chin high. "May the best woman win."

"Or, you know, *man,*" Chef said. His poker shirt read: *Jack*King Off.*

"*Definitely* man," Milo said, wearing his own lucky poker shirt: *I Don't Even Fold My Laundry.*

Stella pulled off her cardigan, under which was her poker shirt: *Poker Is Like Sex—If You Don't Have a Good Partner, You Better Have a Good Hand.* She looked at Jameson. "You need a shirt to play. Hold, please." She vanished into the back and returned with a pink bedazzled tee that read: *I'm Just Here for the Pot.* "Here. It's a large, it should work."

Jameson held it up and eyed it, expression blank.

Everyone looked at him with varying degrees of amusement. Luna didn't know what they were thinking, but she was thinking that the shirt wasn't going to be nearly long enough.

With a shrug, Jameson pulled off his shirt.

The rest of them sucked in a collective impressed breath. Even Luna, who'd rubbed herself all over that body of his just last night.

"Lucky bitch," Chef whispered to her.

Jameson pulled on the pink bedazzled tee. It was a little snug and a lot short, so there was a gap between the waistband of his jeans and the bottom of the tee, exposing a strip of taut skin.

The room was mesmerized for a long beat as Jameson casually, and as comfortable as you please, sat at the table. "Who deals first?"

"Don't take this the wrong way," Milo whispered to Chef, "but I think I'm in love."

Luna rolled her own tongue back into her mouth and sat across from Jameson so she wouldn't be tempted to lick him like a lollipop.

Poker night was always BYOB, so they each pulled out their drinks of choice. Each time they got together, they used a different currency theme, which they had voted on at the previous poker night.

Tonight's theme was candy. Everyone had brought plenty of their personal favorites, which they took very seriously. Plus, they were all competitive and hated to lose. They had a saying here on the farm. You could leave out a pot of gold and it won't be stolen, but don't leave out your candy or it'll be gone.

Obviously Jameson didn't have any, so Luna divided her stash of Skittles in half—keeping most of the reds for herself since they were the best ones—and pushed half over to him. "Don't make me sorry."

He grinned. "Thanks."

Two hands of five-card draw later, Luna was quite pleased. She'd won both hands and had a pile of candy in front of her, but better yet, everyone was miffed.

Except Jameson. He sat there in that ridiculous pink bedazzled tee, mouth serious, eyes amused. She didn't understand why, especially when she went on to win two out of the next three hands as well.

It wasn't until the final game of the night that she understood—right after he'd taken the entire pot in a single hand and then casually collected his loot.

Stella had to give him a bag to hold it all. "I'm so impressed. You're a con man, and I totally missed it. We're going to have so much fun together."

Chef was shaking his head. "I'm good at reading people. I mean, I'm *real* good. And you came out of nowhere. I looked you straight in the face and your eyes told me you didn't know what you were doing. Damn." He fist-bumped him. "You got skills. And by skills, I mean lying skills."

"I never lied."

Chef grinned and clapped him on the back. "See what I mean? Good. You're good."

Milo was shaking his head mournfully. "My entire stash of Hershey's Kisses . . . gone."

Willow rolled her eyes. She was the only one who hadn't lost anything because she'd folded early every hand. "You've got to know when to get out."

"Lock up for me?" Stella asked Luna, and when they were all gone except Jameson, she watched as he separated out a pile of Skittles, making sure to give her all of his reds. "For fronting me."

"Show-off." She flicked off the lights, moved to the door, and paused, closing her eyes to enjoy the little shiver of the best kind when Jameson stopped right behind her, so close she could feel the delicious heat of him.

"What are you doing?" he asked.

"Nothing."

"Now who's the liar?" He sounded amused again. "If you wanted me closer, all you had to do was say so."

"I try not to be bossy."

"Since when?" he asked on a laugh.

She turned to face him. "Just out of curiosity, if I boss you around, you'd do what I say?"

"In bed? Absolutely."

She laughed. "So first I get serious math whiz Jameson, then sexy Jameson, and now funny Jameson?"

"I have my moments," he said modestly, and ran a warm finger along her temple, trailing it softly down the shell of her ear, making her shiver again. "I'd really like to kiss you," he said. "But—"

She gave him a two-handed push to the chest and sighed. "Why is there always a but when it comes to wanting me?"

His eyes never left hers. "There is absolutely no *but* when it comes to me wanting you."

As far as admissions went, that felt like a doozy. "Then what?"

"We need to talk."

Oh boy. "Just so you know, those words are the opposite of romantic."

"We have a meeting with the bank in two days."

"Neither are those."

"I'm sorry, but we're barreling down on that balloon payment," he said, eyes apologetic. "We need an extension."

She got hopeful. "That's a possibility?"

"We're going to find out."

"*We*? We're a we?"

His fingers were playing with a loose wave that had fallen against her jaw. "We are most definitely a we."

"In business." Damn, was that her voice, all light and breathless?

He smiled, then opened the door and gestured her out ahead of him, taking the keys and locking up for her. They walked back to her place in the dark, both of them silent until they were in her kitchen. They'd spent a lot of time in this room together now, which meant it was filled with memories of late-night talks over quesadillas.

"Would you like one?" he asked, reading her mind.

The thing was, those usually ended with deep, drugging kisses, and a whole bunch more. Amazing as it'd all been, she was now in danger of being in so deep that there was no turning back. Because partners didn't sleep together. And women who were broken inside, like she was, didn't have what it took to take things to the next level anyway. "I'm not hungry."

And because he looked far too delectable standing there, she drew a deep breath. Ah, hell, what would one more night hurt? "At least not for food."

He gave her a slow, sexy smile and she knew she was done for.

CHAPTER 19

Willow was second in line at the coffee shop, with a whole bunch of people behind her also needing their fix—er, coffee.

Luna was one of them, two people back, not attempting to talk to her. Willow's own doing, so there was no use getting butt-hurt about it. But she still did. It was the first time Luna hadn't tried to approach her.

When the line shifted and she was up, Mandy looked right through her to smile at the man behind her. "What'll it be?"

Willow scowled. She needed coffee stat or there would be dead bodies. "Are you kidding me?"

"Your usual?" Mandy asked the man.

Hell no. Not today. "Seriously, Mandy? You dated Shayne *one* night *twelve* years ago when we were on a break and you're *still* mad? He's mine, get over it."

Mandy handed the man behind her his order and then smiled at Luna. "Looking good, babe. You working out?"

Luna laughed. "Does carrying baby goats around count? Because then yes, I'm working out."

"No, it's not that," Mandy said. "You've got a certain . . . glow."

Willow whipped around and stared at Luna. And damn, Mandy was right. Luna was *definitely* wearing a certain glow. Just how long had she been wearing it while Willow hadn't been paying attention during her long pity party for one? But then her phone rang and distracted her because she had trouble finding it in her purse.

Finally she got a hand on it and looked at the screen. It was Eddie, one of Shayne's firefighter buddies. "Let me guess," she answered. "He can't find his keys. No, wait—his wallet, right?"

"Willow." His tone, unusually serious, alerted her before his words. "There's been an accident. Shayne's on his way to Sunrise General."

Her heart had stopped, but her body was halfway to the door so she must still be breathing. "How bad?"

He paused.

"Eddie, how bad?"

"We're not sure . . ."

Oh, God. "If he let you guys take him to the hospital, it's bad. I'll meet you there." She was running to her car when she realized someone was right alongside her.

Luna, who took Willow's hand, redirecting her to Luna's truck, pushing her into the passenger seat before running around the front to get behind the wheel. "Which hospital?"

Willow could barely hear over the blood whooshing in her ears. Nor could she speak past what felt like cut glass in her

throat. In fact, for a beat, she thought she might get sick as Luna
started her truck.

"Willow?"

"Sunrise General," she managed.

Luna whipped out of the parking lot. Willow had to grab the
oh-shit bar as Luna took the next turn on two wheels.

"What do we know?" Luna asked.

We . . . She sniffled. "Do you have any tissues?"

Luna opened the center console, pulled out a small stack of napkins, and shoved them into Willow's hand. "He got hurt at work.
I don't know how bad." Her biggest nightmare coming true . . .

Luna reached across and squeezed her hand. "He's going to
be okay."

"How do you know?"

"Because you'll kill him if he's not."

She choked out a laugh. God, she was so relieved she wasn't in
this alone. She'd been such a bitch, and Luna was still willing to
be her rock. If Willow hadn't been so panicked, she'd have been
swamped with gratitude, but she couldn't think about anything
other than Shayne right now. Why hadn't she pressed Eddie for
details? It could be anything. Shayne had once screw-gunned
his hand to the ceiling while trying to install a fan above their
kitchen table and had refused to go to the hospital, saying he just
needed a Band-Aid for the hole through his palm. Another time
he'd been playing touch football with the guys and had twisted
his ankle, which had ballooned to triple its normal size, and
hadn't gone to the hospital for that either. So this . . . this must

be bad. "What if . . ." She closed her eyes. "What if something happens and he doesn't know how much I love him?"

"He knows." Luna weaved around a car going ten miles an hour under the speed limit. "I promise you that."

Willow wasn't so sure. She'd let her fears of losing him guide her, and it was possible she could lose him anyway. "I pushed him away. Why did I do that?"

Luna glanced over at her, eyes tight with worry but still managing a smile. "Because men are dumb and he took the job here in Sunrise Cove without talking it through with you."

Right. Only now that didn't seem like as big a deal as she'd made it out to be. "He's impulsive. I knew that about him when I married him. There's traffic, turn left onto Lake Drive, it'll be faster."

Luna didn't turn.

"What the hell are you doing?"

"Okay, first, yelling at me isn't going to make the truck go faster. And second, they're repaving Lake Drive. Trust me, this is the best way."

Willow sagged back against the seat, hands to her quivering stomach. She hadn't had breakfast yet, not even the coffee she'd never gotten, and her belly was revolting. "I feel sick."

"Breathe slowly. In through your nose and out your mouth—"

"Pull over."

"What?" Luna whipped her head to her. "Why?"

"For the love of God, just pull the eff over!" she yelled, and started gagging.

Luna jerked the truck to the side of the road. Willow barely

got the door open before she was throwing up. When she'd emp-
tied her already empty stomach, she straightened weakly.

Luna handed her some more napkins, a water bottle, and a
piece of gum, not saying anything until Willow had caught her
breath. "Are you okay?"

"It's stress. Everything feels out of control."

"Not everything," Luna said, and squeezed her hand. "You
okay to get going again?"

Unable to speak, she nodded. And five minutes later they were
running into the ER. At the front desk, Willow panicked. But
Luna slipped an arm around her and spoke to the guy behind
the glass, telling them they were here for Shayne Green, and that
Willow was his wife.

"Just a moment," he said, and vanished into the back.

Willow waited in numbness.

"This is Shayne we're talking about," Luna said, rubbing her
back. "He's going to be okay."

Willow nodded, then shook her head. "Remember when he
was hurt in that flood rescue and almost drowned?"

"And you made him promise to get out of that Swift Water
Rescue unit, and he did. Hold tight, I'll be right back."

Willow's knees felt wobbly, so she sank on her haunches and
put her hands over her eyes, trying not to throw up again. "This
isn't happening. This isn't happening. This isn't happ—"

"Willow."

Luna crouched in front of her and pulled her hands from her
face. "Come on, let's go see him."

"You got us in?"

"Yes." Luna pulled her upright, keeping a hold of her hand.

"Where is he?"

"Bay number four." And though neither of them knew this hospital well, Luna led her there and Willow felt so grateful she almost started crying. Which was annoying because she hated to cry.

They hustled down one corridor and then another, and then Luna stopped in front of a closed curtain. Willow's heart was thundering in her ears, but the rest of her had frozen.

Appearing to understand she'd turned into a helpless idiot, Luna squeezed her hand and used her other to open the curtain.

Shayne lay on the bed, eyes closed, face gray. He had stitches across his forehead and his left cheek. He was bare chested, which allowed her to see that his ribs were wrapped and the rest of him bruised and cut up.

Taking a deep breath, Willow straightened her spine and walked over to him, taking his big hand in hers.

He immediately opened his eyes. "Hey." Lifting his other hand, he ran the pad of his thumb over her cheek, swiping a tear away. "I'm okay."

"You're in a hospital and you've got stitches and God knows what else, so no, you're *not* okay!" Spent, she very carefully dropped her head to his chest.

One of Shayne's big hands settled on the back of her neck. "I'm going to need more Advil if you plan to keep yelling at me."

She both laughed and cried, then lifted her head. "What happened?"

Shayne drew a deep breath, but didn't speak. He closed his eyes briefly, and Willow, hating seeing him in pain, leaned in close, gently pushing his hair back from his face just as Eddie spoke. She hadn't even seen him in a chair on the opposite side of the bed.

"It was a Swift Water Rescue gone fubar. Some idiots thought they could raft the Truckee River with the current at an all-time high from that surprise storm."

Willow stilled, then looked at Shayne. "But you don't do Swift Water Rescues anymore. That was the deal."

"Babe—"

"No." She pulled back. "Don't babe me."

"We were stretched thin," Shayne said. "I was the only one trained to lead the rescue."

Willow took a big gulp of air and instead of screaming, let out a completely involuntary half-hysterical laugh.

Shayne looked relieved. "Thanks for understanding—" He broke off when Luna gave him a warning headshake.

"Dude," Eddie said. "When a woman laughs during an argument, it means the psycho part of her brain has been activated and you should abort."

"Thanks, man," Shayne said, eyes never leaving Willow.

Her knees were weak again, but for a different reason entirely now, and she dropped into a chair.

"How can I make this okay?" he asked her.

"Stop changing the rules on me."

"The rules? What rules?" Eddie looked confused. "The captain always takes lead on these rescues."

Willow pointed at him. "Not now."

Eddie shrugged, then stood to offer Luna his chair. "How's it going, Chica? You never returned my calls."

They'd met at one of the station's fundraising events. That particular one had been held at the Olde Tahoe Tap, where Eddie and Luna had danced. Nothing more had happened, which Willow knew because up until the past months, she and Luna had shared everything.

"Work's just really busy right now," Luna said.

Eddie waggled a brow. "Maybe we could try again sometime when things slow down for you."

"Look," Willow said over the span of Shayne's bed. "This isn't about you right now, okay? In case you haven't noticed, I'm in the middle of a breakdown here. Respect for the breakdown, please."

A nurse poked her head around the curtain, looking stern. "You all need to keep it down in here."

"Absolutely," Luna said. "Apologies."

Willow looked at Shayne. "No promises."

Shayne grinned at her, and dammit. That smile. It was going to be the death of her. Unable to help herself, she brushed a kiss to his bruised jaw. Then lightly across his lips.

The nurse was taking his blood pressure. "Huh," she said.

"Huh what?" Willow demanded. "Is it too high? Is he going to die?"

"No." The nurse smiled. "It's lowered since you got here."

Shayne took Willow's hand in his and stared into her eyes. "My wife lowers my blood pressure by walking into the room."

Willow wanted to both hug him and murder him. How was that even possible? "Tell me everything."

When Shayne didn't speak, she looked at Eddie.

He nodded. "A kayaker got into trouble on the river. And don't get me started why he was even on the water since we were under a wind advisory, plus the recent snowmelt on top of spring runoff. Suffice it to say, every mistake this guy could've made, he did. And our boy here paid the price. Victim nearly drowned Shayne trying to crawl over him to the shore."

Shayne turned his head and stared at Eddie.

"Right," Eddie said. "Keep my trap shut about the rescue details. I remember now."

Willow was trying to take deep breaths to dissipate the image of Shayne drowning. "Oh my God. You could've died."

"But I didn't." He looked at the nurse. "So when can you break me out of here?"

"You're staying overnight. Everyone out except one person of his choosing."

"Obviously that's me," Eddie said.

Willow gave him her impressive Evil Eye and he laughed. "Call me if you need anything, Cap. The rest of the guys'll stop by later."

"He needs rest. Tell them to wait until tomorrow," Willow said. "Unless they're bringing food." Then she settled herself into a chair for the long haul, because She. Wasn't. Leaving.

She was only vaguely aware of everyone filing out of the room, including Luna. Willow was too busy looking Shayne over.

Belying his injuries, he snagged her arm and pulled her to the bed at his hip, holding on to her tight. "You always yell at me right before you kiss me."

"There will be no more kissing today," she said. Probably.

"How about tomorrow?"

CHAPTER 20

Late the next afternoon, Luna sat in Jameson's car, not making a move even though he'd parked in the bank's lot and cut the engine two minutes ago. "I'm going to need something sweet after this," she said. "Tell me we'll get something sweet when we get home."

"I'll get you anything you want."

"But will it be sweet?"

He turned to her, his eyes heated. "I've been under the impression that you like spicy, but I can definitely do sweet."

"Variety is nice."

He smiled and brushed his lips ever so gently across hers and she couldn't help but remember that morning when they'd woken up to DZ and his sisters staring at them from their perch on the foot of the bed.

Jameson had sat up, then gently scooped up DZ and set him on the floor. Next he'd reached for Pearl but she'd bared her teeth.

"Don't worry," Luna had said. "She isn't the biter. That's Mini."

So he'd scooped Pearl up and . . . she bit him on the hand. Not hard enough to break the skin, but he'd sucked air in between his teeth.

"That wasn't a bite," Luna had said. "That was a love tap."

He'd slid her a look. "Maybe you should show me the difference."

"I think I've shown you plenty."

Holding the goat against his bare chest with one arm, he ran a finger over her jaw while the air went electric around them. "You can't sweet-talk this away. You know that, right?"

And she'd known he wasn't talking about the baby goat.

Now she looked into his eyes and knew the accuracy of his statement.

As if he was remembering the same thing, he kissed her again. Then they walked toward the bank side by side, Jameson looking confident, relaxed, successful, and effortlessly sexy. It made her want to push him into a closet and rumple him up. She wanted to loosen his tie, untuck his shirt, slide her fingers into his hair, pull his head down to hers and—

He glanced over at her, and at whatever was on her face, his eyes warmed with amusement and something else that had the nervous butterflies in her belly giving way to excited butterflies.

Leaning into her, his lips brushed the shell of her ear. "I love the way you wear a pair of jeans, but you look edible in that dress."

She'd planned to re-wear her visit-the-lawyer outfit, but she'd gotten ketchup on it at the bar that night she'd met Jameson and hadn't gotten to the dry cleaner. Yep, it'd been a month.

Whatever. Her dress from date night with Chef had been accidentally slept on by Sprout, who shedded like it was his job. So she was in her only other dress, a strappy little sundress turned into pseudo business wear by adding a jean jacket and leather boots. She hadn't been at all sure she'd pulled it off, but the adjective "edible" suggested she'd gotten close.

Her phone buzzed with an incoming text from her grandma. Jameson looked over at her and she showed him the screen.

GRAM: How do I text "bite me" in an emoji?

LUNA: To . . . ?

GRAM: Your mom. Who else?

LUNA: You don't. Not if you want to ever have any holiday at any family dinner ever again. Now repeat after me, I will not text her.

GRAM: I'll try.

LUNA: Try hard.

Jameson smiled and shook his head. "You hit the lotto with her." He opened the bank door for her.

They were asked to wait. Sitting in the reception area, Luna felt completely out of her element. She didn't even realize she was bouncing her leg until Jameson gently put a hand on her thigh.

Finally, a man came and got them, escorting them into an office.

"I'm Stan Lawrence," he said. "I understand you're interested in a loan to pay off a debt owed to your investors."

"Yes," Jameson said. "I've brought our financial records to show our longtime good standing with this bank, and—"

"Sit tight," Stan said, cutting him off. "I'll need to run this past my manager."

When he was gone, Luna turned to Jameson. "He didn't even listen to you."

"It's a tactic," he said, and shrugged like he understood it.

"It's rude."

"It's part of the game."

"Game?" she asked. "This is a *game*?"

He took her hand and gave it a squeeze. "He's an underling. He doesn't have the authority to help us."

She looked around, her nerves in her throat now. "If they tell us no . . ."

"We're not making a huge profit, but we chug along just fine. It's good business for them to say yes."

"And if they decide it's not good business?"

He squeezed her hand again. "Your grandfather's company worked with this bank for years. We have a well-established working relationship. There's no reason to turn us down. They've already invested in the farm with that line of credit Silas procured a decade ago to use as needed. My point is, they should want us to succeed." He started to say something else, but Banker Dude strolled back in, rubbing a hand over his mouth, like he was uncomfortable.

He sat behind his desk, and without meeting either of them in the eye, he said, "I'm sorry. We can't help you."

Luna sucked in a breath and looked at Jameson. Sitting at ease, he didn't give a thing away, not a single thought, remaining his usual unperturbed, impenetrable self. He kept his eyes on Stan but spoke to Luna. "It's because they're owned by a larger bank, a private one that the group of investors run, a fact that should have zero bearing on this. But apparently with Silas gone, they no longer have to play nice."

Oh this was bad. So bad.

"We'll use the line of credit then," Jameson said.

Stan shook his head. "The line of credit is closed."

"Since when?"

"Since, as you said yourself, Silas is gone. Everything he had with us is now liquidated, and he's no longer a customer. So unfortunately, we have to go off the farm's financials. The debt to credit ratio on the farm is just too high."

Jameson shook his head in disbelief. "Silas worked with this bank for decades, and now that he's gone you're choosing to cut the farm off at the knees instead of letting things take their natural course?"

"Honestly, I'd love to help," Stan said quietly. "But this isn't my call. It came from above."

Jameson stood, pulling Luna up with him. "Come on. We're done here." He walked Luna back through the bank, his hand warm and reassuring in hers. She was upset, confused, but . . . she wasn't alone. And in that moment, it meant more than anything she could think of, having him at her side, in the trenches with her. "Jameson—"

"Not here," he said, and two minutes later they strode out and into the sun that was way too cheery and bright for how she felt. Jameson opened the passenger door of his vehicle for her and then slid behind the wheel, phone in hand. His eyes, when he glanced over at her as she buckled in, were dark and stormy. He was angry, she realized. Really and truly angry. The cool calm was still there, but she bet she could make popcorn from the energy coming off him.

"You don't have to do this," he said into the conference call with as many of Silas's old cronies as he could get on the line, including Brett. "You don't have to force us to fail by convincing the bank to be on your side. If we're not a good business, we'll fail all on our own." He sounded so logical and in control, and he listened, then said, "I wouldn't count on us going down for the count."

Whatever they said to him after that, he shook his head, disconnected the call, and set his phone aside.

"You didn't expect to be turned down," she said.

"No. But this isn't a business decision. There's something else going on."

"What does that mean?"

He turned and faced her. "It means they want the farm, no doubt for the land. And they're going to get it over my dead body."

She sucked in a breath. "I'm really hoping it doesn't come to that. I like your body just as it is." And then her stupid eyes filled.

With a low sound of regret, he pulled her into him. "It's going to be okay."

Pressed up against him, his strength became hers. She drew a deep breath and nodded. Jameson didn't lie. She was going to believe in him. They would be okay.

CHAPTER 21

She liked his body just as it was. Jameson let the words sink in, let himself enjoy a rare moment of personal pleasure. Well, maybe not so rare, as ever since he'd come to Tahoe, he'd had more of a life than he could remember ever having, thanks to the woman next to him.

And he'd failed her. "Luna—"

"Turn left out of the lot," she said, and then gave him directions on the road until they were at a secluded spot at the lake.

"Come on," she said. And just as he'd done at the bank, she came around and took his hand, sweetly squeezing it.

Comforting *him*.

She led him past the wild grass to the edge of the sandy beach.

It was seventy degrees outside, the sky a blue so pure it almost hurt to look at it. White puffy clouds drifted slowly by, reflected in the unusually still waters of Lake Tahoe. All around them, sharp, craggy mountains covered in a blanket of green pines and still capped in snow provided jaw-dropping vistas. Small swells lapped against the sand. Birds tweeted to each other. From somewhere in a tree overhead, a squirrel chided them.

Luna plopped right down on the sand and wrapped her arms around her knees. Then she looked up at him expectantly.

Shaking his head on a low laugh, because who else on the planet could make him do something he wasn't sure he wanted to do, he sat.

She gave him a small but sweet smile. Then they stared at the water in blessed silence.

"The water's my favorite color," she said softly. "It's because water as crystal clear as Lake Tahoe tends to absorb red light, leaving just the rich azure blue . . ."

He nodded, but all he could think was that he'd failed. He'd failed Luna. He'd failed her crew. He'd failed every part of the farm, down to Dammit Ziggy. He had no idea what to do with that. For the first time in his life, he was on the other side of things, and he wasn't a fan.

The thing was, in his job he'd *always* played fair. Every. Single. Time. So not only didn't the bank's decision make sense, it was as if he'd just been told that one plus two equals four.

"If you're talking to me," Luna said, "I can't understand angry male inarticulate muttering. You'll have to translate."

"I'm furious," he admitted. "It just makes no sense for them to—"

"What? Decide not to help us?" She shrugged. "At the end of the day, it's their money to do with as they please."

"No, it's not that. I'm angry because it wasn't a level playing field." He could see she didn't understand what he was saying.

"Look, money, facts, spreadsheets . . . it's my language. I understand it because it's about analysis, not emotions."

"And it's like someone just cursed at you in your own language?"

He let out a short laugh. Okay, so she did get it. Maybe better than he did, which was a revelation. "Yes. Exactly. And they've threatened our livelihood on top of it."

Her expression softened.

"What?"

"You keep saying that 'we.'"

He realized she still hadn't quite bought into the *trust Jameson* program yet. Which meant he had work to do there. But first things first. "Because we *are* a we. Through thick and thin."

She stared at him, listening to his words in a way that he found to be a huge turn-on, though he couldn't have explained that to save his life.

"You feel a sense of injustice that they would attempt to make us fail," she said.

"Yes, and why do you sound surprised by that?"

She smiled then, the kind of smile that stopped his heart. "Did you know that when you first got here, I thought you were just a robotic numbers nerd, and that I wasn't at all sure I liked you?"

Now it was his turn to laugh. "This is not a news flash."

"Then maybe this is—I was wrong. I do like you. I like you a whole lot."

"Did you really just decide that?" he asked with a rough laugh. "Because I let you see me angry?"

"Yes." She met his gaze. "It's like the old adage, you don't know someone until you've seen them deal with slow internet. I couldn't know you all the way through until I saw this, you all pissed off and fighting mad." She paused. "You're human."

He had to laugh. "What were the other choices?"

She just shook her head. "Look, I know we're in trouble. But I also know we're not going down without a fight. I'm just really glad we're in this together."

Staggered by that, he used his thumb under her jaw to tilt her head up. A small smile played at the corner of her mouth as he leaned in closer, and God, he loved it. He kept his eyes on hers until he could feel her breath on his skin, and then closed them as he touched his lips to hers. The kiss was slow and sweet while his entire being breathed for her as they built on whatever this tentative thing between them was.

"One more stop," she said, standing up, leading him back to the car before directing him to the Olde Tahoe Tap.

Turning off the engine, he looked at her. "You're hungry?"

"Well, I do like to eat my feels." She hopped out of the car. It took him longer; he stayed seated, drawing deep breaths, one after another, but it didn't help. He was wound tight, on edge.

Luna opened his car door, again taking the lead. If he were her, he'd probably not be speaking to him. After all, he'd been so sure, so damn sure he could turn all of this around. It was a bitter pill. But he wouldn't let it end here. If it took everything he had, he would find a way to fix this. And if Brett thought this little stunt would bring him over to their side, it'd backfired.

Inside the tavern, he followed Luna to a large booth in the

back, where the rest of the crew sat, unusually muted. Clearly, Luna had texted them all. He'd never cared much about what anyone thought of him, but he certainly cared now. And it sucked.

Luna slid into the round booth, looking up at him when he just stood there.

"Give me a call when you're finished here," he said. "I'll come get everyone."

Stella grabbed Jameson's hand and tugged him into the booth as well. "Give you a call? What, you think you're not welcome here?"

"You already know what happened," he said.

"Of course. But honey, it's not your fault. And it's all going to work out."

For the first time he wanted to believe she actually could tell the future, that the world wasn't just spreadsheets and analytics and math. "Because you read my palm?"

She laughed. "No, silly. Because I believe in you. We all do."

This wasn't good news. Still, it kind of stunned him, that the sheer support they always gave each other had been extended to him. He wondered if they were aware of how rare and amazing it was. But of course they knew. They'd found each other. They'd built relationships together. A family, more real than any blood tie could be.

A waitress brought over a couple of pitchers of beer. Luna poured everyone a glass, then looked at them all. "Stella's right. We'll find a way."

"I don't get it," Milo said. "How could they do this to us?"

"It doesn't matter," Luna said. "We're going to rally like we always do and find another way to make that balloon payment. We'll up our game somehow. We'll get help."

Jameson didn't have the heart to correct her. And he certainly had no intention of telling her that she'd already had help just breaking even every month, but that her help had passed away.

"So what's the plan?" Chef asked.

All eyes, including Luna's, turned to Jameson. Great, *now* they were listening to him. He racked his brain for something constructive to say. "Well, for starters, we'll try other avenues for a loan. Maybe new investors."

Luna perked up. "Yes! Once upon a time, this was one of the biggest farms in the region. We're the heart of the community. That means something to the town. They'll want to help."

Milo raised his hand. "I can also get social media influencers and bloggers to post about us, and link to a donation page I'll put up on the website. They love a good cause."

"I've got a long-distance friend who'd be willing to invest in this place," Chef said.

"Is that your ex?" Milo asked, eyes narrowed. "The so-called app developer you once had a long-distance relationship with because he was too busy to come out here? That guy was so catfishing you."

Chef patted his hand. "Honey, green is not a good color on you."

Catfishing aside . . . "These are solid ideas," Jameson said.

"We could get people to adopt a tree," Jeb said, using air quotes for *adopt*. "With a donation, they could each get a plaque with their name at the base of the tree. Or we could add benches out in the orchards, which would also be available to have plaques on them. With hundreds of trees, it'd be a great moneymaker."

Everyone stared at him in shock.

"I've never heard his voice before," Milo whispered. "Very manly."

"I'll say," Stella said, and winked at Jeb.

"Hey, just because I don't speak doesn't mean I can't," Jeb said. "It's just that you all chatter so much, half the time I can't get a word in edgewise, so I don't bother." He looked at Jameson. "But I like this job. I want to help."

"Your idea is fantastic," Jameson said honestly. "And easy to implement, thank you." He looked at Stella. "We'll make the benches wood, not stone."

"My hemorrhoids thank you," she said.

"Shayne and his fellow firefighters will all want in," Willow said.

Jameson nodded. "How's he doing?"

"Shockingly good. The man's made of steel. He was released from the hospital and is resting at the firehouse being spoiled by his guys, all of whom love to cook. They are great at raising money. Just last month they raised forty K for the library. I know they'll want to help."

Luna smiled at her. "That would be amazing."

Willow didn't exactly smile back, but her eyes warmed and Luna looked relieved and grateful.

Stella waved her hand. "My BFF's sister's husband's brother is a big VC. That's short for venture capitalist. I bet he'd invest."

"Didn't you marry him?" Luna asked. "Back in the sixties?"

"Yes, but it was my own bad luck that I divorced him before he got rich. We're still friends though. Oh! We could have a moon harvest festival!"

"No." Luna shook her head. "Last time your friends came over for a moon festival, they went moon-clad and we got cited for indecent exposure."

"Hey, that was only because one of the girls' husbands was a cop," Stella said. "He stopped by, and when his captain caught him here, he got in trouble and *had* to cite us. It was really just a big misunderstanding. Probably if he'd kept his clothes on, it would've been fine. Hindsight being 20/20 and all."

Jameson was speechless. But not Luna.

"*No* moon harvest festival," she said firmly. "But . . . I do think we're on the right track here. We've got a month left to pull this off. By then some of our plans will have come into play already, like Willow hosting those two weddings next month. But what if we also do some sort of big quarterly moneymaker gathering? We could invite local craftspeople in to display their wares with pop-up tents, and any interested artisan or shop. We go as big as possible with it and hold the first one next month, right before the balloon payment is due. Invite the investors out to give them a taste of what we're doing here and how much it means to the community."

Jameson nodded, not wanting to rain on their parade but needing to be realistic. "But I think it's unlikely we could get the permits we'd need for an event like that in time."

"Luna can," Stella said confidently.

Luna smiled and reached for her hand. "Thanks, Gram." She paused then, clearly thinking. "We could invite the entire county and charge an additional fee to get into the orchards, letting them pick tulips and cherries. We could have an ice cream food truck, a petting zoo, and I know the local animal shelter would want in. We could have a kitten adoption room, a puppy adoption room . . . hell, we've got Sammy and his two brothers, Dozer and Ninja, so we could do a tortoise race. And a bake sale! We *definitely* need a bake sale . . ."

"Love it," Chef said.

Luna smiled. "And pony and horse rides . . ."

"How do we keep the cost of this event down?" Jameson asked. "And by down, I mean next to nothing out of our pocket, or it will defeat the purpose."

There was a beat of silence.

"I'd be willing to toss all of my profits for the weekend into the kitty," Chef said.

"Me too," Milo said. "I mean, I know I don't actually work here, but I'll add a percentage of my upcoming book profits into the mix. A *small* percentage, of course, but it's going to sell gazillions, so . . ."

"And I'll even charge people for tarot card readings," Stella said. "Just like you taught me, Jameson. No more free readings."

Luna turned to Jameson, who was, quite frankly, speechless. "It's going to work," she said with utter confidence.

He wasn't so sure, but he knew them now, and as a collective, they were the very definition of stubborn. There would be no swaying them. This thing would happen whether he was behind it or not. Realizing all eyes were on him, and that those eyes were all warm and accepting—the opposite of what he'd always found on his jobs—he could do only one thing. "Let's start planning."

Everyone clapped and cheered, simply because he was on board. Fucking humbling.

They shared pizzas and a few pitchers of beer as they talked, but eventually they broke it up. Luna held back, waiting until it was just the two of them. She put her hand on his arm and looked him in the eyes. "Okay, now tell me what you *really* think about the plan."

He gave a rough laugh and scrubbed a hand down his face. "It doesn't matter. My job is to make sure this thing is profitable and we make that balloon payment."

"*All* of us will make sure it's profitable so we can make the balloon payment." She brushed a kiss along his jaw. "It's not just on you, Jameson. You've got a whole crew behind you including me."

He was grateful for the sentiment. They were actually alike in a lot of ways. They'd both been abandoned early in life. Were self-made. Worked really hard, and out of that had come a good life. Which meant that Silas had been wrong. It wasn't just about getting what you want. It was also caring about other people.

Luna was watching him quietly while he thought this all through. "For once, I want to build something," he said. "My entire career has been taking things apart and selling them off piece by piece. And I know what it feels like to be one of those discarded pieces."

At that, her eyes glittered with both affection and, if he wasn't mistaken, a fierce sort of protectiveness. Which was ridiculous. No one had ever felt both of those things for him. Not ever. But he knew something she didn't—that she had the ability to kick him out of his new self-made family. She had the power to hurt him.

And surprisingly, so did this place, this small town and the farm in it. He'd spent time here now. It was no longer just a number on a spreadsheet. It required a crew willing to show up and work every day, and he'd made connections with those people instead of just the analytical facts. How ironic that the more he worked the land to make the property a success, the more he made his personal life a success as well. Building a business instead of tearing it down was giving him a life filled with good people.

Like the woman sliding her hands up his chest, entwining her fingers in his hair, and pulling his head down to hers to kiss him, long and deep. When she finally pulled back, he was dumbstruck. "What was that for?"

"For you being you."

CHAPTER 22

Luna and Jameson settled up the tavern bill and headed outside. She knew he had huge reservations about her plan. She got that. But she also knew that he'd back her in spite of it—a thought that warmed her from head to toe.

And just having a plan had eased her panic.

As they walked out the door, she realized everyone was still there, standing beneath the overhang staring out at the pouring rain, in varying degrees of tipsiness, probably waiting on Ubers.

Jeb stood stoic. Chef and Milo were holding hands and smiling a little drunkenly at each other. Stella was on her phone, swiping through a dating app, muttering "too big, too little . . . ohhh, this one looks juuuuust right."

Jameson's hair was slightly mussed, like it always was when he was stressed because he tended to run his fingers through it. But she knew he wasn't tipsy, he hadn't had more than one beer. She suspected that was a control issue. Right on top of that thought came another—what it would look like to see him lose control.

In bed . . .

Since that took her mind to a place she couldn't go right now, she walked up to Willow, who was looking perfect, as always. "I know. We're still not talking." She held up a hand when Willow started to say something. "First, is Shayne really okay?"

"Unbelievably, yes. The doctor hasn't cleared him for duty yet, but there's no keeping that man down."

Luna nodded. "And you? Are you okay?"

Willow took a deep breath. "I'm okay because he's okay."

"Good." Luna then hesitated.

"What is it?"

"I'm going to spend the day in town tomorrow drumming up interest in our fair. I'm putting you in charge at the farm."

Willow straightened up. "Are you serious? Like, I get to be Head-in-Charge-of-Everything?"

"Yep. I'm handing over the proverbial key to the kingdom and you're queen for a day."

Behind Willow, Chef was giving Luna the knife across the throat motion.

Milo had his head in his hands. Unclear whether that was because he was drunk or worried.

Jeb was his silent, imperturbable self.

"God help us all," Stella whispered, and made the sign of the cross even though she wasn't Catholic.

Willow was jumping up and down and clapping. "I've always wanted to be Queen Head-in-Charge-of-Everything!"

"Let's call in sick tomorrow," Milo whispered to Chef.

"Don't you dare," Willow said, pointing at them. "I want all my minions."

Chef gave Luna puppy dog eyes.

"It's going to be fine," she said, and watched as they all piled into two Ubers. She waved them off and then turned to Jameson, finding him watching her pensively.

"Sometimes," he said, "no matter how badly you want something to work out, life throws you a curveball."

"Not this time." She was certain of it. Almost one hundred percent. Okay, maybe seventy-five. They got into Jameson's car and she watched him drive for a moment, trying to clamp down on her curiosity but couldn't do it. "Have you had a lot of curveballs?"

"Yes."

"What was your very first one?" she asked.

"Probably when my dad walked away from me and my mom."

She sucked in a breath. He'd never mentioned his dad. "How old were you?"

"Five." When she gasped at that, he lifted a shoulder. "He remarried and started another family. Wasn't interested in me after that. I think he just didn't want a reminder of his past."

She hated that for him, hated how alone he'd been after his mom had died. She already knew him to be strong, inside and out, but she was only beginning to realize the depths of that strength.

"What about you?" he asked.

"What about me?"

He glanced over at her. "Tell me a curveball you've had." He smiled at what was undoubtedly panic on her face. "We've been through this. Turnabout is fair play."

True. "Well, today felt a whole lot like a really big curveball."

"Yes, but since that was a curveball for both of us, it doesn't count."

Right. Drawing a deep breath, she went with her usual surface answer. "Well, I did fall in love with a man who turned out to be gay, blah blah blah."

He made the sound of a game show buzzer. "Something I *don't* know, Luna."

"Uh . . . I'm ridiculously stubborn?"

He didn't smile. He wasn't playing.

Luna let out a laugh that sounded a little shrill to her own ears. "You already know everything, and would you look at the time?" By that point they were back at the farm, and she got out of the car and they walked to her cabin, where she bounded up the porch steps.

He was right with her, and caught her before she went inside, gently turning her to face him, slowly pulling her closer, his hands on her hips. It was a dark night, but she'd left the porch light on, so she could see him in the warm glow. He hadn't worn a jacket, and raindrops clung to his hair and face. He had at least three days of stubble going, which for some reason was a huge turn-on. She wanted to touch him, and then wondered why she held back. So she didn't. Lifting her hands, she let her fingers brush along his jaw.

"Tell me something I don't know," he repeated softly.

Her gaze was locked on his mouth, the memory of how it felt

on hers always there in the back of her mind, day and night. "Okay, well, I really want to kiss you right now."

That got her a smile, which was when she decided the hell with it and kissed him.

He kissed her back, and it was somehow both hot and sweet. And then . . . just sweet because he pulled back entirely, looking at her with those eyes that seemed to compel her to let him in.

"Fine." She had to rack her brain because she'd been hiding for a long time. "So . . . my parents didn't tell me."

"Didn't tell you what?"

"That I was adopted."

His brows shot up. "What?"

"Yeah, I found out at school from a kid when I was thirteen."

He shook his head. "That is . . . not okay."

"It was a pretty devastating plot twist," she agreed.

"Did they say why?"

"Not really." She shrugged. "Just that they'd planned to tell me when I was old enough to understand and not freak out."

He shook his head in stunned disbelief, and she felt some of her tension drain. He got it. He got her.

He cupped her face. "Thank you for trusting me with that."

Unlocking the front door, she pulled him inside, not turning on any lights. "I've got something else I might want to trust you with."

"Name it."

She pulled off her wet denim jacket and they moved to the couch, where she gave him a little push down to the cushions. "Some things a man should find out for himself."

"A game." His voice was low and sexy as he pulled her down

beside him. "I'm good at games." He slid his hands to her waist and tugged until she lay flat on the couch, lots of lean muscle and highly motivated and determined male testosterone pinning her there. He kissed the soft, sensitive skin just beneath her ear, eliciting a gasp of pleasure from her.

She felt him smile against her skin as his mouth went on a hot, wet, thorough tour to the hollow of her throat, making her writhe beneath him for more.

Her hands slipped inside his clothes, trying to get him naked. "Jameson."

His fingers nudged the straps of her sundress off her shoulders, and with one tug, she was bared to him. "Mmm, and the way you taste . . ." Lowering his head, he kissed everything he'd uncovered before making a home for himself between her thighs. "And I especially love the way you look like this." Rising up, he pulled off his shirt while she undid his jeans. Thankfully he'd taken to having condoms on him after a late-night foray in the barn one night that had been one of the best, most erotic nights of her life, even when they'd finished to discover a very curious Estelle the Emu watching them.

It made her chest warm with affection that he didn't question the crazy in her world. He just accepted it, at every turn.

"Still with me?" he asked, a hand cupping the side of her face.

"Like you don't know just how with you I am."

He smiled. "Admit it, you're charmed by me."

"Just about everything you do charms me," she admitted. "In fact, I was charmed a couple of times as recently as this morning, so I don't know why you're trying so hard here."

"Because you're worth it."

They maneuvered into a good position, bumping into each other, laughing and swearing as they lined things up. "I want you to remember tonight for this," he said. "Not for what happened earlier at the bank."

"What bank?" she murmured, making him laugh against the hollow of her throat, which tugged a low moan from her. "Jameson?"

"Yeah?"

"Are you too good to be true?"

"I'm exactly what you see." He took her hand. "Let's go to bed, where I'll show you again, and then again, until you believe."

CHAPTER 23

Willow went to bed early but the bed felt too big. Also in the too big department was the house she and Shayne had bought when they'd moved back to Sunrise Cove. Too big and cold and . . . empty.

Why hadn't she insisted Shayne recover from his accident here?

"You're fine," she muttered to herself from under three layers of blankets as she shoved her fifth consecutive mega-stuffed Oreo in her mouth and readjusted her beanie with the baby Yoda ears. She reached for her Sleepytime tea that might or might not have been laced with a tiny dollop of whiskey.

For medicinal purposes.

Normally, she'd call Luna, who'd come over with McDonald's fries and shakes and they'd watch TV and laugh and talk.

But that would involve admitting she was wrong, and she wasn't ready to do that.

Instead, she turned off the lights so she could wake up and be Head-in-Charge. Not of her life, of course. That didn't feel possible. But the farm . . . that she could manage.

Only when morning came, she woke feeling . . . off. Probably the Oreos. But then again, she wasn't a morning person. Some might argue she wasn't a night person either, but whatever. She was who she was. And that person really missed waking up to Shayne in bed.

Because Shayne in bed was . . . *magic*.

But Shayne out of bed? When they weren't naked and she could think past the pheromones and testosterone that leaked out of his pores, making her stupid . . . *out of bed* he was the man who'd dragged her around to fulfill his dreams while hers floundered.

It's not all his fault. You don't tell him what you need. You expect him to read your mind . . .

She'd dismissed the words when Luna had said them to her, but deep, deep down, she suspected Luna was right. Luckily she had zero time for self-reflection this morning. She was Head-in-Charge today, which brought her a rare early morning smile. Being Head-in-Charge would be as much fun as Shayne being in her bed.

Well, almost.

Hurrying through her morning routine, she was momentarily stymied by what to wear. When she worked in the gardens, she wore jeans and work boots—with sexy lingerie beneath because, well, a girl's gotta feel good about herself, right? Standing in front of her closet in her favorite ivory lace satin bra and panty set, she eyed her clothes. Even though Luna wore jeans while being Head-in-Charge, Willow couldn't do it.

So she wore her favorite peach sleeveless, belted pantsuit. She'd be cold, but the look was worth it because nothing said boss like *looking* like a boss. As she was heading to the offices to grab Luna's daily planner, her phone rang. The way her body vibrated in sync with her phone's vibration told her it was Shayne. "Are you okay?"

"One hundred percent," he said.

She sagged in relief. "I don't have time for a booty call. I've got a big day."

"I've never asked you for a booty call."

Because he sounded insulted, she sighed. "I know. It somehow just happens every time we see each other. What I meant was that I don't have time to, you know, 'see' you."

He chuckled, and the sound made her want to "see" him more than ever. "I just wanted to say kick ass today," he said.

She smiled down at her new ankle boots. "Oh, I will."

"And . . ."

Her heart stilled. Her smile dropped. "You said you were okay."

"I am. I wanted to talk to you about something else. I—"

"You're seeing someone."

"No. Well, yes—"

"Who is she?" Her heart stopped. "If it's Mandy, I'll—"

"It's you." He was chuckling again. "I'm trying to see *you*, Wills. I'm trying to ask you out."

"A date?"

"Yes."

Do not melt. Do not melt. *Do not melt.* "Would this date include dinner?"

"It'll include whatever you want it to include. Except for sex. We're not doing that anymore."

"Says who?"

"Says me." He paused. "I feel like I'm giving away the milk for free."

She burst out laughing.

He did too. "I swear I have a point. And that is, if we're doing it all the time, it makes it easy for you to not deal with your emotions. So you get back to me on when we can go out. I'll text you my schedule so you know when I'm not working."

Her insides instantly chilled, her reluctant affection turning to anger in a single beat. "Tell me you're not back at work already."

He sighed.

"Omigod, *you're back at work*?" she cried.

"Light duty, of course. I've been cleared by my doctor, the department's doctor, *and* HR to do paperwork and manage the guys. I'm good."

"You almost died!"

"But I didn't. Babe . . . this is what I do."

"Piss me off? Yeah, and you're good at it," she said tightly, closing her eyes for a beat, seeing him so still and pale in that hospital bed. And that brought back why they were in this situation in the first place. He hadn't been honest with her about the job. Clearly, he felt he had to manage her and her responses. All she wanted was him alive, dammit. Was that so wrong? "I gotta go."

"Willow—"

She ended the call so hard she broke a nail, and now felt even worse. She strode into the farm's office building and down the hall toward Luna's office. Halfway there, she heard someone talking on a phone in the staff room. Poking her head in, she found Jameson at the table, which was covered in cans of baby formula and tins of oatmeal that had been donated to the farm for the rescue baby animals.

He'd eked out a tiny corner of the table, big enough for just his laptop. The chair was too small for him so his long legs were bent, his knees bumping up against the bottom of the table. His elbows were in close to his body to avoid toppling cans off the table as he hunted and pecked away on his keyboard.

She nearly smiled. Nearly, but not, because she didn't feel good and she suspected she was hangry. "Why aren't you using Luna's desk today?"

"You'll need it. It's okay," he said when she opened her mouth to protest. "I'm fine. I've worked with way less."

She wondered what his life had been like, always on the move. Then she had to laugh because she knew exactly what it felt like since Shayne had moved her five times in the twelve years they'd been together.

"What's so funny?" he asked.

"Not funny, exactly." She took a stack of cans near his elbow and put them on the counter next to the coffeepot, repeating that for his other elbow, giving him more room to work. "I just realized that maybe we have a lot in common."

"You mean because the people in our lives think we're emotionally bankrupt since we're not open books?"

She choked out another laugh. "Um, no. I meant because neither of us has had much of a choice about moving around all the time."

He shrugged. "I chose this life."

"Well, I didn't."

He met her gaze, his own non-judging but frank. "But you sort of did, right? I mean, you chose to stay with your husband. We're all in the driver's seat of our own life."

Well, hell. She felt that little kernel of wisdom hit her right between the eyes. How was it that someone she barely knew appeared to know her better than anyone? "Are you always this bluntly honest?"

"It serves no purpose to be anything but."

She snorted. "You might have a point there." She headed to Luna's office, grabbed the day planner that Luna had told her she'd need, and then stared at a fat pad of notes labeled *READ ME FIRST!*

With a sigh, Willow sat, but no sooner had her butt hit the chair than her phone rang. It was Stella, who answered the farm's phone, mostly because she was the nicest and had the most patience.

"Hey, honey. The electrician's out at the barn. He's got questions for Luna."

"Electrician?" Willow asked, putting the notes aside and flipping through the planner. A meeting with Tony was listed. "Is it a guy named Tony?"

"Yeah, and he's in a hurry. Sorry, gotta run!"

"But—" But nothing, because Stella had ended the call. Awesome. She rushed out to the barn, lugging the heavy planner. Shep looked relieved to see her, and it didn't take a genius to see why. He was literally the pied piper with a line of ducks behind him, quacking.

"It's feeding time," he said apologetically, and bailed on her.

She turned to the man in overalls with a patch on a pec that read *Tony's Electrical*. "Hi, how can I help you?"

He scowled. "You're not Luna."

"I am today." She offered a hand. "I'm Willow."

The guy sighed, took off his baseball cap and scratched his head before jamming it back on. "I'm supposed to be fixing some faulty wiring. I need to know if there's been any sparks or rolling brownouts."

Well, hell. She'd left the pad of notes back on Luna's desk. "I'm sorry, I don't know the answer to that off the top of my head, but I can go get Luna's notes—"

"How about flickering or total outages?"

She squelched a grimace. "Again, I'm not sure, but—"

"Can you just call Luna? She'll know."

Damn. Willow pulled out her cell and hit Luna's number. It went right to Luna's voicemail, which said, "If you're calling me from the farm, talk to Willow. She's got everything you need. If she doesn't, then improvise. If it's an emergency, call 911. If this is Willow, then read the damn notes."

Willow ground her back teeth. She would call Luna again over her dead body.

Looking resigned, Tony went hands on hips and looked down at his shoes for a long beat, either contemplating an existential

crisis or trying to figure out if he could get away with strangling her. Her phone was buzzing in her pocket. "I'm sorry, I
have to—"

"Just have Luna call me when you guys have your shit together," the guy said, and then stalked off.

Willow was halfway back to the office when she almost plowed
into Buddy, their favorite local carpenter, who always came to fix
whatever needed fixing. "Hello," she said. "What are you doing
here today?"

"I've got a meeting with Luna."

How many meetings does Luna take in one day?

"We've been going over the empty coffee shop, deciding what
needs to be done for the new tenant coming in next month."

Willow pulled out Luna's thick day planner and flipped
through to today. Sure enough, there was a meeting with Buddy
listed. Beneath that it said: *walk through space and get bid*. "I can
take you over to walk the space—"

"I know the space. I looked at the space already. Now I need to
go over everything with Luna."

"Can you leave the bid?"

"Nope. I sent her a few options, and I need to talk to her about
them."

"I'm sorry, she's not here, but I've been left in charge—"

"We're running tight on time. If you want this place finished
before the tenant moves in, I need you to approve one of the
three layouts I've got."

"Uh . . ." Her phone rang, and grateful for the interruption,
she held up a finger and answered her phone.

"I need you to come to my cabin right away!" Milo shouted in her ear. "But first call the plumber!"

"What's wrong?"

"We've got a toilet leak and it's a doozy. We're talking brown trout swimming wild and free."

Oh dear God. But at least there was a list of contacts in the planner. "What's the plumber's name?" she asked, running her finger down the list.

"I don't remember. He's on Luna's contact list."

"Okay, but I don't know which one he is."

"His name is Louis. I think. Call Luna and ask."

"I'm not calling Luna! I've got this under control." She ran back to the office, past a brows-up Jameson, and grabbed Luna's notes. She skimmed through each of the eighteen pages of handwritten notes—front and back!—and found Louis on the very last freaking page. The note said:

Call Louis if you need a plumber. He's grumpy AF and always says he doesn't have time for us, but if you sweet-talk him, he will come.

Welp, Willow didn't know if she had any sweet talk in her, but she called his number.

"The answer is no," he said in lieu of a greeting.

She blinked. "Is this Louis? Louis the plumber?"

"Who's asking?"

"This is Willow from Apple Ridge Farm. We've got a plumbing emergency—"

"You guys *always* have a plumbing emergency."

Here was the thing. Willow spent all her time at the gardens. She rarely paid attention to the goings-on beyond her corner of the farm. She didn't even really know why, other than she'd been very busy pouting over having to move back, asking Luna for this job in the first place, and the state of her marriage. "I don't know about that," she admitted. "I just know that we have a problem right now, and you're Luna's auto-call."

"Tell Luna to lose my number."

Sweet-talk him, Luna had said. So she drew a deep breath and smiled so that he might hear it in her voice. "Luna says you're the best plumber on this side of the Sierras."

He snorted. "I'm the best in the *country.*"

"Of course," Willow said. "Luna tells everyone that you're worth every penny, and no one knows how to fix our problems like you do. She says she'd never even *consider* going to another plumber . . ."

"You mean because none of the other plumbers will touch your place since the plumbing's ancient and you guys can't afford an entire renovation?"

Willow dropped her forehead to Luna's desk. "Please? *Pretty please?*"

"No."

"Oh, for God's sake! You're acting like this isn't your chosen profession! Like we won't pay you out the nose for your emergency services!"

"You want me there, then have Luna call. She's better at sucking up than you are." Disconnect.

"Dammit!"

Milo came running into the office looking deranged. "How do we turn off the water? When is the plumber coming?"

"I don't know and he's not." Dear God. Had she really been green with jealousy over Luna being manager of this place, and even worse, 50 percent owner?

Milo groaned. "We're screwed. Please call Luna?"

"I said I'll handle it, and I'll handle it!"

"Jeez," Milo said. "Luna's strict sometimes, but she never yells at us."

Willow called Jeb. "Do you know how to turn off the water to, say, Milo's cabin?"

"Yep."

She waited for more info, but the line remained silent. "Jeb?"

"Yeah?"

"*Can* you turn off the water to Milo's cabin?"

Disconnect.

Okay, she was going to assume that was a "yep" too. She then googled plumbers and started making calls. Eight plumbers in, she found someone willing to charge them an arm and a leg for a visit today. She ran to Milo's cabin and dear God. She was helping him mop up when her phone fell into a suspiciously brown puddle.

"Oh shit," Milo said.

Literally.

An hour later she'd welcomed the new plumber and was heading back to the office. She was completely done in and it wasn't even noon yet. There were guests milling around, petting Kong and Miss Piggy, who were lying in a sunspot together looking adorable. She took a deep breath, which smelled like spring and pines and very faintly of the amazing scents coming from the Bright Spot. It should've made her mouth water, but for once she wasn't hungry.

Stopping in the main square, she tilted her head skyward, wondering how to survive the rest of the day, but something about the way she moved her head had her entire world tilting on its axis. Suddenly so dizzy she couldn't even see, she sat hard right there on the ground.

Jameson came running from the office building. "Hey, someone said you fell. Are you okay?"

Was she? She was still trying to decide when he crouched at her side and put a hand on her arm. "Willow? Should I call Shayne?"

"*No!*" She didn't dare shake her head. "No," she said more softly. "I'm just tired." Exhausted, really. "Do you know what my husband needs to fall asleep? Like eight seconds and a very flat, old pillow. Do you know what I need to fall asleep? Four fluffy pillows *minimum*, a fan, a pitch-black room but with the door slightly cracked open so I can hear any monsters coming, three hours of mental checklists, and heart-racing anxiety. How is that fair?"

Jameson's concern hadn't faded. "Uh . . ."

"Oh, never mind."

"Maybe you should come inside. I'll get you a chair and some water—"

"No need, I'm totally fine." More like stark raving mad, but whatever. She caught his hand in hers, the one reaching for his phone. "Don't you dare call Shayne!"

"Willow—"

"I'll fire you," she warned.

He just looked at her.

"Right." She sighed. "Okay, so I can't fire you because I guess you're *my* boss and all that, but I'm Head-in-Charge today, re-member?"

Jameson studied her and rubbed his jaw—the universal tell for wary male. "Please don't take this the wrong way, but we all know you're Head-in-Charge because you keep shouting it to the moon."

She sighed again. "Are you trying to say I let the power go to my head?"

With a small smile, Jameson held up his thumb and index finger just a smidge apart.

"Oh God." He was right. "I'm sorry! I just can't seem to stop myself. I mean, how does Luna even do this crazy job?"

"I've got no idea. I think it's that she's a natural with people, whereas you and I are more comfortable behind the scenes, making things happen for her."

"What do I make happen?" she asked miserably. "All I do is plant plants."

"Are you kidding? I've been researching everything about this place. I know what it was like before you, and after you. The gardens were struggling, but now they're . . . *stunning*. Look around, you've planted pots and pots of flowers from the gar-dens and spread them throughout the Square, Stella's barn, the entrance area, even the parking lot. You've brought color to the entire farm."

"Well, I try," she said. "But the baby goats and Kong keep eating the flowers right out of the planters."

He smiled. "Regardless, you've created a gorgeous, colorful setting here like I've never seen anywhere else. And then there's that extra thing you always do, the thing no one asks you to do but you do anyway. Like how you're planning each quarter forward so that the colors are seasonally themed. Genius."

She was surprised to find herself hanging on his every word. Maybe because the man was certainly no bullshitter, and he was also hard to impress. But probably because she was feeling extra pathetic today.

"Working here clearly makes you happy," he said. "It shows in your work, and then it makes the people who come here happy as well."

"Okay, and I appreciate you even noticing. But how about my skills as manager? Because that's what I've always dreamed of doing, running the show."

"But dreams change, right?"

She narrowed her eyes.

He shook his head like he was searching for words. "Look, it's hard to say to yourself, 'Hey, maybe that dream I had when I was younger isn't the right dream for me now. Maybe my dream's changed.' Especially when you get—"

She held up a hand to stop him. "If you're about to say 'older,' I swear I won't be responsible for my actions. I'm only twenty-eight, you know." She squelched a grimace. "Okay, fine. I'm thirty. Whatever."

"You're missing my point."

She tossed up her hands. "I'm still waiting for your point!"

He laughed wryly. "Sometimes letting go of what you think your life should be, in order to accept what it actually is, can be . . ."

"Crushing?" she whispered. "Like the picture of the life you had in your brain doesn't exist anymore?"

Eyes sympathetic, he nodded. "So you have to take stock around you and go, okay, what do I want to do now? What is actually the thing that's going to make me happy?"

She'd always, *always*, envisioned herself as her own boss. But lately, and especially today, that dream was scooting over, making room for something else, something she wasn't ready to put a name to. But the realization didn't bring calm. If anything, it brought the very opposite, leaving her off-kilter because she couldn't take any more upheaval at this point. She just couldn't. "I really thought I was jealous of Luna. Because she's got all this success, but . . ."

"But?" he asked, seemingly willing to sit on the ground with her in the middle of the Square, with guests milling around, for as long as she needed.

She drew in a deep breath. "You're right," she said softly. "My old dream is making me miserable."

"Hand me your phone," he said. "I'm going to put in my contact info so you can call me if there're any more issues you need help with today."

"My phone's out of service."

He looked surprised.

"I dropped it into a puddle of poop at Milo's."

Jameson appeared to try and hide his smile, but he failed. "I guess that would do it."

Willow blew out a breath and put a hand to her belly, which was still upset. "It's been a day."

"I bet I can improve on it."

"Only if you've got a private jet ready to fly me to a deserted South Pacific island."

"Sorry, no," he said on a laugh. "But a call came in right before I came out here. *Better Homes & Gardens* magazine wants to do a spread on your botanical gardens."

Disbelief warred with excitement. "*Better Homes & Gardens* magazine?"

"Yep."

"Like THE *Better Homes & Gardens*?"

He smiled and nodded.

"*Better Homes & Gardens* magazine," she repeated again. "You swear?"

"I do."

She opened her mouth to say something, and . . .

Threw up on Jameson's shoes.

Mortified, she gasped out, "I'm so sorry!"

He gently patted her back while calmly making a call. "Can someone bring me a bottle of water and paper towels to the Square?"

Stella showed up less than two minutes later with the requested supplies. Jameson twisted the lid off the water for Willow. She expected him to use the paper towels for his shoes, but he handed those over as well. She wiped her mouth and mopped her sweaty forehead, overcome with humiliation. "I'm really so sorry."

He shrugged, like shit happens. "Let's get you home for the day."

Here was the weird thing. She was feeling one hundred percent better. "I'm okay. Honest," she said, while both Stella and Jameson just looked at her with concern. "But . . . *Better Homes & Gardens*?" she asked Jameson again.

He nodded.

She grinned. "*Better Homes & Gardens*," she repeated, just to hear it again.

"Yes," Jameson said warily. "Are you in shock? Are you going to throw up again?"

"No and no." She reached for her phone to call Shayne before remembering two things. One, she had no phone. And two . . . she was still mad at him. She thought of Luna, but . . . well, they weren't really talking yet either, and an emotion swamped her. She was pretty sure it was loneliness mixed with sorrow. Here she'd just had a huge milestone happen and she didn't have her peeps to share it with.

She'd asked them both for time and space, and that's exactly what she'd gotten.

CHAPTER 24

Jameson spent the next few days seeking financial options for the farm, optimizing the books he'd finally finished entering into an actual accounting program, and going through the reports analyzing the places where they were especially vulnerable or actually bleeding money, as well as where they were solid and in the black.

He spent his nights in Luna's bed. He was pretty sure what they'd been doing to each other wasn't just sex, and knew Luna felt it too. Something had been established between them now. There was no going back—though he had no idea what that even meant for going forward.

This was why he loved math. Everything had its place, and numbers balanced. Always. He appreciated the order and efficiency and logic. His nights with Luna had none of that, and he'd loved every single second anyway. At first he'd told himself the chaos was rubbing off on him and he'd lost perspective. But the joke was on him, because he'd fallen for the farm, the people in it, *and* their incredible leader, Luna Wright.

He stood in her kitchen making them a late dinner because she was working even later than he had. She'd put Willow in charge again because, as she'd explained it, she didn't want her to feel defeated or to give up on a bad note, and then had spent the day in meetings at town hall, still working on getting the permits they needed for their event.

He had Sprout tucked against his chest with one arm, the other hand stirring his spaghetti sauce when someone knocked on the door.

Since he could practically reach the front door from the kitchen—or anywhere in the tiny cabin for that matter—he opened up with Sprout still in his arms.

"Hello," Stella said brightly, brushing a kiss to his cheek and then Sprout's before pushing past him. "Are you cooking for us? Smells *amazing*."

"Us?"

Chef and Milo entered behind Stella. Chef gave him a half hug and a wink, and Milo handed over not one but two pitchers of . . . "piña coladas," he said. "Sorry ahead of time for the incoming circus."

Stella laughed. "It's poker night. Of course it's a circus. Luna forgot to mention she's hosting tonight?"

"Yes, but she's been swamped."

"Too swamped," Stella said. "And of course you'll join us." She gave him a sassy smile. "Last time was beginner's luck, is all."

An emotion filled his chest, and it took a moment to label it. He felt accepted, a new and alien feeling that he had to admit he liked.

What killed him was that Silas had had access to all of this, these wonderful experiences and people, including his own granddaughter, and he'd chosen to hold himself apart. Jameson couldn't imagine how he'd managed to do that. And yet . . . he'd been that person too, before Apple Ridge Farm. He knew he could either stick to his pattern of being disassociated emotionally, or he could step into the ring.

"You're feeding us, you've got to play," Stella said.

Everyone looked at him expectantly, and he realized they actually wanted him to join them. "Deal me in."

There was a cheer and he found himself smiling. "What are we playing with today, pretzels? Peanuts?"

"Oh honey." Stella patted his cheek and took Sprout to cuddle him into her. "It's Dollar Night." She took Jameson's hand, turned it over, and looked at his palm. "Huh." She bent over it to take a closer look and Sprout took the opportunity to lick his fingers.

"You're at a crossroads."

"Me or Sprout?"

Lifting her head, Stella didn't smile. Instead, she eyed him intensely for a beat. "You can take the turn. It might be a little scary and uncomfortable, but you'll be happy. Or you can keep going on your current path and miss out."

Since that felt far too close to his truth, he tried to joke it away. "Are you telling me to bet big tonight?"

She didn't smile, instead remaining uncharacteristically serious. "I'm telling you to go all in."

The door opened and Luna stepped inside, and everyone turned to her hopefully.

Her face was carefully blank, and the air suddenly filled with tension and anxiety. "Oh, Jameson, I'm so sorry. I forgot about poker night."

"Forget that," Chef said. "Tell us what happened today."

Luna carefully set her bag on the small wooden bench at the front door, then slipped out of her coat and hung it on a hook before turning to them all. "The mayor said she can't give us a permit on such short notice for a fair or festival."

Everyone stared at her with varying degrees of sadness and worry.

"But . . . if we call it a Founders Day and agree to do it annually, *and* give a small portion of the proceeds to the local Boys and Girls Club, she's willing to pull strings. She also said she'll work on getting us a permit for future quarterly events, like we wanted to do. Now deal me in." She sat at the table.

Everyone continued to stare at her. "I'm sorry," she said. "Did you not hear me?" She beamed. "We're good to go."

Everyone sagged in relief, then cheered and began talking at the same time. Jameson sat next to Luna and smiled. "You're amazing. You made it happen."

"Of course she did," Chef said. "She's Luna."

She looked around. "Where's Willow?"

"She had another long day, honey," Stella said. "And she got nauseous again. I think it's her anxiety. She threw up on her brand-new baby tulips. She went home to get some rest."

Luna opened her mouth, then closed it, like maybe she was holding something back. She looked at Jameson. "I hope it was the loafers."

"Nope," he said.

"There's always next time." Luna turned to the rest of the table. "How did she do today with the actual managing?" she finally asked.

The entire table groaned.

"Oh, come on," she said. "It can't be that bad. The place is still standing."

Chef coughed into his hand and said "barely" at the same time.

"She tried her hardest," Stella said diplomatically. "Oh, and regarding Founders Day, I've already designed the flyers and created the landing page for Milo to put up on our website."

Luna's jaw dropped. "What? When?"

"I had it ready to go, because I had no doubt we'd need it." Stella turned her phone toward Luna and showed her the design. "I'll call it Founders Day and have them printed tomorrow and hung up all around town right after."

"Send me the design," Milo said. "I'll take out ads on the Sunrise Cove Facebook page and local papers and sites like the town's webpage."

"And I've got a menu planned," Chef said. "People are going to go nuts."

Jameson, who hadn't been able to take his eyes off Luna, smiled when she looked his way. "Not bad, partner."

She put her mouth to his ear. "Last night you used the words 'mind-blowing.'"

He felt a grin split his face. "And I can't wait to come up with new adjectives tonight."

"As long as it's better than 'not bad, partner.'"

Lightning quick, his teeth sank gently into her earlobe, smiling when she shivered. "I think I can manage that."

JAMESON SLID OUT of Luna's bed at dawn, then looked back at her sprawled on her belly, sleeping like the dead, hair in her face, breathing slowly and deeply. It gave him a Neanderthal thrill to see her so completely sated. A thrill that was weighted with something else.

Regret.

Guilt.

He'd made a promise to Silas, but lately that promise had felt like an albatross around his neck. And the more time he spent with Luna, the heavier that promise felt.

Fact was, it'd become a burden. It no longer felt right to carry it, and if he was being honest with himself, it hadn't for a while. He wished he'd been smart enough to figure this out before he'd slept with her, because he'd sealed his own fate by waiting. Now when she found out, and she would because he was going to tell her himself, she'd kick him the hell out of her life.

And she'd be right to do so.

His heart gave a little jump at that, but it wasn't productive to worry about it now. Instead, he gave in to his need to watch her sleep for another moment, imagining waking her up by running his hands down her spine to her perfect ass, lifting her hips from the bed and—

She sighed and turned her head away from him. Knowing he needed to go before he gave in to urges he didn't have the luxury of satiating, he quietly made his way out of the bedroom, planning on making her breakfast. Halfway there, he stopped short at the large lump on the couch, which should've been empty since *he* was no longer occupying the spot.

The tall lump moved and then sat up. It was Chef, who pointed at Jameson. "I know what you did last night. Or should I say *who . . .*"

It wasn't often that Jameson found himself speechless, but he was now. They hadn't tried to keep this to themselves, but they hadn't taken out an ad either. "Uh—"

"Sorry about the company." Chef yawned. "The piña coladas really got to me, so when Milo told me he was taking an Uber to spend today with his mom, I stayed, which, FYI, I've done a million times. Luna's never minded before, but then again . . ." He chortled. "She's never had an overnight guest here before either."

Jameson thought of the things he and Luna had done to each other in the night, heart-pounding, incredibly erotic things, and tried to remember how loud things had gotten.

"Don't worry, I didn't hear a peep from you," Chef said, reading his mind. "But either you kept forgetting your own name, or Luna really, really likes saying it."

Shit.

A large throw on the chair in the corner began moving too, and Stella emerged. Her hair looked like the top of an ostrich's head and her makeup had shifted from her eyes to the rest of her face. "Sorry," she said, not looking sorry at all. "I wasn't sure I could get home either."

"It's like twenty-five feet from here," Chef said.

"Okay, I didn't want to miss anything." She smiled at Jameson. "I see you picked a road and figured it all out."

Chef divided a gaze between them. "What did he figure out?"

"That he and Luna speak different languages. Her love language is actual words, which, no offense, isn't your strong suit, Jameson. That's not the real problem though. The problem is that *your* love language is actions. Actions are all that matter because you can't always believe words. How am I doing so far?"

Shockingly accurate.

Chef took one look at Jameson's face and grinned, then rolled off the couch. "Fascinating, but I like living—something that if she finds us talking about her would definitely be over for me." He stopped and turned back. "Oh, and some advice? Don't let her get away with not sharing. She held back big-time with me, and I'd bet my last dollar she's doing the same with you. She's afraid to open up and not be accepted as is."

"You giving him relationship advice is like the blind leading the blind," Stella said. "But in this circumstance, I agree with you."

Chef nodded. "And now I really gotta go." He made it to the door before Luna's bedroom door opened. Jameson turned just as she came straight for him, wearing his T-shirt and possibly nothing else. Ignoring both Chef and Stella, she slipped beneath Jameson's arm and snuggled in, making herself comfortable. She then offered him an adorably sexy smile before turning her eyes to Chef.

The guy lifted his hands. "I saw nothing, I heard nothing, I speak of nothing."

"*I* heard plenty," Stella said. "But my lips are sealed too." She blew Luna a kiss and met Chef at the door.

"Hey," Luna said.

They both turned back.

"I don't care who knows," she said softly, and looked up at Jameson with an open expression that should've terrified him but didn't because he suspected he was looking at her in the exact same way. He gave her a "good morning" squeeze, bringing her in even closer.

Chef smiled. "Happy looks good on you, babe." He nodded to Jameson and then he was gone, pulling Stella along with him.

CHAPTER 25

Willow woke up to knocking in her head. Odd, since she hadn't gone to poker night and hadn't had any alcohol. The knocking started up again, louder this time, and she realized it wasn't her head, it was the front door. At 6:00 a.m.

Someone was going to die.

Even though she was wearing baggy sweats she normally wouldn't be caught dead in, she staggered out of the bedroom and whipped open the front door prepared to blast someone with morning breath. "*WHAT?*"

Luna shoved a small bag into Willow's hands.

Okay, so if it was a blueberry scone, she'd forgive Luna on the spot. She opened the bag and stilled. *Not* a blueberry scone. She lifted her head and stared at Luna. "You're kidding."

Unusually serious, Luna shook her head. "You threw up on Jameson's shoes, and also on your precious tulips. Chef says you've been light-headed a couple of times. We both know math isn't my strong suit, but in this case, one plus one equals you with a baby on board. You're taking that pregnancy test if I have to pee on the stick myself."

"Yeah, cuz that's *exactly* how it works." Willow's sarcasm didn't quite cover the fact that her voice was shaky. Hell, everything was shaky. She staggered back a step, shaking her head. There was no way. No possible way. "I'm on birth control."

"Yeah, well, you and Shayne have been boinking like Energizer bunnies, and birth control is only ninety percent effective."

The bag was trembling. Oh, wait. That was her. *She* was trembling. Which was ridiculous. "I'm not pregnant, Luna."

"Then you won't mind peeing on the stick."

"I don't have to pee."

Luna pulled a thermos from her backpack. "Drink."

"This isn't funny, Luna."

"Do I look amused? You acted like the Queen of Hearts yesterday."

"Yeah, well, your crew misbehaves when Mom's gone. I think they wanted me to fail."

"You know that each and every one of them loves you. Now take that test right now so I can kill you where you stand if you're not pregnant."

Willow whirled on a bare heel and headed to the bathroom, not realizing Luna was right on her until she tried to shut the door on her nose. "Stay!" she demanded, and slammed the door.

Carefully not looking at herself in the mirror, she peed on the damn stick, then finished her business. The entire time she washed her hands she never glanced over at the potential life bomb on the counter. She refused to look. Couldn't. "Luna!"

Luna opened the door so fast that Willow knew she must've been plastered up against it.

Willow thrust the peed-on stick at her. "Watch that."

Luna gingerly took the stick with the tips of her fingers. "Okay, but this is some seriously sister shit here. If this doesn't prove I love your mean, stubborn, crabby ass, I don't know what will."

"Just look at the stick! What does it say? Is there a plus or minus sign?"

Luna looked at the stick, her face revealing nothing.

"*Well???*"

Luna looked up, still giving nothing away. "What do *you* want it to say?"

Willow opened her mouth, then closed it again. When she spoke, she was surprised to hear herself lie. "Not pregnant, obviously. Do you not know me? Have we not been best friends for over twenty years?"

Luna bit her lower lip, reminding Willow without words that *she'd* been the wedge between them.

"Just tell me what it says."

Luna's eyes got suspiciously misty and Willow's heart stopped because Luna never cried. A positive test. *Pregnant.* "Shit." She grabbed another test from the bag. Peed on it and watched the stick herself.

It lit up with a plus sign so fast her head spun. "Oh my God." She tossed it to Luna. "*Another test, quick!*"

"Stop throwing your pee sticks at me! And are you a water hose or what?"

The third one came out positive as well.

"Stop," Luna said.

"I can't!"

The fourth was also positive. Willow looked at the sticks lined up on the counter, all positive. She felt her eyes fill up.

"No, don't cry," Luna begged. "Please don't cry. I'll go to another store!"

Willow shook her head. "There's no point."

Luna, who'd already started toward the door, stopped and faced her. "You sure?"

"Yes," she said, ignoring the catch in her voice. She and Shayne had always said that thanks to how they'd each grown up feeling like an afterthought, they never wanted kids.

Never.

Ever.

But there was a funny thing about saying never ever, and that was you couldn't tell your heart what or how to think. Or that it wasn't allowed to change its mind.

Because Willow's heart had definitely done exactly that, changed its mind. Yes, she felt inadequate. Yes, she knew she was too much like her mom and Luna's grandfather, tough and distant. She'd make a horrible mom. So it made no sense that this was *exactly* what she wanted.

Luna pulled a food container from her backpack. Willow opened it and stared down at the two blueberry scones. They swam as tears filled her eyes. As far as love languages went, with her and Luna, food was the epitome of unconditional love.

Luna patted her pockets and came up with two napkins, and

in that moment, Willow knew she couldn't have asked for a better sister of her heart.

They ate, and when the sugar hit Willow's bloodstream, she sighed.

"Are you okay?" Luna asked softly, like how one might speak to a person holding the detonator to a bomb.

"I don't know." She took another bite of the scone. "I'm still tired from yesterday's tired. And I've already used up tomorrow's tired."

"I meant the baby. Are you okay about the baby?"

Willow sat on the floor and leaned back against the wall. "I was just going to wait for *you* to have kids. I was going to be that cool aunt who never settles down, and ruins every family party by drinking too much. And I was okay with that." She sighed. "This is all Shayne's fault."

"Yeah? And who kept dragging him into a closet, bathroom, cabin, wherever?"

Willow jabbed a finger at her. "That's *not* the point. The point is that you're supposed to be on my side."

Luna came over, sat on the floor too, and hugged her. "Always."

"How is this even possible?" Willow whispered.

"Well, when the birds and the bees—"

Willow choked out a laugh and dropped her head to Luna's shoulder. "I can't be pregnant, Loo."

"Okay, but you are."

"I've chased my husband away, and we both know the truth— I'll make a terrible mother, single or otherwise."

"You're going to make a *great* mother."

"I don't even know what a good mom looks like."

"Hey, that doesn't have to be a bad thing," Luna said. "You won't make the same mistakes your mom made. You're going into it with a clean slate. And personally, I think you'll make an amazing mom."

"But what am I going to tell Shayne? We agreed a long time ago—*no* kids. Now I've changed the game on him."

"There were two people in that closet. And everywhere else you two jumped each other."

Willow thought of how great Shayne was with his nieces and nephews. "He's going to be better at being a parent than me."

Luna choked out a laugh. "How is this a competition?"

Willow pleaded the fifth by taking another bite.

"And we've been through much worse than this," Luna said.

"We have?"

"Okay, maybe not."

Willow managed a laugh, and Luna smiled at her. "It's going to be great. You'll see."

Willow shook her head. "I've got zero idea how to handle myself, much less myself, a job, *and* a baby."

"You're an excellent multitasker."

Willow gave her a look. "Are you kidding? Ask anyone how I handled being Head-in-Charge."

"Oh, believe me, I heard."

Willow thunked her head back against the wall. "This killing them with kindness is taking a lot longer than I thought it would."

Luna snorted. "I think you forgot to add the kindness part."

"Yeah, well, it's the thought that counts." Willow sighed. "I don't know how you do it, how you make everyone love you, while also getting them to do what you want them to."

"Bribery, mostly." Luna met her gaze. "What can I do to help?"

"Figure out how I'm going to tell Shayne."

"Tell me what?"

Shayne appeared in the doorway, propping up his tall, leanly muscled, and perfect bod against the jamb like he had all the time in the world. He was in soft, faded jeans and a navy T-shirt, which meant he was off duty, and his eyes were hooded. Her fault.

Willow looked at Luna, feeling completely betrayed. "You texted him."

Luna rose to her feet. "You might be mad at me now, but I promise you, this is what a best friend does." She walked out of the bathroom, but then her footsteps stopped, like maybe she would stay to referee in case Willow needed it.

And just like that, Willow felt the ball of emotion clog her throat. Gratitude, because she didn't deserve Luna. Nerves, because Shayne was silent and watching her in that calm way of his, and she knew she didn't deserve him either.

But *he* deserved answers.

She was still sitting on the floor, but now she had two fistfuls of the sticks in her hands. She hadn't even had a chance to process this, and now she had to tell him that she was carrying his baby in spite of their long-ago promise to each other.

Her husband pushed off the doorway and crouched next

to her on the floor before nudging his chin toward the sticks. "Something you want to tell me?"

"I tested positive, but not for Covid."

He sat at her side and nudged a shoulder to hers, his smile saying that maybe her holding the positive sticks was the best thing he'd ever seen.

"Everything's *terrible* and you're smiling?" she asked in disbelief.

His smile spread and she shook her head. "What's wrong with you?"

"A lot of things," he said. "But not this—I'm excited."

She stared at him. "Are you crazy? You didn't want kids."

"What are you talking about?"

"We always said no kids."

He shook his head. "We maybe said it once, like when we were what, eighteen?"

"And?"

"And . . ." He cupped her face. "I had no idea those words were even still standing between us. I mean, at the time I wasn't even legally allowed to drink."

"And yet we did. That very night as I remember."

He smiled. "True. But I don't think I should be held accountable for what I said when we were both drunk."

"What are you saying?" she asked softly. "That you think this is a good idea?"

He took her hand in his big, warm one. "Yes."

She was boggled. She'd counted on him freaking out too. "But we aren't even together. What kind of world would I be bringing this baby into?"

"We," he said. "What kind of world would *we* be bringing this baby into. We're in this together, Wills."

That gave her a flutter, the good kind, which meant she turned to sarcasm to cover her discomfort. "Really? Are 'we' going to push a bowling ball out *your* va-jay-jay?"

"No, but I'll do everything I can to make it as easy as possible for you."

She just looked at him, so filled with questions and emotions and feelings that she couldn't speak. "Why aren't you freaking out? Why am I the only one?"

He just kept smiling. "Because I love the idea of a baby with you. I hope they have your eyes, your laugh, your sweet, sunny nature."

She snorted and shook her head, a little stunned to realize his excitement was contagious. "We're not together," she whispered again.

"And why is that again?"

Willow opened her mouth to tell him all the reasons why, only none of them seemed to matter in the moment. "Honestly? I have no idea." She swallowed. "I think I got caught up in a cycle of unhappiness, and I blamed it on you. And Luna."

"I accept your apology," Luna said through the door.

Shayne brought Willow's hand to his mouth so he could kiss her palm, and she dropped her head to his chest. "I'm still mad," she whispered. "Except when I'm this close to you I forget why."

Luna's voice came through the door. "It's because he hurt your feelings when he didn't tell you about the job offer before he accepted it."

"Thanks, Luna," Shayne said dryly.

"Don't blame her." Willow looked at him, into his beautiful face. "She's right. We need to talk about stuff more. Especially if we're going to have a . . ." She couldn't say the word. She literally couldn't get it out.

And then Luna, knowing her better than anyone, and permanently cementing her BFF status in Willow's life, said through the door, ". . . a T. rex. You're having a T. rex."

Shayne grinned. "I love T. rexes."

Unbelievably, Willow felt herself smile. "Oh my God. We're having a T. rex." Which seemed *way* less scary than an actual human baby.

Very gently, as if she were made of the finest china, Shayne lifted her off the floor and settled her onto his lap. He ran a finger along her temple, pushing a loose strand of hair off her face. "How do you feel about this? For real."

"For real? *Terrified*." She set her head down on his shoulder and breathed him in. "You know that I have no idea what a happy household looks like."

"I always thought we had a happy household."

"We did." She paused. "At least until I screwed it all up."

"No," he said gently. "*I'm* the one who screwed it all up. Luna's right. I should've come to you about the job offer. I acted on impulse, like I always do. I'm sorry, Willow. So sorry."

"And it's not like it didn't work out," Luna said through the door. "It brought you back here, to me!"

Being angry took a whole bunch of energy. In fact, it'd taken *all* her energy, and she was tired of carrying it around with her, letting it invade every corner of her life and every relationship. It was time to let it go and create room in her heart for a new dream. A dream her body had already moved on to. Her hands went to her belly as she let that sink in. She'd been fighting against change, against letting herself be happy, and she wanted to be done with that. "Luna's right."

"Of course I am."

Shayne's gaze held Willow's. "Remember our first date?" he asked. "At the last minute you got cold feet, and I had to work my ass off to charm you into changing your mind and giving me a shot. You never even noticed how nervous I was."

"You were not nervous. You never get nervous. You've got nerves of steel. You run into burning buildings for a living."

Shayne laughed. "I hate to argue with the pregnant lady, but I was incredibly nervous on our first date, and I'm nervous now."

This surprised her. "Come on."

"I am. I did this to us. I moved us around to earn more money and move up the ladder faster, but I hate what it did to our relationship. I hate the distance it put between us." He cupped her face. "I miss you, Wills." He smiled. "You complete me."

She snorted. "I don't know if I could ever complete someone. But driving you batshit crazy sounds doable."

He grinned, but it faded quickly. "I love you, and I want my best friend back." He took one of her hands and placed it against his chest so that she could feel his heart racing beneath her palm. Unbearably touched, she did the same for him and they stared at each other.

"Can you ever forgive me?" he asked.

"Yes," she said, one hundred percent sure. "If you can forgive me for hiding myself and my feelings from you, when deep down I knew I could trust you with them. With everything. Because I love you too, Shayne. So much. I can't imagine my life without you in it." She cupped his face. "I want you to come home."

"Thank God." He pressed his forehead to hers. "The guys at the firehouse have nicknamed me Goldilocks because I hop beds to whichever one's empty."

She found a laugh. "Good thing then that our bed is just right."

"It's perfect. You're perfect." He slid a hand to her still-flat belly. "Our life is perfect."

This made her snort. "It's not."

"It's perfect for me. I can't wait to see you become a mom, Wills. You're going to be so good at it. Our T. rex is lucky to have you."

Her eyes were leaking again. "I'm sorry. I don't know why I'm crying."

"It's the pregnancy hormones," Luna said through the wood.

"Makes sense," Willow said. "But why do I get the feeling pregnancy is going to be like a high school group project, where one of us is going to do all the heavy lifting while the other one shows up fifteen minutes late with his coffee and just takes the *A*?"

Shayne laughed. "But I'll rub your feet whenever you want."

"Well, okay then." Reaching past him, she opened the door for Luna.

Luna waved her phone. "I've been googling pregnancy. Apparently you're going to cry all the time and get horny. Oh, and your boobs are going to hurt."

Willow winced. "Is there anything good on that list?"

"Didn't you hear the horny part?" Shayne asked.

Willow gasped.

Shayne smiled. "I know, right?"

"No! I forgot to tell you guys something! Something big! *Better Homes & Gardens* wants to do a spread on the botanical gardens!"

"Of course they do," Shayne said. "You're the best of the best."

"That's so great," Luna said. "I told you that you are amazing. And, not to change the subject or anything, but . . . we're all okay?"

"Correct." Willow burped and scrambled off Shayne's lap. "But you both need to back up, like back *way* up. Our baby wants to throw up now."

CHAPTER 26

A *baby*. It was the middle of the night and Luna lay in her bed staring up at the ceiling instead of sleeping. Willow and Shayne were having a *baby*. It boggled, it'd come out of nowhere, but it also felt so right for them, and she felt the smile curve her face.

At her side in the dark, the only light being a faint sliver from the moon slanting in the window, Jameson came up on an elbow and peered into her face. "I'd like to claim credit for that smile, but I'm not sure it was me."

She pulled him down for a quick but hot kiss. "Oh, it's you too."

His smile heated, probably, like her, remembering how they'd just taken each other apart and put each other back together again. "And . . . ?"

"And it's also Willow and Shayne. Willow's pregnant."

"Explains the intermittent barfing. Are she and Shayne going to be okay?"

"I think so, yeah."

"And you? Are you and Willow going to be okay?"

She met his gaze and saw the genuine interest, and more than that, worry and affection. For her. "I think so," she repeated softly.

With a soft smile, he leaned in, but just as the kiss got interesting, her stomach growled so loudly it sounded like a geyser about to blow.

Jameson laughed and got out of bed. He tossed her his shirt and then pulled on the pair of soft, clinging pj bottoms he'd left on the floor. She stared at the sight of him in nothing but the pants that rode indecently low on his hips. "What are you doing?"

He pulled her from the warm bed. "Feeding the beast." But he didn't move, instead took her hands in his and spread them out to her sides, looking her over with a low groan.

"What?" she asked.

He took a long, purposeful breath. "I was unprepared for the sight of you in my shirt, showing off your long legs and your pretty cherry-red toenails." His gaze dragged back up her body. "Nowhere is safe to look. You're so beautiful, Luna."

She bit her lower lip, never quite seeing that herself, but hell, if he wanted to believe it, who was she to disavow him of that notion?

"You still don't know what to do with a compliment," he said, looking amused.

She shrugged. "I was born with commitment issues mixed with trust issues. Sometimes I think my commitment issues and trust issues have gotten married and had babies."

His laugh was rueful. "Same. But somehow with you, my fears fly out the window. Luna . . . I know I'm leaving, and that my job keeps me gone a lot, but I'm thinking of making Sunrise Cove my home base."

She blinked. "When did you decide that?"

"I think maybe it's been in the back of my mind since the day I arrived." He gave another short laugh, like he was surprising himself. "But I didn't let myself really believe that it could work until this very minute. Which doesn't make it any less true." He met her gaze. "So if you ever decide you want to be with me, we could make it happen."

"It?" she whispered.

"Us. And it'll be good, I promise."

Wow. She drew in a shaky breath before nodding.

He smiled and nodded back. "Now let's feed you."

In the kitchen, she turned to the fridge, but he caught her and lifted her onto the counter, where he kissed her stupid. Pulling back, smiled into her dazed face. "Cute," he said. "Oh, and before I forget, there's a message on the farm's Facebook page. Someone complaining about the fact that we're going to have snakes at Founders Day. I located the problem. There's a typo on the flyers around town. 'Snacks' somehow autocorrected to 'snakes.'"

"Oh my God." She whipped out her phone and went to Facebook. Finding the typo, she sighed. Then made a new post:

ATTENTION

There will be no snakes at Founders Day! There was a typo on the flyer that said we would have snakes. We will NOT

have snakes. We will have *snacks*. (Not that we have anything
against snakes. In fact, snakes are awesome!) So, to summa-
rize: **NO SNAKES at Founders Day.**

Jameson read the post over her shoulder, a hand running
lightly up and down her arm. He laughed softly, kissed the shell
of her ear, and then proceeded to cook her a quesadilla.

She watched, feeling like a silly, smitten kitten. She was in his
shirt, which still held his delicious scent and body heat. She'd
just had the best sex of her life, and everything in her world felt
good. She and Willow were okay. Founders Day was coming together, everyone was working as a team, and she had an honest
and good man in her life.

When he handed her a plate, she took a bite of yummy, gooey,
perfect quesadilla and moaned.

His eyes darkened a bit. "That's a sound I usually have to work
hard for," he murmured.

"Well, you're *almost* as excellent in the bedroom as you are in
the kitchen."

He choked on his quesadilla. "Almost?"

She grinned.

He smiled, but didn't say anything. Unusual even for him. She
watched him stop eating and realized . . . something was off with
him. And if she thought about it, maybe something had been
off for a few days now. How had she missed it? She blamed the
orgasms. "What's wrong?"

He stepped between her legs and ran his hands up her bare
thighs.

"Oh no," she said. "I recognize the distraction technique. I *live* the distraction—" She broke off on a soft moan when he lowered his head and nuzzled that soft spot just beneath her ear, giving her the shivers of the very best kind. "Don't even try it."

She felt him smile against her skin. "But distracting you is so much fun."

She set her hands on his chest and gave a nudge so she could see into his eyes. "Just say it, Jameson. Whatever it is. I can take it."

He paused, and oh dear God, *déjà vu*. She'd been a part of this dog and pony show and she knew what came next. "You're dumping me."

"What?" Looking horrified that she'd jumped to that, he leaned back into her. "No. Are you kidding? Luna, you're the best thing that's ever happened to me."

She let out the breath she'd been holding. "Then what? What's wrong? Is it about the books? Our numbers?"

She watched him draw a deep breath. "I've run and rerun the numbers," he said. "The ticket sales are coming along, but unless we bring in a profit of at least fifty K during Founders Day, we're not going to make that balloon payment."

"We could still do it."

He cupped her face. "I love that about you. Your ability to hope and believe in something that's intangible, something that can't be balanced at the end of a spreadsheet. It makes me feel like there's more to life than I've been living. But—"

"But what? Because maybe the event's going to be better than we can imagine."

"Maybe. But I haven't been able to get a bank interested in giving us a loan. I'm worried that without your grandfather at your back fudging the monthly numbers as needed, without him floating us on this, I'm not sure it's possible."

Luna felt herself go still with shock as she replayed the words that couldn't possibly mean what she thought they meant, and pushed him away from her. "Fudging numbers? *Floating us?*"

Jameson scrubbed a hand down his face before meeting her gaze. "I never wanted to have to tell you, but this is what Silas did for you, Luna. He funneled money into the farm when you needed it, via the line of credit the bank closed down after his passing."

"Wait." She slid off the counter and stared at him, unable to quickly process the words suddenly. "*What?*"

"I know, it sounds crazy. And it was. It went against everything he'd ever taught me to do."

Luna actually staggered back against the counter like she'd taken a hit. It certainly felt like it. "I never asked him for help. In fact, I never ask *anyone* for help, for this exact reason. I never wanted to be beholden to anyone, *especially* him."

Jameson reached for her, but she shook her head and lifted her hands in the universal "stop" gesture, unable to handle him touching her right now. Turning away, realization after realization bombarded her. Silas had let her think this job had come to her on her own merit, but it hadn't. He'd let her think she'd *earned* the job of farm manager, but she hadn't. He'd let her think she was succeeding, when she hadn't done that either.

"I know what you're thinking, Luna."

"That he was a liar? That he pitied me?"

"Silas didn't do pity. He loved you."

"That's another lie." She whirled to face him. "If he loved me, how did he justify not telling me who he really was? Or how he let me think I was succeeding, when in actuality, I wasn't? And while we're on this, just exactly how badly was I not succeeding?"

Jameson hesitated, damn him. "*Tell me.*"

His voice when he spoke was very gentle. "First, you have to understand that farming in general is in trouble, not just Apple Ridge. It's nearly impossible to make a decent profit at this. Second, I handled all of Silas's business accounting. All of it, except this farm. He always insisted on doing it himself."

She stared at him. "Because you wouldn't have approved of him cooking my books?"

"I didn't approve of him letting you think one thing was happening, when it was another entirely."

She calmly nodded, even though she felt like screaming. "How long did you know?"

"Not until last season's taxes. He accidentally left the farm's forms accessible to me. But even then I had no idea how much he'd been doing behind the scenes. I didn't know until I got here and recognized the shoe boxes of receipts and put it all together."

"So just how bad was it?"

He shook his head.

"*Jameson.*"

He studied her for a beat and then sighed. "If you put all the numbers into a spreadsheet, the spreadsheet would actually turn blood red and your laptop would blow up."

"Oh my God." She took a step back and sank onto one of her chairs. She had a hand on her heart, which had just been handed back to her in a box with a shiny ribbon made of betrayal. Her grandfather had been cooking the books because she'd been that big a failure, just as her parents had always thought. "I'm such an idiot. I actually believed I was running the farm on my own merit, that Silas believed in me as a manager. That you and me . . ."

"We're real, Luna," he said softly. "You and me."

"Maybe, but you holding back the truth makes everything all the messier, and deeply affects my ability to trust you."

"Luna—"

"Don't." Her ego had just been kicked and destroyed. "Show me what he did."

He looked pained. "You don't need to see it."

"Oh, I need to see it."

Jameson reluctantly opened his laptop and typed something on the keyboard before turning it to face her. "Okay, so here are the numbers with the money he funneled into the accounts from the line of credit as needed. And here are what the real numbers would've been without that." He paused while she looked at the shocking discrepancies and felt sick to her soul.

"Tell me again you don't think that man loved you," he said quietly.

"I don't think *lying* is love." There was a lump in her throat she couldn't swallow. Or breathe past. "So is this why you're here?

I mean, you could've hugged your fifty percent to your chest at night from anywhere. Or hell, sold me out to the investors." At his silence, she turned and looked at him and, to her shock, caught him mid-grimace. "Oh my God. There's more."

"Do you remember when I told you there are things you don't know about me?"

"Yes, but you said you weren't a murderer and that you recycle."

His smile was mirthless. "You never pushed me for what I really meant."

He was right, and she cursed herself. "I guess I was afraid to look too closely because I liked you too much."

He winced a little, presumably at her use of past tense. "Silas asked me to come here and stay for two months. To look out for you and make sure you were okay, and to help steer this, whichever way you decided you wanted this to go."

And the hits kept coming. "And you didn't tell me that *why*?"

"I made a promise, and I couldn't break it, not to Silas. Not even for you."

Noble, she thought. But she didn't give a shit about noble at the moment. "You just did."

"Because it no longer felt right to keep it. Because even though you're doubting that this between us is real, it is, Luna. More real than anything. So much so that I couldn't let it go another day without telling you everything."

She wasn't going to be moved by that. Where she'd been warm before, now she felt only cold. "But you're only here because Silas sent you here to babysit me."

He shook his head. "You're missing the point. You know what my job is, Luna. And Silas taught me everything I know. But for you, he was literally doing the opposite of all of that. He broke his own ironclad rules for you. He wanted to know you were going to be okay."

"Without him manipulating things from behind the curtain, you mean."

He looked pained. "Yes."

"And you want me to believe that was love."

"Just because love doesn't come the way you think it should doesn't mean it's anything less than love."

Luna narrowed her eyes. "The way I think love should come is without lies. And speaking of lies, you knew all this, the whole time, and you kept it to yourself until now."

"Luna, I *owed* Silas. I owed him . . ." He shook his head. *"Everything."*

She let out a mirthless laugh. "A promise to a dead man. That was more important to you than being honest with me."

"At first, yes," he said, surprising her with his honesty.

Shaking her head, she turned away.

"Luna, look at me. Please?"

It was the "please" that did it, *not* that low, husky voice of his, she told herself. Reluctantly, she met his gaze, hers undoubtedly filled with everything she was feeling because she was shit at hiding that.

"I don't make promises lightly," he said quietly. "In fact, I've never met a promise I couldn't keep."

"And yet you promised me I could count on you for your

honesty. You told me I could trust you." Even worse, her greatest fear had come to life—she'd been dependent on someone, grandfather or no. And now she was also dependent on Jameson, or at least her heart was. Stupid heart. Scared and anxious about how very much she felt for him, maybe more than she'd ever cared about another man ever, she closed her eyes. *When would she learn?* Right the eff now, she decided. "You know what, Jameson? I can't do this."

"This?"

"*Us.*"

He looked stunned. "What are you talking about? You're going to end our relationship over an argument?"

"No. I'm ending this relationship that was never a real relationship since relationships are built on trust. And I don't think I can trust you ever again. In fact, I know it."

"Okay, yes, I held some information back because of a previous promise," he said. "A promise that I kept out of love, by the way, but—"

"*No.*" She remembered him sitting in her office closet to work, his knees up to his ears, reassuring her it was going to be okay. But he'd lied about that too. Because nothing was okay. Feeling like her whole world was crumbling in on her, she shook her head. "You're wrong."

"The facts are never wrong. Facts that I gave you because I think you deserve to have them."

Everything was falling apart, and worse, her heart felt . . . broken. "It's too late. It's all too late." She turned away and then whirled back, because apparently she wasn't quite done being furious. "You know what kills me? You made me tell everyone the truth about Silas leaving me fifty percent of this place. 'Be honest,' you said, and yet you've been lying from the beginning."

"And believe me, I'll never forgive myself for that," he admitted. "But before you get on the soapbox, I wasn't in this alone. You kept plenty from me."

She gaped at him. "Like what?"

"Only just about everything of yourself."

She shook her head, confused. "What are you talking about?"

"I opened up," he said. "I shared things with you that I've never shared with anyone else."

"I did the same."

"You gave me the bare minimum, while holding back everything else, like the most important parts of you. Those you kept to yourself. So no, Luna, I didn't break your trust, you never trusted me to begin with."

Shocked, she stared at him. "That's not true. I . . . sh—sh—shared with you." Shit. She'd actually tripped over her tongue trying to say the word "shared."

He gave her a get-real look that put her on the defensive. "Okay," she admitted, "maybe not my whole life story, but my life story isn't something I like to revisit. I lived it once, why live it again?"

"It's called opening up with the person you sleep with every night. Instead, you managed me, just like you manage the farm. You managed every little nugget you gave me of you."

For some reason, it was that which amped up her panic and anxiety more than anything else. Had they slept together every

night . . . ? She thought back, to all the long, dark, delicious
hours they'd spent in her bed exploring each other. Her bed,
her shower, her kitchen counter, the floor in front of the fire . . .
Damn. What had she been thinking? She'd let him into her bed
and then into her heart, which kicked hard at the realization.
Worse, the fear was closing her throat now, mostly because he
was right on the money. She *had* tried to manage him. Hell,
she managed *everyone*. He wanted her to open up? She had no
idea how, any more than she knew how to share the load, or let
him in. She also had no idea how to say it was all too much. So
instead her mouth said, "I'm done with this right now."

"Okay." He nodded. "Let's get some sleep, and in the morning
we'll—"

"No. There is no more 'we.'" Somewhere in the back of her
spinning brain she was well aware it was the worst thing she
could possibly say to him, but she couldn't seem to stop herself.

He sucked in air at the words, then his eyes went hooded as
he nodded. And with his usual calm and grace, he said, "Understood." He headed to the door, then stopped, his hand on the
handle. "If it means anything, I'm sorry, Luna."

She hugged herself and nodded. And then in the next beat, he
shoved his feet into his shoes and grabbed his jacket, pulling it
on over his bare chest before walking out of her life.

CHAPTER 27

Even though it was one in the morning, Jameson went in search of a place to bury himself in work. So he couldn't think about what had just happened. The office building held no appeal, so he wandered around the farm. He'd never seen it so still in all his time here.

Estelle the Emu lifted a sleepy head as he passed her pen. She stuck her curious little face over the fencing but she couldn't goose him from her enclosure. Something in his favor tonight, at least. He gave her a face rub, which got him a soft happy emu sound, and kept going.

He ended up in the tack room of the rescue animal barn. He sat there at the table surrounded by gear and with a baby goat on his lap, like he hadn't just had his dreams crushed hard.

"Numbers will never fail you," he told Dammit Ziggy, who had no comment. "Never."

DZ looked Jameson in the eye, then slowly and gently nudged him in the chest with his knubby head. He might not understand English, but he knew bro code.

Jameson took in the spreadsheets on his screen, but the numbers were a blur. Luna had been right. He'd lied by omission and broken a promise to her at the same time. He could still see the look of devastation and betrayal on her face, and his chest had been aching ever since she'd said she was done.

He'd warned himself, but still he'd delayed telling her the truth because he'd known it would blow them up.

He'd been right.

At some point he must've fallen asleep because he woke to the sound of animals stirring in the early dawn light, and then Stella poked her head into the tack room. "Interesting choice for an office," she said. "I like it. Oh, and you've got a . . ." She gestured to his jaw.

He lifted his hand to his face, and a pen, the one he'd fallen asleep on, fell and hit Dammit Ziggy, still perched in Jameson's lap, on the head.

Stella smiled. "Just wanted to tell you that Sunday brunch is starting."

This was the weekly staff brunch that had nothing to do with work. These people actively wanted to spend time together. "Thanks, but I haven't showered or anything."

"No shower required. Come on." She pulled him up, took him by the hand, and began walking him out of the barn, toward the café.

"I don't want to make things awkward."

"You mean because Luna dumped you?"

He let out a rough laugh. "She told you?"

"No. I eavesdropped on Luna's call with Willow when she was in the office a few minutes ago."

Wonderful. "So does everyone know?"

"Yep. I'm sorry my granddaughter is so shallow."

He went still. "What do you mean?"

"Well, because she broke up with you because of your . . . issues."

"Issues?"

"Your snoring, how you leave the toilet seat up, you've got an extra toe . . . oh, and you fart in your sleep. Which, honestly, who doesn't?"

Jameson just stared at her. "What?"

Stella patted his hand. "Don't you worry. Your secrets are safe with us. And just so you know, none of us think that any of those things are deal breakers."

Jameson wasn't sure if he was shocked that Luna hadn't ratted him out, or horrified at the reasons she'd made up for dumping him instead of telling the truth. "How in the world did everyone else find out?"

"Oh, because I told them. I really thought I'd taught Luna better than this."

He shook his head, not willing to let her take the fall for what had happened between them. "Look, you guys are her family and I won't get between that. There are things you should know—"

Stella stopped walking and turned to face him. "Oh, honey, don't you get it yet? We're your family too. Now get your cute patoot in gear. If the bacon's gone, I'll kick your ass."

They entered the Bright Spot and stopped at the "family" booth. Everyone was there but Luna, all of them treating him the exact same as always.

He'd just decided that maybe this was going to be okay when Luna walked in. When she pulled off her sunglasses, it was clear she'd been crying.

That was on him. So was the punch to the gut from just looking at her.

She eyeballed the full booth, clearly trying to decide which side to squish in on. Jameson was in the middle, and he realized belatedly he'd been outmaneuvered by Stella, probably so he couldn't leave. And yeah, he would have if he could have because Luna's unusually stilted body language said that if she'd known he was here, she wouldn't have come.

No one scooted over for her.

Luna crossed her arms and went brows up.

"You do know you fart in your sleep too, right?" Chef asked Luna.

Luna gave Stella a long look.

"You know there are no secrets here. And brunch is canceled today."

"Seriously? You're all literally sitting right here."

Her grandma slid out of the booth and gently set her hands on Luna's crossed arms. "Sweetheart, I know you've never been sure how to conduct yourself in a relationship, but—"

"*Excuse me?*" Luna asked in sheer disbelief.

"You don't dump a good man for having an extra toe," Stella said. "A bad man, maybe, but not a good one."

Luna let out a choked sound. "You used to con rich men for a living." She then turned to Chef. "*You* let me think you loved me for three years." Milo was next. "And you. You dumped your last lover via a TikTok video." She ignored Jameson entirely when she looked at everyone. "Stop judging. I'm not the jerk here."

Stella kissed her on her cheek. "I know you actually believe that, but we took a poll. And the jerk is you."

Jameson stood up. "No, she's right. I'm the jerk."

Luna's gaze flew to his, like she was shocked he'd stand up for her, which just about killed him. "Listen," he said to everyone, "the truth is—"

"No," Luna said quickly, shaking her head at him.

She didn't want him to spill on what had really happened. Why? "Can we talk?" he asked her. "Privately."

She lifted a shoulder in clear indifference. Ouch. He looked at the group. "Excuse me."

No one moved to let him out.

"I will climb over all of you," he warned, and with some grumbling, everyone dramatically scooched over and got up to let him out.

"I hope you're not going out of earshot range," Milo said.

Luna pointed at him and he sighed. Then she walked out of the Bright Spot.

Jameson followed. "Where to?"

She shrugged. "This is your meeting."

He gestured to an empty bench in the Square. They sat among the gorgeous, fragrant spring flowers Willow kept so beautifully in those big clay pots. Birds tweeted. A cow mooed. He looked over at Luna and found her watching him. He hated the uncertainty and unhappiness he saw there. "Luna—"

"I didn't want them to hate you," she said. "You're an owner too, and I don't want what happened between us to jeopardize your authority here."

Stunned, he stared at her, his throat tight at her generosity. He had never deserved her. "I'd like the chance to explain some things to you. Things I should've told you when I first got here."

"About my grandfather?" She lifted a shoulder. "I heard you. You made a promise."

"Yes. But—"

"Oh, don't second-guess yourself now." She looked at the sky as if it were the most interesting thing she'd ever seen.

"... But," he repeated softly. "It left me with a moral dilemma."

"Me or Silas." She nodded. "And you chose the man who took you in. I get it."

He doubted that. "I chose wrong, Luna. I should've told you everything up front, like a true partner would have."

"It doesn't matter now."

He was really hoping that wasn't true. "Silas was a complicated man, and a hard one. But he had one soft spot."

She snorted, and he gave a wry smile. "I know, it's hard to imagine, but it's true."

"If you're about to tell me that I was his soft spot, I won't believe you."

"Even if it's true? Luna . . . He didn't tell you when he first hired you because he wanted to give you time to find your way. He wanted you to fall in love with the place so that you wouldn't want to let go of it, just like he couldn't. I know it's hard to believe, but think about it. The farm was never particularly profitable and he kept it anyway. He kept it for you."

"And you," she pointed out.

He nodded at the truth of that, not telling her he'd already started the work to reverse that. "My point is you earned your half."

"I didn't *earn* anything. He lied to get me here to save something he loved. The end." Shaking her head, she looked away.

He struggled to find the right words. "It was literally *you* in this place that he loved so much. He got to see you be happy from afar. *You're* the thing he cared about here, Luna. He had zero idea how to be a grandparent. He always said it was Rose who made him human, and without her, he knew he was terrible at it, and nothing even close to what you might have needed. So he did this instead. He gave you the best part of him. And you literally saved this place. You earned every bit of what he gave you and more."

She drew a ragged breath. "Thank you. But the truth is, I'd have rather had *him*, flaws and all. I'd have rather had the truth than be left feeling like I do now, with my love of this place tainted by the knowledge that he manipulated me here."

"Luna—"

"No. I don't want to hear any more, Jameson. Knowing what I know now about the financials, I realize some hard truths. He never believed in me." Her laugh was rough, and far closer to a sob than amusement. "I never got this job on my own merit. And I certainly didn't make the farm succeed."

"Listen to me," he said. "No one could've made this place run like you do."

Shaking her head, she looked him in the eyes. "Thank you for that. I think I even believe it. But while we're being honest, you should know that I'd have rather you'd just kept your secrets and taken them with you."

Each word was like a knife to his chest, but he nodded his understanding. He'd probably have felt the same way in her position. "For what it's worth, Luna, I'm really sorry."

"Me too." Then she got up and walked away.

CHAPTER 28

Luna walked fast and blindly since the chances that she was about to lose it were a twelve out of ten. Since she was far closer to the office building than her cabin, she sneaked inside via the back door, going straight to the staff room for her tub of double fudge ice cream and a big wooden spoon. Hearing voices, she quickly slid into the storage closet and silently shut the door before sliding down the wall to sit on the floor.

Her phone vibrated in her pocket with an incoming text. Unable to ignore it in case it was work related, she looked at the screen.

GRAM: You okay?

LUNA: How is my life such shit?

GRAM: I think you'll find that the outcome is in line with your self-destructive tendencies.

Luna choked out a half laugh, half sob, and put her phone away. This place, this farm, was . . . *everything* to her. She'd pulled the little community of people she loved together: an ex-boyfriend, adoptive grandma, her BFF, another close friend . . . and more recently the first man she could see forever with, all because she'd had a need for a family who loved her unconditionally. One of her biggest fears had always been that she would somehow blow it all up.

A self-fulfilling prophecy, as it turned out. Oh, she knew she could've told everyone the truth. But then they might've turned on Jameson. And if there was anyone who needed their little self-made family as much as she did, it was him.

She was still sitting on the floor eating ice cream when she heard footsteps stop right outside the closet door. "*Go away.*"

Willow opened the door and joined her in the closet, and Luna stared at her with narrowed eyes. "That's the opposite of going away."

Hands on hips, her BFF eyed the ice cream. "Nice breakfast."

"I thought it was a beautiful day to get fat and tell everyone to go to hell. But now I just feel like throwing up."

"Sorry, that's my thing now."

Luna tipped her head back to the wall and stared at the ceiling. "Everyone hates me."

Willow sat next to her. "Hate is such a strong word."

Luna sighed.

"And they don't hate you, Luna. They love you. They just also love Jameson."

"I think he broke my heart." Blindly, she reached out for Willow's hand and pressed it to her chest. "See? It's not even there anymore."

"Okay, no more ice cream for you. It's Mama's turn. Mama needs some sugar."

"You hate ice cream."

"Yeah . . ." Willow snatched the tub and started eating it. "But apparently the T. rex loves it."

Luna gently patted Willow's nonexistent baby bump. "Good T. rex, taking after her auntie already."

"Jameson told us everything," Willow said around a huge bite.

The implication of that, of him risking alienating the crew, was huge. He hadn't cared about what they thought of him. He'd only cared about her.

"I get why you're upset, but it was up to Silas to do what he wanted with this place when he was alive. That's not on Jameson. And neither is the fact that Silas asked him to come here and not tell you about it."

"By not telling me, he lied."

"He *omitted*." She turned to meet Luna's eyes. "And isn't that exactly the same thing you did when you didn't tell me about Silas being your grandpa? Or when he told you not to give me a promotion. And I still love you, so . . ."

Luna sighed. "I'm *failing* this place." *And* the people in it . . .

"Babe, you're the glue of the farm and we all know it. But it's up to you to believe in yourself."

"Well, excuse me, but it's hard to believe in myself when my own grandfather had to cook the books in order for us to continue operating." She grabbed for the spoon and took another bite.

Willow growled and grabbed it back. "Now see, Silas not telling you all that is on *him*. If he'd told you, you could've adjusted, done things differently."

"I'm adjusting now, and things are still a disaster."

"You're selling yourself short. Look at what you've pulled off. You've procured the permits for our event, got the locals on board, and are about to pull off the best Founders Day we've ever had."

"It will be the only one we've ever had."

Willow waved the spoon around. "Semantics. The advantage is that there are no expectations."

"It's in a week," Luna said in disbelief. "We have presales. There are *plenty* of expectations. For one thing, we have to make enough to cover the balloon payment or we're all out on our asses."

"It's going to happen." Willow peered into the now nearly empty tub. "Is there more in the freezer . . . ? No?" she asked when Luna just stared at her. "Fine, whatever. Let's get to why you're really in the closet, because it's not about the farm or Founders Day."

"Uh, pretty sure it is."

Willow smiled knowingly. "Okay, let's pretend for a moment that you're right."

"Gee, thanks?"

Willow wasn't deterred. "For reasons I can't understand, you love this job."

Luna gaped at her. "For reasons you don't understand?"

Willow shrugged. "Well, as I've learned the hard way, dreams change."

A wave of guilt washed over Luna. "About our B and B—"

"Shh." Willow took her hand. "I'm going to say this with all the love in the world, since you let me be Head-in-Charge for not one but *two* days." She drew a deep breath. "Your job is terrible."

This startled a laugh out of Luna.

"It is," Willow said. "When I first started here, I remember hearing you on a call. You said something like 'sure, but your *other* solution is doing what I suggested in the first place.' And then you just hung up. It was beautiful, and I knew I wanted to be you when I grow up. But . . ." She shook her head. "It turns out, I don't. I don't want to be Head-in-Charge. I know I was jealous of what you do for a long time, but the truth is, I don't want to ever be the boss, not even for our someday dream of the B and B. I mean, your phone *never* stops, and if I was you, even caller ID wouldn't be enough. I'd need to know why someone was calling me up front. I'd even pay extra every month for caller justification."

Luna choked on another laugh.

"I'm not kidding. While I was you the other day, someone told me signing emails with 'best' was passive-aggressive, so I switched it up to 'see you in hell' just to eliminate any confusion. Turns out that's just *aggressive*-aggressive. Oh, and apparently I'm no longer allowed to answer the phone with 'for fuck's sake, what now?'"

"I'm going to pretend you're joking," Luna said, and sighed. "But I hear you. I know the job is terrible, and I love it anyway. I love it so much. Even if someone gave me a million dollars to walk away, I'd still be here. This is still what I'd be doing."

"And Jameson?"

Luna had to take a deep breath. "That's over."

"But if it wasn't?"

Luna slid her a look.

"I'll reword the question," Willow said. "Would you still be doing it with Jameson?"

She went for light, because otherwise she'd cry. "Well, he is *really* good at it, so . . ."

Willow laughed, but wagged a finger. "No. I'm not going to let you joke this away."

"You're not going to *let* me?" Luna asked in amused disbelief.

"I'm trying out my mom voice. What do we think? Do we like it?"

"It needs a little work." Luna's stomach growled in spite of the ice cream. She wished she'd eaten before she'd stormed off. "Jameson's nature is to tear things apart, not put them back together."

"What Jameson are *you* talking about?" Willow asked. "Because the Jameson I know has done nothing but help you build this place up. Luna . . ."

When Willow didn't finish her sentence, Luna turned to look at her.

"Be honest. If he'd told you the truth from day one about Silas funneling you money for the farm or the promise he extracted from Jameson to look after you, would you have even let a friendship with him happen, much less fall for him?"

Luna sighed. No. No, she wouldn't have. If he'd told her from the beginning, she'd have felt like such a failure that she'd never have let herself get attached to him. And attached she was. And then there was the business. Without him, there'd be no upcoming Founders Day. She'd never have been brave enough.

Which meant that the farm would have failed for certain.

"He's a man of his word, Luna. He's proven that."

"You're right," she admitted. "And he made the promise to Silas before he met me. I know he regrets that."

"So then . . ." Willow went brows up. "Who are you really mad at?"

Luna closed her eyes.

"Let me help you," Willow said. "You're mad at you."

"Yes," she whispered, throat thick. "I used the situation to back off from him, when the truth is I got scared."

"Bingo." Willow smiled brilliantly. "Which I only know because I did the same with Shayne, and I nearly lost him because of it."

"But now you've got a get-out-of-jail-free card," Luna said, looking meaningfully at Willow's stomach.

Willow snorted. "He should've run while he had the chance. I'm telling you, pregnancy hormones are not for the faint of heart. I bounce between being a needy five-year-old who can't control her emotions, to a teenage rebel who makes poor life decisions, to an eighty-year-old woman who's tired and needs a nap."

Luna grinned.

"It's no joke. It takes a plastic bag over one hundred years to break down, and it takes me only one minor inconvenience."

Luna laughed and leaned her head on Willow's shoulder. Right there on the floor of the closet, she knew that no matter what happened, whether they saved the farm or not, whether she and Jameson worked things out or not, that at least she and Willow were going to be okay. "I've been so scared," she said softly. "Scared to blow up the farm and have everyone here lose their jobs and livelihood."

Willow reached out to hold her hand. "You've done your best. If the worst happens, it won't be your fault."

Standing, Luna pulled Willow up as well. "You know what? I'm not going to let this do us in. If Silas was willing to go as far as cooking the books so we could stay open, then I have to turn this around. For him. For all of us."

Willow smiled. "*There* you are. And just in time to make Founders Day a success and save all our asses."

Luna felt her stomach jangle and the heart she thought decimated skipped a few beats.

"No." Willow pointed at her. "Don't you dare let the doubts back in. Sure, you messed up a really great relationship with a really great guy, and you pretend you're an island of one when you're not, but one thing you're never wrong about? Your instincts. So go with them. The event, plus everything else we're implementing, is going to work. Now repeat it."

"It's going to work."

Willow smiled serenely.

"Are you going to be this scary for nine months?"

"And beyond."

THAT NIGHT, AND the next handful as well, leading up to the last night before Founders Day, Luna didn't even try to be okay.

And maybe it was this new strategy—letting herself wallow and grieve and overthink—that let some answers come to her.

Such as she was suddenly getting what Jameson—who'd moved back into cabin number seven—had been trying to tell her. Maybe Silas hadn't been a warm, cuddly man. He hadn't held a sweet side, or kept a roomful of bunnies and rainbows. That hadn't been him. He'd understood that about himself, and well aware of his failings—messing up his marriage, and his relationship with his daughter, and not coming clean to Luna out of fear of messing up her life as he had those of everyone else he loved—he'd still tried to do the right thing by her in the only way he'd known how.

To a man like Jameson, also self-made and self-taught, that had been the very best part of her grandfather. After all, he'd taken in a street kid without qualm. He'd then gone on to give Luna a place to go when she'd been floundering in life without a direction. Looking at it that way, Silas had actually been far more sentimental than she'd given him credit for. And wasn't that part of being a family? Understanding that everyone in it could be different? After all, they too had different love languages. Silas's had been "I don't know how to love you in the way you need, I'm scared to ruin another relationship or hurt you, so here's a farm."

Thinking about it hurt her head. And her heart. So she didn't even pretend to be okay. Instead, she went over and over the plans for tomorrow's Founders Day, making sure they hadn't missed anything.

All while not looking at the empty spot next to her in bed.

CHAPTER 29

On the morning of Founders Day, Jameson got up early, determined to do his part to make it a success.

The farm was hopping. Vendors were preparing their booths and activities: mini-zips, jump pads, face painting, private farm tours, goat yoga, tortoise races, and more. The creativity involved amazed him.

But that was all Luna. On top of being a great leader, she was creative, flexible, a problem solver, and held an open mind. She'd taken everyone's ideas and made them happen. She was incredible.

Employees had the petting zoo pen in place and the barn doors wide open. The Humane Society had brought kittens and puppies available for adoption.

The farm animals watched the spectacle with brimming curiosity, their energy matching that of the people around them.

Jameson moved about assisting wherever he could. He secured pens, set up line management, and prepared the entry gate with money boxes so they could make change, then went over the protocol for how much money they could collect before they needed to call him to come empty the kitty and take the cash to the office safe for safekeeping.

After that, he stopped by the two food trucks, and Chef ambled over. "So. I might have a confession to make."

Jameson couldn't imagine what that might be. "Okay."

"The other day you were using the back booth in my café as your office."

"I was."

"And you walked away for a minute, leaving your laptop open. I came by to give you a refill on your soda just as an email came through. Hey," he said at Jameson's look. "This is what I do, stalk her ex-boyfriends. I did tell you about what I did to the last guy's phone. Anyway, the email was from your attorney."

Well, hell.

"Yeah," Chef said. "Want to explain?"

"You want me to explain a private email?"

Chef smiled. "I can see why you're so efficient. You use that no-bullshit, I-could-kick-your-ass-if-I wanted-to voice and people back right off."

"But not you."

"Nope," Chef said. "So let me make sure I've got this straight. You spent I don't even know how many years with Silas the Grinch, working your very fine ass off, and yet you're willing to give up your ownership, something you legitimately earned, to make sure Luna understands how you feel about her?"

"That and more," Jameson said softly. "Not that I expect anyone to understand."

"You'd be surprised. You forget that Luna and I go way back. She's easy to fall in love with and nearly impossible to get over. So yeah, I understand perfectly."

Jameson nodded and, from fifty feet away, his gaze met Luna's. For a brief beat, he saw what no one else probably did: She hadn't slept, and she was hurting.

He'd done that.

But then he stopped breathing because she was walking toward him. He continued to not breathe as she was stopped a bunch of times by people needing questions answered or just wanting to talk to her.

Then she was right in front of him, and because they were chronic idiots, they stood there staring at each other.

"I'll just . . ." Chef gestured vaguely over his shoulder and then made himself scarce.

Luna was in her usual uniform of jeans, work boots, and Apple Ridge Farm jacket, hood down, hair up, eyes hidden behind dark sunglasses, and he sucked up the sight of her. "Hey," he said softly.

"Hey," she said just as softly. "Thanks for helping set up. I didn't expect—I mean now that we're not . . ."

"Sleeping together?" He raised a brow when she blushed. "You think that because you dumped me, I'd walk away from saving this place?"

She winced and looked away. "I'm sorry, that was thoughtless. I should have known you'd still want to help protect your half."

He thought about what Chef had discovered on his laptop.

He wanted to tell her, but had no idea how. "I want today to be a huge success, for the employees, and for you."

"And what about you?" she asked.

He shrugged, trying to keep his expression even. He'd have thought he was used to being cut loose, that he'd be impervious to the pain, but he wasn't that lucky. "It's not about me. Never was." He turned to go.

"Jameson?"

He looked back.

"I need to talk to you about something, but I want to do it in private. Do you have time when today's over?"

He nodded, and she went back to running the show. He stayed still for a moment, knowing this was it. She was going to tell him it was okay to go back to his world early. Definitely for the best, he told himself, and then tried to believe it.

But the truth was, he loved the pace of life here, which was to say frenetic, wild, and crazy. The opposite of his usual cutthroat and vicious. And he didn't want to leave.

Twenty minutes later, Luna gathered the entire staff in the courtyard. Standing on one of the planters, she announced that their think tank ideas had all started to bring in money, how grateful she was for their help, and that they couldn't have pulled this off without each and every one of them.

People seemed genuinely touched by her words, and Jameson had to admit, he was as well. Then she asked anyone if they had last-minute questions.

Willow raised her hand, then walked up to Luna and handed her a check. "Here's the money I've put aside for our B and B."

Luna shook her head. "Willow—"

"Please accept it. It would mean so much to me to be able to add to the save-the-farm kitty."

They hugged for a long moment, but what Willow had done started an avalanche of people walking one by one up to Luna and handing her checks, cash, and, in Shep's case, an actual honest-to-God piggy bank that he had to pull to her in a little wagon because it was so heavy with change. Chef had money from his ex, proving he hadn't been catfished. Stella had a check from one of her ex-husbands, the venture capitalist. Shayne, who'd stopped by to leave a big, shiny red fire truck for kids to see, also had a check from their firehouse fundraiser.

And for the second time that day, Jameson found himself stunned by these people putting everything on the line for a company they didn't even have a stake in. Two months ago, he'd actually believed that he alone would have to save this place. He'd carried his laptop with his spreadsheets around, speaking a foreign language that no one was interested in. Still, he'd persevered, coming up with some viable solutions for how to save money. But mostly, the joke was entirely on him because Luna and her merry band of wonderful misfits were going to save themselves.

As if to prove it, they opened the front gate at 10:00 a.m. sharp to a long line of people waiting with eager smiles on their faces.

To JAMESON'S SHOCK and relief, hours later, the place was still packed. People had turned out in droves on droves. The farm was always a bustle of activity, but today took it to a whole new level, all of it managed by employees and volunteers consisting of members of the town council and their families, and friends of the farm.

Between the booths, stations, petting pens, crowd control, line control, you name it, it was a huge endeavor, and a successful one. The food trucks, one a handmade ice creamery, the other a burger and hot dog truck, also volunteering their time and food, all had lines. Milo was managing the photo booths, which were busy. So was Stella's Place. She sat in front of the barn at a table, reading fortunes. She looked at him and winked. "You want to be next?"

"No thanks." He already knew what his future held. And it wasn't good.

Someone came up behind him and threw their arms around him.

Willow.

She was beaming. "Guess what?" She didn't wait for his answer. "Just finished the magazine shoot and they weren't here for just the botanical gardens—they came for me! Can you believe it? *I'm* the main focus of their piece! Me and my work!"

He *had* known it, and so had Luna. They'd agreed to keep it their little secret as a surprise for Willow. Her eyes went suspiciously shiny and she waved a hand in front of them. "Ignore me. I think I'm going to be crying for the next nine months. I'm just so happy!" And she flung her arms around him again and hugged him hard.

He was trying to gently untangle himself when Shayne came up and rescued him with an amused "Babe, you're strangling the poor guy."

She kissed Jameson on the cheek, then wrapped herself around her husband, beaming. "I'm going to throw up on you later."

Shayne laughed. Willow grinned at him and then looked at Jameson. "So . . . you look fine, and you sound fine . . ."

"Uh, thank you?"

"It's just that I'm really hoping it's an act."

"Why?"

"Because Luna needs you to love her. But if you do, you'd be devastated right now. So . . . which are you, devastated or fine?"

He looked into her eyes and saw worry and concern for her best friend, which was the only reason he answered about something so personal to him. "Door number one."

She nodded. "Good, because she's been through a lot. She needs you."

He let out a choked laugh. "Pretty sure she doesn't let herself need anyone, much less me."

"Then you're not paying attention."

He met her gaze. "Okay, you're right. I should've said she doesn't *want* to need me."

"Well, duh. Like I said, she's been through a lot. Doesn't trust her emotions. But be patient. She's worth it."

He knew that much to be true. What he didn't know was how to make her want *him*.

He kept moving. Mostly because whenever he stopped, he became aware of the pain in the region of his heart. Incred-

ibly aware of Luna also moving through the crowd, stopping
to rescue the mayor from DZ, who was attempting to eat the
woman's hair. They were laughing, and he loved the way her
entire face lit up when she laughed. He loved the way her eyes
sparkled, the way she talked so animatedly with her hands,
even when those hands were full of baby goat. He loved . . .

Damn.

He loved *her*.

As the day went on, the crowds never let up. He'd been pulling the cash in hourly, taking it to the office safe. He was walking
down the main strip, halfway between the office and the front
gate, heading back there to check on things, when he heard his
name.

Turning, he came face-to-face with Luna. She strode right up
to him, nearly toe-to-toe, then tilted her head back to look at his
face. Or so he assumed, as her sunglasses were dark and mirrored.

He said nothing.

She said nothing.

They stared at each other for an uncomfortably long beat, but
Jameson was getting used to being in uncomfortable situations.
Finally, she blew out a breath. "You're going to make me ask?"

"Ask what?"

"Omigod, don't play with me right now. How much money
did we make so far? *Did we come close?*"

He pulled off her mirrored sunglasses. "Better."

She stared at him some more, then, as he'd hoped, she read
him like a book and let out a big smile, giving him a tap on the
chest that was maybe more of a shove. "We did it!" She looked

around, seemed to realize they were surrounded by people, so she grabbed him by the hand and pulled him around to the back of the barn and pushed him up against the side of it.

He couldn't help it, his heart stuttered. And maybe some other reactions happened as well. Nothing sexier than a woman taking what she wanted. Even if she'd kicked him to the curb.

She had her hands on his biceps and was looking at his mouth, like maybe she'd forgotten what she'd dragged him over here for, which gave him a dark sense of satisfaction. "If it's breakup sex you're after," he murmured, "it's probably best to wait until some of the people leave our general area."

She rolled her eyes. "*Say it.*"

He smiled. "Adding in all the donations you got this morning, plus from the Founders Day till so far, we've made more this week than we have in any previous quarter in the farm's history."

"Oh," she breathed, and then smiled. "Enough to make the balloon payment?"

"Enough to make the balloon payment and then some, which we can save for the slow months."

With a whoop, she threw herself at him. He managed to catch her as she wrapped her legs around his waist, shoved her fingers into his hair, and kissed him, one long, hot, wet smooch that had him so dizzy it took him a moment to realize she'd let go of him.

"I'm sorry," she said softly. "I mean, I wanted to do that, but didn't know how to ask."

"Luna, you don't ever have to ask for what you want with me. Or be afraid of wanting too much. Just take it. It's yours."

Her eyes went misty and she looked away for a minute, like

whatever she was feeling was just too much for her to take. "I've been afraid you'd run once you saw how messed up I was inside. So I ran first."

He gave her a ghost of a smile. "You do know you're not the only one who's messed up or afraid to believe, right?"

She studied him, then returned his small smile with one of her own. "Yeah. I think I'm getting there." She swiped under her eyes, removing the few tears that had escaped. "How do guys get through shit without crying?"

"Easy. We bottle everything up until we die of stress-induced heart failure in our forties like real men."

She laughed, and this time their silence didn't feel nearly as awkward.

"Maybe my messed-up-ness sort of balances your messed-up-ness," she said quietly, pulling out her phone, which had been going off steadily. She finally answered it, listened for a beat, then sighed. "I'll be right there." She gave Jameson an apologetic look. "I'm needed at the barn. You still free later to talk?"

"Yes."

"Meet me at the office?"

He nodded, and then watched her walk off to keep doing all the billion little things she needed to do to keep everything running smoothly. For a hot minute she'd let him in and it'd been the best minute of his life. Just as falling for her had been the easiest thing he'd ever done.

He wasn't going to regret that. Or how he'd found a place where he belonged, even if he was going to leave because he refused to put Luna through any more than she'd already been through.

He was about to go figure out who might need his help when his phone rang.

"Your circus made the local news," Brett said in his dry voice. "There's a reporter walking around getting footage of some baby goat named Dammit Ziggy, and some palm reader who was telling fortunes. I'll be shocked if you don't get an offer to be a reality show by the end of the day."

"You want to know if we made enough money to pay you off," Jameson said.

"No, actually. We want to know if you're going to say yes to a reality show. There's a shit-ton of money in those dumb things."

Jameson rolled his eyes so hard he nearly saw his own brain. Luna would've been so proud. "Let me guess. You want a new deal."

"Damn-A straight. Forget the balloon payment. We'll rework and extend the loan."

"For . . . ?"

"A piece of the TV deal."

Over his dead body. "I'll have to check with my partner and employees," he said. "But expect the balloon payment to come in on time."

"The employees?" Brett asked. "What the hell do we care what the employees think? I'll need your answer by—"

Jameson disconnected.

He couldn't have even said what he did for the rest of the day, but at the end, when all their guests were gone and everything had been broken down and put back together so that it was just the animals and employees again, he headed to the office building. Inside, he felt like a dead man walking as he made his way down the hallway. He stopped at Luna's office, but it was empty.

"Down here!" he heard her call out.

He found her standing at the end of the hallway in front of the storage closet. She'd changed into leggings and a soft-looking sweater that clung to her sweet curves, looking like the best thing to ever happen to him.

"Thanks for coming," she said.

Milo peeked out of the staff room. "Make sure you tell him that him being a part of this family isn't predicated on you two being together."

Chef stuck his head out too. "Agreed. We want to keep him."

Willow's face appeared next to Chef's. "All of that," she said. "Love you to the moon and back, can't stress that enough, but we love him too."

"*Bleeeat*," Dammit Ziggy said in Stella's arms.

"Clearly, DZ agrees," Stella said.

Luna pinched the bridge of her nose. "Can we please have a moment here?"

Everyone nodded and retreated.

Luna drew a deep breath and looked at Jameson.

"I'm so sorry," he said. "I never should've kept what Silas wanted me to do from you—"

She shook her head. "You already apologized, and you're forgiven. First, I want to thank you again for all you did today. We couldn't have done it without you."

"Today's success was all you, Luna."

"Wow," Milo said from behind the staff room's closed door. "That hurts."

"Shh," Stella whispered. "It'll get good as soon as they get the pleasantries out of the way, and I don't want to miss anything."

"They don't do anything good at work," Chef said. "Luna won't mix business with pleasure. Especially nekkid pleasure."

An almost smile lit Luna's eyes. Jameson had a much better poker face than she did, but even he had a hard time not smiling at the memory of them taking each other apart in the barn while being watched by a very curious Estelle.

"Oh my God," Willow said. "I saw that smile, Luna! And you told me I couldn't do it with Shayne while at work."

"Everyone out of the building," Luna said. She took a deep breath and looked at Jameson. "I'm sorry about them. That we even had this event today was because you taught me how to respect the bottom line. Then you gave me the courage to make it happen by simply believing in me, when, to be honest, I didn't believe in myself."

He drew a deep breath, feeling . . . well, everything. Because here it came. The "but."

"*Awkward*," Milo whispered.

"Oh my God, for the last time, *OUT*!" Luna yelled.

There was muttering, but the sounds of footsteps and then the front door to the building opening and shutting told him they were alone.

He didn't know whether to be relieved or terrified.

CHAPTER 30

"Just say what you want to say," Jameson said.

Luna sucked in some air, because how did one eat humble pie without making a bigger mess? She put a hand to her chest. "Give me a minute. My heart's pounding and I'm sweating in places I shouldn't be sweating."

Jameson's eyes softened very slightly. He seemed braced, and she couldn't blame him. He also looked hot as hell in another pair of jeans, an actual T-shirt, one of their own, which melted her heart. So did the way he was looking at her like maybe she meant a whole lot to him.

"Since when are you afraid to tell me something?" he asked.

"I'm not. I'm just so nervous I might throw up." She paused, then quickly said, "I mean, not the kind of throwing up Willow's doing. I'm not pregnant or anything."

He smiled. "You ramble when you're nervous."

"Always." She looked into his face and Stella's words flooded back to her. *Sometimes what we need the most is the one thing we keep pushing away because we're afraid.* "I'm trying to work on myself to be better," she said. "But it's a steep learning curve. The simple truth is, I'm sorry. For a lot of things." She drew a big breath for courage while he stood there waiting with warm, curious, patient eyes. Okay, well, here went . . . everything. "I thought I hated quesadillas because sometimes they have peppers in them," she said. "But you don't use peppers, because as it turns out, you don't like them either, so there's that."

He smiled, but also looked a little confused by the direction of this conversation.

"Another thing is that I like to be the big spoon," she said. "Also, I don't like it when the blankets on the bed are loose so my foot sticks out. My feet have to be covered so the monsters under the bed can't eat my toes."

He smiled. He already knew this. "You're trying to tell me something."

"Yes." She drew another deep breath. "Sushi used to be my favorite food until I got food poisoning last year and threw up for three days. And I don't understand why people like roller coasters." She racked her brain for more. "Oh! In the third grade I cheated on a spelling bee off Brian McDonald and when I got caught, I blamed it on him."

"You're opening up without being pressed to do so," he said softly, looking incredibly touched. "You're opening up willingly . . . to me."

"Trying anyway." She took a beat to breathe. "Jameson, you *are* a part of this family. An important part, and I'm sorry I ever let you think otherwise. You're . . . family." She paused. "But to be clear, not the kind of family I can't sleep with, because I'd really like to go back to sleeping with you." She paused. "The inappropriate kind of sleeping, in case I wasn't clear. I know I told you I was done, but that was a lie. I'd talked myself into believing I didn't deserve you. I don't know why exactly, except maybe it's because growing up, I felt I had to . . . I don't know . . . conform, I guess, in order to be loved."

He stepped closer to her, his eyes both soft and fierce. "No one should have to change who they are to be loved."

She waved a hand in front of her face while simultaneously staring up at the ceiling. "I'm going to cry. And I really, really, really hate crying. The truth is, I *want* you to crowd my space and be all up in it. I'm so sorry I screwed us up so spectacularly. It wasn't until after you said I never opened up to you that I realized you might be a little right."

He smiled. "Just a little?"

Her smile was rueful. "Okay, a lot right. Don't get used to that."

"This isn't a contest. We can both be wrong." He leaned in to kiss her, but she put a hand to his chest.

"Wait," she said. "There's more."

He gave a gallant head bow and a hand gesture for her to continue.

She put a hand to her pounding heart to keep it inside her chest. "The very first guy I was ever with . . . it turned out that he only slept with me because of a dare."

He sucked in a breath and whispered her name as he again reached for her, but she held up a hand. "I have to say this,

Jameson. All of it. As you know, my first real relationship, and the first man I ever loved, turned out to be gay. There was someone after that, but he doesn't deserve a mention. The second man I fell in love with . . . he kept something from me, something big."

He went still as stone. "Luna—"

"A secret that was his right to keep. And yes, I hid myself from you because the truth is, I've never lived up to expectations. And no matter how hard I try, I'm never quite enough—"

"I'm going to stop you right there," he said, tipping her face up to his.

"But maybe I have more deep, dark secrets—"

"I don't care. Because you *are* enough, Luna. You're more than enough, you're . . ."

She cocked a brow. "Don't even try to say 'perfect.'"

"I was going to say the most amazing pain in my ass I've ever met. Is that okay?"

She had to laugh. "No one's ever told me that."

"That you're a pain in the ass?"

She rolled her eyes, but a very small smile curved her mouth. "You know what I mean."

Stepping into her, he slid his hands up her arms to cup her face. "Let me repeat myself. You're enough, you're more than enough, you're the most amazing woman I've ever met." His face was so serious, so intense as he looked down at her. "Now it's my turn to tell you some things you should know. I love your courage. I love how you light up a room when you walk into it.

I love the way you'd do anything for your friends and family. I love how your eyes flash when you know someone's bullshitting you. I love seeing your face first thing in the morning, your hair all crazy beautiful."

She tried to look away, but he held on to her. "I love the way you think, and the way you refuse to compromise the things that are important to you. I love the way I feel when I'm with you."

She just stared at him, shocked at his list, its length, and the way he said it all with genuine emotion.

"Luna, you're the most amazing woman I've ever met."

She must've looked like maybe her brain couldn't upload that, because he said it again, his mouth brushing against her ear. And then again against her mouth this time, kissing her like his life depended on it, and hell, she was pretty sure hers did as well. "I love you, Jameson. So much." The words slipped out naturally and without thought.

His eyes closed for a quick beat, then opened again, revealing surprise, affection, and . . . a much deeper emotion. "Luna, when I look into your eyes, I finally, for as long as I'm holding you, feel peace. Refuge. A sense of home." He dropped his forehead to hers. "I love you so very much, and have since you walked into my life and told me you didn't date suits."

She nearly collapsed with relief. "You know you're crazy to love me, right?"

He grinned. "Maybe I'm just crazy for you."

Marveling at that, she shook her head. "So what does it all mean?"

"That's easy, honey . . ." This from Stella, who clearly had decided not to leave. "It means your auras are intertwined and the universe is in favor of this joining and merging of souls."

"Gram, you're going to make him go screaming into the night."

Instead, he pulled her into him. "I'm tired of taking things apart and leaving. I want to stay, but I think there should be a change."

Her heart skipped a beat. "A change?"

"I take it you haven't checked your email yet today."

She shook her head, confused. "No time. Why?"

"Check it now."

She pulled out her phone and waited for her emails to download. One of them was from Silas's attorney. She opened it, then her heart skipped another beat as she lifted her face to Jameson's. "You signed over your fifty percent ownership to me?" She took a breath, then shook her head. This couldn't be real. *You signed over your fifty percent to me?*"

He smiled. "One hundred percent looks good on you."

She shook her head again, feeling sick. "Jameson, I can't let you do this. You deserve half—"

"I don't need it. I know I belong here, with or without ownership. It doesn't change anything for me, Luna. I still have an emotional stake in this place. And you."

"I don't know what to say . . ." She lifted her face to his, knowing her eyes were shiny with unshed tears. "Jameson—"

"Say I can stay," he said softly. "With you."

Head spinning, she nodded. "I was really hoping you were

going to say that, because . . ." She bit her lower lip, nervous all over again. "There's one more thing I need to tell you. Actually, show you." And with that, she opened the closet door—which was no longer a walk-in storage closet. She'd stayed up late clearing it out completely. All the shelves and all the things that had been on the shelves were gone. So was the layer of dust, the holiday decorations—including a life-size Easter Bunny. She'd removed everything and painted the walls white—the only paint she'd been able to find on-site, but it made the space seem bigger. She'd left the small window open to vent out the fumes and had rush-ordered a desk and chair, still in their boxes. The only other thing in the room was a key ring lying in the middle of the desk.

Jameson looked at her, then moved to the desk and picked up the key ring. It was brass letters that spelled HOME, and held two keys.

"One's to the door of your new office," she said. "The other's to my place. Which I think of as our place. Hence the key." She waited until he looked at her. "There's space for you here, Jameson. You truly belong here, with us. It's your home too, and I'm sorry I ever let you think otherwise."

He gave her his crooked smile. "Is this a romantic gesture, or do you just want me to keep doing the books?"

With a laugh, she wrapped her arms around him and planted a hell of a kiss on his lips. "Actually, I have a list of things I want you to keep doing, but the books is at the *very* bottom."

He grinned. "Well, you know how I love a good list. Maybe we should get started."

"Do you think they're talking about sex?" Chef asked Milo.

Milo shrugged. "I didn't know old people could still do it."

"Seriously," Luna yelled back to him. "I'm only three years older than you! *And* I asked you all to leave!"

"Can *we* make a list?" Shayne asked Willow, sounding hopeful.

"I'm still in the middle of the consequences from the *last* list we had," Willow said.

Stella came to Luna and Jameson and hugged them tight. "I'm so happy for you both. And for me too, since when you decide to get married, I'll be the officiant and all. Don't worry, my charge for the services will reflect how much I love you. Four figures tops."

"Gram," Luna said. "We're not engaged."

"But you will be, someday."

Luna looked at Jameson, seeming horrified that her grandma was putting them on the spot, but he just smiled. "Yes," he said, never taking his eyes off her. "Someday. When she's ready."

Stella whooped with glee. "I knew it. And four figures is a deal, you know. You might want to lock me in."

Luna shook her head, but also laughed. "*No* fee and I'll buy you a new dress."

"Sold," Stella said, and winked at Jameson. "You may now kiss your bri—"

"*Girlfriend*," Luna corrected.

Jameson smiled into her eyes. "Don't mind if I do."

And then to Luna's delight, he did just that, and their deal was sealed.

EPILOGUE

One year later, after the second annual Founders Day

Luna and Jameson sat at a table in the Square, basking in the glow of another successful event when a squawk from the region of Jameson's chest had them both going still. They both very slowly stared down at the T. rex, whose face was scrunched up in displeasure.

"Don't move a muscle," Luna whispered. "Willow said if we wake her, she'll kill us."

Jameson cupped a big hand under the baby strapped to him by some sort of complicated sling contraption that Willow'd had to put on him because they'd bungled it so badly. "Shh," he whispered to three-month-old Lily Rose Green, gently jiggling her. "I've got you, shh . . ."

Lily Rose relaxed, her face smoothing out, her mouth falling open as she fell back into a deep sleep.

Luna lifted her head and looked at Jameson in shock. "What was that?"

He shrugged. "Gas maybe?"

"No, I mean you soothing her in two seconds flat."

He smiled over the baby passed out cold on him. "Maybe I've just got the touch."

Wasn't that the truth. Before she could say so, a woman joined them at the table, smiled at the baby, and pulled out her laptop.

Allie was the architect for the house Jameson planned on building only a few miles from the farm. Up until now, they'd been living together in her tiny cabin, but he'd been wanting something bigger, a real home, he'd said.

He never said "his" home, he *always* said "our home," but her mind autocorrected it every time to "his" home because she still, after all this time, tended to default to the worst-case scenario.

That being that he might yet decide she wasn't enough and would no longer want her in his life.

She looked into his face now, and when he caught her staring at him, he smiled and reached for her hand. And her brain, for the first time, didn't autocorrect anything.

He loved her. Like the forever kind of love. And she believed it.

"Here's what we've got so far," Allie said, turning the laptop to face them. "Scroll to the right to see the close-ups of each room."

As Jameson did just that, Luna's breath caught. It was going to be beautiful.

"Do you like the main bedroom?" Allie asked Luna. "We have some room for adjustments."

Luna looked at Jameson. "That's up to you."

Jameson held her gaze. "Allie, would you mind giving us a minute?"

"No problem," the architect said. "I'm going to get a hot dog. I've been looking forward to that all day."

When they were alone except for the blissfully sleeping T. rex, Jameson turned to Luna. "I want you to be happy in our new place."

She bit her bottom lip.

"Talk to me."

She drew a deep breath. "I have no idea what makes a house a home."

Leaning in, he slid a hand to the nape of her neck and kissed her softly. "The only thing I care about being in there is you."

"What about a bathroom?"

He gave a rough laugh. "Luna."

"See?" she asked, tossing up her hands. "You *do* care."

Instead of getting ruffled or frustrated with her, he held her gaze, his own warm and amused. "Okay, fine. I'd like to have a bathroom *and* you in the same place."

She laughed. The past year had been . . . amazing. He'd taught her to trust her inner strength, and she'd taught him how to lighten up and enjoy life, which made them better together than either of them could ever be apart.

Realizing that, she smiled against his shoulder. Home was where your soul resided. Her grandma had told her that. "So," she said lightly, "I want to be your wife. What do you think?"

He went still in her arms. "I think you're nuts." He gently tugged on her ponytail until she lifted her head so that he could look deeply into her eyes. "I also think I want to be your husband so bad it's killing me."

She kissed the baby and then Jameson. "I love you," she said with an ease that at one time would have been impossible.

It was strange to her now, how saying those three little words had once been so hard for her to say. And though she still didn't say it often, when she did, there was no mistaking how deeply she meant it.

A slow smile spread across his lips and he leaned down, brushing a soft kiss against her forehead. Then her cheek.

And finally her mouth.

"And I love you," he whispered against her lips. "Are you ready to look at the plans now? Help me make this house our forever home, together?"

Forever. She liked the sound of that. "Yes," she said. "To all of it. To everything, with you."

The next stand-alone book in the Sunrise Cove series
will be available in Summer 2024.

The
Summer Escape

Read on for a sneak peek!

CHAPTER 1

At the ripe old age of eight, Anna Moore decided she knew enough about engineering and physics to design a cape so she could fly. It went without saying that jumping off their second-story deck into a pile of soft, spongy Tahoe snow, which had in fact been neither soft nor spongy, had gone badly.

As an adult, she understood the ridiculous plan had come from the part of her brain responsible for stupid ideas. Older now, and hopefully wiser, she'd long ago locked that part of herself away and given up being a wild child. It'd probably taken her longer than it should've, but eventually she'd accepted it was safer to live life by the book.

She still tended to learn lessons the hard way though. Or as in today's case, the *really* hard way. She'd told Mari, her entire support staff at her private investigations firm, that she didn't need backup today. So here she stood, alone in the alley of the bar she'd been staking out for a client who thought her husband was cheating. Only she'd accidentally run into the pissed-off ex-husband of a *different* client, who was as big and mean as the Sierra Mountains behind him, *and* had a knife in his hand.

Some days it didn't pay to get out of bed.

She had her back pressed to the brick wall behind her and her hands out in front of her, signaling she came in peace, wondering how to reach the Mace in her back pocket without him noticing. Problem was, the guy towered threateningly over her, close enough to inflict damage if he wanted, but not quite close enough for her to administer a well-aimed knee to the crotch.

So yeah, hindsight being 20/20 and all, she could've used backup. And where the hell was everyone anyway? It was broad daylight, and the bar, part of a beautiful little shopping village, sat right across the street from Lake Tahoe. Normally on a gorgeous July day like this, there'd be people swarming everywhere. But today . . . not a soul. Seemed her luck was on point as always. "Okay, Gerald, you've got my attention. Let's talk this out."

"You testified against me in court and Tish got custody of Brownie."

Brownie was a nine-pound Shih Tzu. "Yes," she said. "Because you went off the rails during mediation and threatened to bake Brownie like, well, a brownie."

Gerald's massive shoulders drooped, and a flash of shame crossed his face. "Ah, man, I never would've done it. Brownie's my baby. I rescued him. Tish didn't even want him." His eyes went misty. "He's all I've got left, and now he's gone too."

From inside her pocket, her phone buzzed with an incoming text, and she knew from the air of superiority surrounding it who it was from. "Listen," she said. "That's my big sister, and trust me when I tell you that if I don't respond immediately, she'll send out the cops, SWAT, *and* the National Guard." This was probably not even a fib. She was twenty-eight, but her sister, only six years older, still tried to mother/smother her on the daily.

"I'm the baby of the family too," Gerald said sympathetically. "I've got four older sisters who never leave me alone. They're always bossing me around and telling me what to do."

"So you understand me," Anna said, trying not to stare at the knife. "And I understand you. See, this is just a mistake, Gerald. Let me go and there's no harm, no foul."

He scratched his scruffy jaw with the butt of the knife as he thought so hard she could almost see smoke curling from the top of his head. "You'll call the cops on me."

"I wouldn't do that to you." Her most impressive investigator skill was lying. "Just walk away."

"Okay. *If* you talk to Tish and get her to agree to joint custody of Brownie."

"Sure. Done." She would talk to Tish, but she couldn't guarantee him a thing. But Gerald studied her, during which she did her best to look confident. Finally, he nodded once and was gone.

She let out a relieved breath. Honestly, she understood some of his rage, if not the method. If an ex had taken Clawdia, the fifteen-year-old feline love of her life currently keeping her bed warm, she'd be devastated too.

Giving up on surveillance, she called Tish, warning her about the knife and the threat, letting her know all Gerald wanted was

Brownie. Tish said she never should've given him that knife for Christmas a few years back—*gee, ya think?*—and also she was tired of Brownie eating her shoes anyway.

With that handled, Anna quickly accessed her texts. One from Mari, checking in. One from her friend Nikki, reminding her that it was Anna's turn to buy drinks this week. And . . . shock . . . three from her pregnant-with-triplets sister.

WENDY: I need you.

WENDY: ???

WENDY: It's an emergency! And this time I mean it!

Heart kicking hard, Anna quickly strode to her car as she called her sister. "What's wrong?" she asked the second Wendy answered. "The babies?"

"They're fine, but I'm not. I need pickles."

Anna sucked in air as her heart settled back in her chest. "You've *got* to stop doing that!"

"I can't," Wendy said. "Not until you forgive me."

They'd had a fight. Yet another in a long line of fights that Anna didn't have time to deal with today. "Do you really need pickles?"

"More than anything except peace on earth and maybe for Ryan Reynolds to be single. Don't tell Hayden."

Hayden being Wendy's husband. "Fine. I'll bring you pickles after work."

"How about on your break? What are you doing right now?"

Besides dodging knife-toting dumbasses? "*Working.*"

"Okay, but I really, really, really need pickles. Like yesterday. Screw work, come over."

Anna thunked her head on her steering wheel.

"I'm sorry," Wendy said, softly now. "I know I'm being slightly bossy again. Ignore me."

If only that was an option . . . Anna loved her sister, but she didn't like being manipulated. "I'll be there."

She went to the store. She was heading toward the checkout, carrying a massive jar of pickles, when a stream of texts came through.

WENDY: I could use a watermelon too.

WENDY: And a steak!

WENDY: Oh, and Raisin Bran!

ANNA: Anna Moore has left this conversation.

WENDY: I know that's a lie . . .

Thirty minutes later, Anna let herself into her sister's house, carrying four bags of groceries. The cute little cabin that Hayden had inherited from his grandmother wasn't too far from the lake. Close enough to walk on a nice day, far enough that the swarms of summertime tourists seemed a world away. Wendy had the perfect life: the cute home, a husband who loved her, and babies on the way.

Telling herself it was silly to be a little envious, especially since she didn't want any of those things right now, Anna left everything but the pickles in the kitchen and walked down the hall to the main bedroom. There she found her supposedly on-bed-rest sister sitting on the floor of her closet, everything she owned scattered around her, reading a book.

"You came!" Wendy said, and then burst into tears.

Anna grimaced. "The doctor said if you keep crying every five minutes, you're going to get dehydrated."

"I know." Wendy was currently twenty-nine weeks pregnant, and the plan was if she didn't go into labor by week thirty-two, her ob-gyn would induce, since carrying triplets for longer than that could get dangerous.

Wendy wore Hayden's sweats, low-slung beneath her massive belly, and a tank top straining to within an inch of its life to hold everything in. There was a stain across the middle because Wendy used her baby bump as her table.

"You're staring at the stain on my shirt, aren't you."

"Nope. Not me. No way."

"No, I get it." Wendy hiccupped. "I'm falling apart!"

Feeling bad for her lack of patience, Anna dropped to her knees next to her sister. "Listen . . . tacos fall apart, but they're still amazing, right? And so are you."

Wendy's eyes watered again. "You still love me."

"As much as I love tacos." Which unfortunately was a whole lot. Anna took in the mess. "Was there a tornado in here?"

"Haha." Wendy blew her nose. "I was cleaning out my closet and found a baby book Hayden had bought me months ago. Did you know that babies get hot lava poops? Hot lava poops! What does that even mean?"

Horrified, Anna shook her head. "I don't know, but it can't be good."

Wendy tossed the book aside and made gimme hands at the massive jar of pickles Anna held.

But this wasn't her first rodeo. Or even her second. Or tenth. "Not until you get back into bed."

It took the both of them to get her there. Finally, Wendy sat back against the headboard, legs crossed, the pickle jar snugged between her legs as she dove right in. "You know what would make these even better? If they were fried."

"I'm not going back out."

"I really am sorry for being bossy. And also for setting you up with my dentist last week. I keep trying because all I want is for you to find a *great* guy and get married and have babies like me. Is it so wrong to want you happy?"

"First, there are all kinds of happy," Anna said. "But also, that 'great' guy ordered the most expensive thing on the menu, and when I pulled out my credit card to split the bill with him, he smiled and thanked me for buying dinner."

Wendy winced. "I'm sorry."

"It's fine, but I'm going to need you to stop trying to fix me because I'm not broken. I'd ask you to promise, but we both know you wouldn't mean it." Anna looked around at the mess again, then stilled at the box of her dad's things, the box they'd never been able to get themselves to go through. A sharp jab of grief hit her in her chest like a hot poker. He'd been gone a year and it still hurt, proving whoever had come up with "time heals all wounds" was full of shit. Turning away from the box, she found her sister still eating pickles.

"I know what you're thinking," Wendy said, licking her fingers.

"I'm thinking you're going to get heartburn if you eat another one."

"A lot you know. I've had heartburn since five weeks into this five-year-long pregnancy."

Anna snorted.

"Laugh now, but you're the godmother. You get these puppies when they turn into teenagers and send me to the loony bin."

"I love puppies." This from Hayden, who came into the room shrugging out of his suit jacket, moving with a smile toward Wendy. "Hey, babe." He kissed her.

"Hey yourself." Wendy grabbed him by the lapels and sniffed at him. "Wait. Why do you smell like your mom's amazing chicken noodle soup?"

"Because I stopped by her house to pick up a whole big pot of it for you."

"God, I love her."

Hayden went brows up.

Wendy smiled. "Love you too, but let's be honest. I married you for your mom."

Hayden didn't look concerned. He was incredibly chill and laid-back. Anna supposed he had to be to deal with Wendy, plus he used that great energy as CFO of the Moore Foundation,

which their dad had started as a way to facilitate getting money
and resources to people and places who needed it most.

"I'm going to shower and change," Hayden said, and kissed
Wendy's belly. "Hi, babies."

Anna turned away from their cuteness, her gaze once again
falling on the box of her dad's things. Kneeling before it, she
took a deep breath. After a year, she should be used to missing
his laughing eyes, the way he smiled at her like she was his favorite person in the whole world, his warm hugs . . .

Maybe it'd help if she had something of his home at her place.
She pulled out a framed picture that sucked the air from her
lungs.

"You okay?" Wendy asked.

Unable to answer, she brought the pic to the bed. Wendy let
out a soft breath as they both looked at the image of a young
Wendy and their pregnant mom at the lake.

"I was almost six here," her sister said softly. "I had a thing
about sand, hated it. Mom said I was such a princess that I
wouldn't even put my toes in it, so Dad had to carry me the
whole time."

A sweet memory, but Anna would give just about anything
to also have memories of their mom. Or even one. Shoving
the sadness where she shoved all her unwanted emotions—
deep, deep down—she distracted herself, this time by taking
another dive into the box. Fixating on the flash of something
shiny rather than facing any more family photos, she pulled
out a small gold coin about half an inch in diameter. "Huh. It's
dated 1853."

Wendy's eyes got big. "Let me see!"

Anna dutifully brought it over.

Wendy stared at it. "What if it's worth a ton of money? We could be like those people on that antique road show who've been sitting on a fortune and didn't even know it!"

"It's probably just a reproduction."

"Are there any more?"

Anna went through the box. "No."

Wendy bit the coin. "It tastes like real gold."

"How do you know what gold tastes like?"

"It tastes like this." Wendy held it up to the light. "You know what we need? A coin expert." She started to push herself to the edge of the bed to get up.

Anna held out a hand. "Stay." And when Wendy rolled her eyes, she added, "Yeah, sucks when someone bosses you around and tells you what to do, doesn't it. Now just sit there and eat the pickles in your lap."

"I can't even see my lap. For all I know, I could've finished all the pickles already. And you don't always have to be the keeper of the rules for everyone, you know."

Anna slid her a look. "If this is where you give me the *live-a-little* lecture, save your pickled breath."

"Come on. Aren't you the least bit curious about the coin?"

She was trying not to be.

"You could even go now. Come on, you're your own boss."

"Yes, but my caseload is overwhelming right now." Another fib. She was low on jobs. And money. But that was another problem entirely.

"Hayden, make her listen to me," Wendy said as he came back into the room, his hair damp, wearing basketball shorts and a T-shirt now. He took the jar of pickles from Wendy and replaced it with a bowl of soup.

"Like I've ever been able to make either of you listen to me."

"Aren't you even the least bit curious in the story behind the coin?" Wendy asked Anna. "And it's not like either of us are rolling in the dough. All of Dad's money went to his humanitarian and philanthropy efforts. My teaching salary's on hold for my pregnancy leave, and Hayden loves his job, but it's not exactly making us rich. An unforeseen windfall could change all of our lives."

Okay, good point. But if their dad had wanted to leave them something other than his reputation, he would have. And call her obstinate—others had used far more derogatory names—but she didn't want anything she hadn't earned.

Unfortunately, Wendy being pregnant threw a wrench in Anna's defiance. This pregnancy was ten years in the making and Wendy's lifelong dream come true. Until her sister safely popped out Thing One, Two, and Three, Anna was going to have to suck it up to keep her happy. "Fine. I'll take the coin in tomorrow. Happy?"

"Yes." But then Wendy burst into tears again.

Anna turned to Hayden. "You're up at bat."

Unfazed, he handed Wendy the tissue box from the top of their dresser.

"I'm sorry," Wendy said soggily. "I'm so tired of crying every time someone does something nice for me."

Anna wisely didn't say that she was *also* tired of the crying, mostly because she wanted to keep on breathing.

LATE THE NEXT day, Anna was back at Wendy's. All she wanted was a loaded pizza, a shower, and her own bed. Okay and maybe she also wanted her laundry magically folded and put away, a car that didn't have its "service needed" light on, and she sure wouldn't turn down an orgasm or two. But she'd brought the coin in to check its value, and there'd been a shock.

"I can't believe there just happened to be a news crew when you were there." Wendy pulled a bag of cheese puffs from Anna's bag.

"Hey, those are mine."

"Finders keepers." Wendy had her laptop open. "I'm searching YouTube for the news segment. They really said the coin was worth over ten grand?"

"Unbelievably, yes. Apparently it's part of a collection that hasn't been seen in years. The guy asked me if I had the rest of the set."

"Oh my God, do you think we do?"

"Where?" Anna asked.

"Good point."

"Listen . . ." Anna confiscated her family-size bag of cheese puffs, aka her dinner. "I know the coin's worth a lot, but I think we should keep it until we know why Dad had it—"

"Found it!" Wendy hit play on the video.

A reporter stood in the coin shop standing next to a very annoyed-looking Anna. "We don't need to see this—"

"Shh! And wow. That sweater you stole from me makes your eyes pop. But . . . did you even brush your hair?"

Anna ran a hand down her always wild and crazy waves. "Well, it's not like I knew there'd be a camera crew there."

"What if you'd run into a cute guy who's into smart-ass, perpetually irritated, brilliant women?" her sister demanded. "And what happened to the emergency lip gloss I put in your purse?"

"You think I'm brilliant?"

"Duh."

The reporter smiled into the camera. "Today we're visiting Sunrise Cove's Rare Coin and Antique Shop, where we came across Anna Moore, who found a rare coin in a box of her deceased father's belongings. Back in the day, Louis Moore made his fortune in real estate wholesaling, flipping before flipping was even a term. Of course he's even more famous for his philanthropy, giving away much of his fortune—"

"Or all of it," Wendy said proudly.

"—and to this very day, Sunrise Cove is grateful to him for donating buildings that became our rec center, the local hospital, and our historic society, among others. Anna, how do you think your dad came to be in possession of the coin? It's rumored he was a cat burglar way back in the day. Any truth to this?"

Wendy sucked in a breath. "*Cat burglar?*"

On-screen, Anna said, "None."

The reporter turned to the camera, blocking Anna out of the shot. "A modern-day mystery. Makes one wonder what other mysteries might be associated with Louis Moore, and if he . . . cat-burgled . . . the coin." She smiled. "Back to you, Doug, and the incoming weather system."

Wendy shut her laptop. "You let her defame dad?"

"Hey, she didn't want to listen—"

Wendy snatched back the cheese puffs. "What if they take his name off the hospital wing? What if this ruins all the good he did? What will I tell the babies? They can't grow up with the whole town thinking their grandpa was a thief, they'll get bullied. You were bullied and it messed you up."

Did all big sisters drive their little sisters bonkers? Or was that just a special skill of Wendy's? "I was bullied because you'd always brush my hair into a squirrel's tail. You're not supposed to brush this crazy hair once it's dried! And you never used any product. Do you have any idea how many products I have to use to keep the frizz at bay?" Anna paused because they both knew in spite of spending a fortune, her hair was still frizzy. "And I'm not messed up. I mean, not terribly."

Her cell phone buzzed with a number she didn't recognize. She wanted to answer with a *thank you for contacting the abyss, your scream is very important to me, but there are 5,493,823 people ahead of you in line* . . . But she controlled herself. "Anna Moore."

"Anna, this is Suzie McNab, a reporter from KQRS. We're running a piece on Louis Moore and I'm hoping to get a quote from you."

Anna's stomach sank. "What's the angle?"

"Whether he was the town savior or an infamous cat burglar. What can you tell us?"

"No comment." She disconnected.

Wendy, who'd obviously been able to hear the convo, had gone still, a cheese puff halfway to her mouth. "Why did you do that? You had a chance to clear his name."

"It didn't matter what I would've said, she'd already made up her mind to spin a wild tale."

In a statement of just how upset she was, Wendy shoved the cheese puffs away from her. "Infamous cat burglar? That implies he was a thief who entered buildings by climbing to an upper story, but Dad couldn't have climbed anything to save his life. His MS made him far too unsteady for that."

"You're remembering how he was in the second half of his life. Early on, he was an athlete and loved to mountain climb."

"Oh my God. You're right." Wendy closed her eyes briefly. "It's been so long, I'd almost forgotten." Her eyes flew open. "You don't think he did this, do you? Stole the coin?"

"What I think is that we need a lot more information."

"That's the investigator in you. But you're his daughter. You can't possibly believe— Wait, what am I even saying? You're the job. No emotions, no feelings, nothing too personal."

Hard to be insulted at the truth, but she managed it just fine. "It'll blow over."

"Only if we fix it." She leveled Anna with a look of despair. "We have to fix this."

"It's just words, Wen. *We* know Dad didn't do this. And anyway, now that he's gone, it doesn't matter what anyone else thinks."

"Of course it matters. What do you think will happen to the

foundation if Dad's name is dragged through the mud? Hayden losing his job is the least of it. We do so much good."

"Okay," Anna said carefully. "I hear you. But I still think you're jumping ahead here. Dad didn't steal anything. He'd *never*."

"We need to prove it," Wendy said softly, hugging her belly.

Anna could withstand a lot of things. Like *a lot* a lot. But Wendy feeling sick with anxiety right now wasn't one of them. The doctor had been very clear. No stress. "Fine. I'll fix this. But don't get excited," she warned when she could see her sister doing just that. "I'm not even sure where to start, when the only person with any answers is dead— Why are you on your phone right now?"

"I'm ordering a GoPro so you can take me along for every step of your investigation. It's got a headband strap and an app that you can download on your phone so if we're connected, I can see everything you see, as you see it."

Anna choked out a laugh. "No. Hell no."

"Listen, do you know what it's like to be the same weight as a whale? Or to have to run with your legs crossed to the bathroom so you don't pee on the floor? No, you do not. Also, I've got one alien kicking me in the stomach, another punching me in the lungs, and every time I move, I . . ."

"You what?"

"Toot."

"*Toot?*"

Wendy threw her hands in the air. "Yes, I fart. All the time. And we're not talking little dainty ones that you can hide either. I've been telling Hayden it's him, but I'm pretty sure he's not buying it—" She broke off to narrow her eyes at Anna for laughing her ass off. "Jeez, I haven't seen you laugh in forever, and when you do it's at my expense?"

Anna swiped at the tears of mirth on her cheeks. "I'm not going to wear a GoPro."

"Are you telling me I'm about to push Midnight, Sunshine, and Eclipse out of my hoo-ha and you can't do this one little thing and bring me along?"

"Wen, if you love your babies, you will *not* give them hippy-dippy names. And as for bringing you along, I'll wear earbuds and keep a line open when acceptable, but that's it."

Wendy hugged Anna so hard it hurt, a perfect euphemism for their relationship. But it wasn't until she drove home and entered the teeny-tiny condo she loved so much that she realized once again she'd caved like a cheap suitcase to her sister.

$\mathcal{D}$on't miss the other books in the gorgeously romantic

Sunrise Cove series

Available now from

HEADLINE
ETERNAL

$\mathcal{D}$iscover Wildstone in the delightfully addictive

Wildstone series

Available now from

HEADLINE
ETERNAL

FIND YOUR HEART'S DESIRE...

VISIT OUR WEBSITE: www.headlineeternal.com
FIND US ON FACEBOOK: facebook.com/eternalromance
CONNECT WITH US ON X: @eternal_books
FOLLOW US ON INSTAGRAM: @headlineeternal
EMAIL US: eternalromance@headline.co.uk